Praise for *When the A*

I thoroughly enjoyed reading *When th*
Bliss and the adventures of a feisty heroine and a
hero who find romance during a tragedy that shook the Cascade
Mountains. I recommended it for your 2025 book list.

—Rita Gerlach, author of *Mercy's Refuge*
and other historical novels

In her latest novel, talented author Lauralee Bliss compels her
characters to wrestle with the age-old question of how we trust
God during a deadly catastrophe. With their differences in social
standing, education, and depth of faith, the seemingly mismatched
hero and heroine face tremendous odds when tragedy strikes.
Their realistic emotional and spiritual journeys pulled me into the
story so that I was happy-sad to reach the end.

—Johnnie Alexander, best-selling, award-winning author of
Where Treasure Hides and *The Cryptographer's Dilemma*

Lauralee Bliss paints with both broad strokes and fine detail the
historical tragedy of the Wellington Avalanche of 1910. As readers
get acquainted with the victims and heroes, they see a portrait
of both the frailty of human existence and the providence of
God. *When the Avalanche Roared* is an admirable and meaningful
work of art.

—Rhonda Dragomir, author of *When the Flames Ravaged*

A DAY TO REMEMBER

When the Avalanche Roared

LAURALEE BLISS

BARBOUR
PUBLISHING

Published by Barbour Publishing, Inc., 1810 Barbour Drive, Uhrichsville, Ohio 44683, www.barbourbooks.com

Our mission is to inspire the world with the life-changing message of the Bible.

 Member of the
Evangelical Christian
Publishers Association

Printed in the United States of America.

DEDICATION

To Dad and Mom, now together in heaven,
who enthusiastically supported my endeavors in life,
including my writing. Their love, determination,
and support guide me this day.

ACKNOWLEDGEMENTS

With thanks for these insightful works:

The White Cascade by Gary Krist

The 1910 Wellington Disaster
by Deborah Cuyle and Rodney Fletcher

Northwest Disaster by Ruby El Hult

My agent Tamela Hancock Murray

Barbour Editors Becky Germany, JoAnne Simmons

Critiquers Steve, Rita, and Sherry.
Thank you for your words of wisdom.

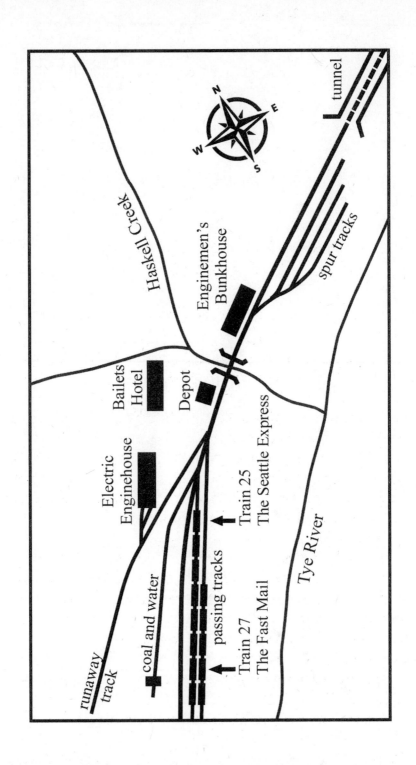

Chapter 1

SEPTEMBER 1909
EVERETT, WASHINGTON

The hand shook in a voiceless plea for help. She strained, trying in vain to grasp the hand, reaching ever closer, nearly there. A cry rose up in her throat for heavenly grace and strength. *Please, oh please. Help me reach. Just a little bit more. Oh God, I must help. Help me!* Again came a rumble in her throat, the effort causing every part of her to cry out. "Help!"

"Lillian!"

Lillian Hartwick awoke with a start, the vision quickly disappearing into the realm of reality with the worried eyes of Mother standing over her. She drew herself to a sitting position. Only a moment ago she had lain back on the settee to think. "I must have fallen asleep." She wiped her damp forehead with her hand. "What a terrible dream."

"I heard you cry for help from the other room. Do you want to talk about it?"

Lillian shook her head, inhaled a deep breath, and tried to put on an air of confidence with a forced smile. "It was just a silly dream," she said, more to herself than anyone. "It means nothing. Nothing at all." She stood to her feet and touched her tousled hair.

"Well, try to pull yourself together. Mr. Travers is on his way here as we speak. He said he has news. Tea will be set up here in the sitting room."

He's coming now? Lillian inhaled another sharp breath and began straightening her skirt. Anthony Travers. Tall, dark-haired, with a thin line of a mustache that to Lillian, denoted an air of mischievous intent. Anthony Travers had been calling on her over the last six months. Everyone expected that they would one day marry. He worked in the timber industry that had grown by leaps and bounds over the last few years, as had the mill town of Everett where they lived. He'd been cordial, taking her to Seattle once for a sumptuous dinner while sharing stories of his work. Lillian had kept her hands folded and back straight while trying to listen to his endless chatter about trees and lumber and shipments, which made her drift into a land of boredom. At times, his work took him to other states. He had plenty of money, as everyone knew, and Father and Mother couldn't be happier if their only daughter found a good life with a prosperous businessman. But what was a good life? Wealth? Prestige? The comforts of a home? Did any of that matter in the grand scheme of things?

Lillian hurried to her room to fix her hair and change her blouse to a rose-colored affair, accompanied by dangly earrings and a sparkling necklace. As she reached for the jewelry, she thought back to the hand reaching out and her straining to help but never able to do so. Her reflection betrayed the seriousness of the dream in deep-set, blue eyes under brows drawn together in concern, accompanied by a curved chin, high cheekbones, and molasses-colored hair caught up in a bun.

"Lillian, Mr. Travers is here!" Mother called up the stairs.

The vision left, replaced by jitters when she thought of Anthony standing in the foyer of their home. She tucked a handkerchief into her sleeve, never knowing if she might shed a tear or pretend to do so—Mother said it looked well to show emotion for a man's work—and hurried downstairs.

Anthony stood in the hallway with his hat parked under one arm, wearing a nicely appointed sack suit of a double-breasted jacket and trousers with polished shoes on his feet. His mustache glimmered in the light from oil to sharpen the curled ends. "Hello, Lillian." Her name glided off his tongue in a friendly manner.

She smiled and led the way to the sitting room, where the maid had set tea out on a gleaming silver tray. "I am surprised to see you calling so late in the afternoon."

He took a seat on the settee, the same one on which Lillian had arisen from tremulous slumber moments before. "Two lumps," he told Lillian as she poured their cups of tea. "I felt I should come as soon as I heard word."

Lillian saw her hand tremble, the spoon nearly dropping the lumps of sugar onto the floor. With a few short breaths, she managed to steady herself. "Is there trouble?" When she gave him the cup, their gazes met. His lips curved into a smile under the mustache.

"Absolutely none. Only good news."

Lillian thought she might faint with the ups and downs of her emotions so far this day. She managed to take a seat in the armchair across from him as he looked at her with wide eyes.

"Are you all right? I assure you it's good news."

Lillian forced a smile. "Oh yes. It's just that I drifted off to sleep a short while ago and had a bad dream."

"I'm sorry to hear that. Can I help?"

"I think you will, by your good news." She reached over and picked up the teacup, sipping on a sickly-sweet brew. She winced. *You don't have to impress him, Lillian*, she told herself. *Including trying to match tea preferences to his.* She actually favored unsweetened tea.

"I've just signed one of the largest contracts for lumber in our company's history," Anthony exclaimed. "It's with a company in San Francisco. Since the earthquake a few years ago, they are deep into rebuilding and require as much timber as possible. Whatever is left can then be shipped where the need is the greatest."

"Oh?" She looked at the lamplight reflecting in the amber liquid in her cup.

"You don't seem very excited. I don't think you realize what this means, Lillian. This contract is worth a fortune. And with it, I can put down a good amount of money on a fine house for us."

The words pierced her heart and made her nearly upset her teacup. She quickly placed it on a nearby stand. "A house?"

"On Rucker Avenue with a fine view of the harbor. In fact, not far from the O'Neills. I know they are friends of your family."

Lillian treasured the O'Neill family, especially dear Berenice who lived down Hoyt Avenue with her husband and young baby. They often gathered for social calls to chat about life. These days, Berenice missed her husband Jim who worked for the Great Northern Railway and was gone on lengthy work trips. "I don't know what to say."

He set down his teacup and pointed to the empty space beside him. "I'd hope you'd say how thrilled you are and how you can't wait for our marriage."

She straightened in her seat and gave what she hoped was a coy smile. "Mr. Travers, you haven't even proposed yet. And have you discussed your intentions with Father? I don't think he likes surprises."

He laughed. "Lillian, you and I were meant to marry. Everyone knows it. And marriage to the chief lumber business operator in Washington State—and maybe even the entire West Coast—can't help but impress dear old Father." He patted the fine cushion of the settee. "So come sit beside me and congratulate me."

Lillian stood and moved to sit beside him where he took up her hand and kissed it. How she wanted to be excited for his news. But she feared what might happen with a marriage to the head of a large company. The same as what happened to her friend Berenice—pining after a love usually absent because of work and obligation and other loves that pulled the husband away. Nevertheless, Lillian submitted to Anthony's kiss and the oiled mustache tickling her cheek, tasting the sugary sweetness of the tea on his lips. She felt certain he loved her. Maybe she would learn to love him in return.

When they parted, his joviality took on a serious tone. "With this new contract though, I must personally oversee the transportation of the lumber shipment to San Francisco. I leave in two days."

"What does that mean?"

"It means that I will be gone for a lengthy time to set up this operation. I'll travel with this shipment and see to its deliveries, along with selling new contracts."

"How long will this take?"

"I don't know. Several weeks. But it could be a few months, depending on where the lumber is needed and if there is enough to even establish overseas transactions. Once everything is running smoothly, I can return and manage operations from here."

Did he really say he could be gone for months? Lillian glanced at the large grandfather clock across the room, ticking methodically. "And what am I supposed to do? Stare out a window and wait?"

"You can write me and tell me you love me, and make wedding plans. When I return, we will marry. It won't be for long."

Lillian inhaled a sharp breath. What could she say to his plans in life? She had no sway in them, especially in business affairs. Nor did she think she ever would. "I suppose you must do what you need to do."

Anthony took her hand in his and kissed it again. "Believe me when I say this will be worth it in the end. We will be apart but only for a little while."

Lillian remembered the look on Berenice's face when she took out the latest letter from her husband, with all the talk of issues on the rail line, and how it kept them apart as a couple and a family. The weight of Anthony's pending absence felt like a burden she must now bear. Did she really want that in a marriage? To have his timber business come between them and even tear them apart? "I hope all goes well," she said, instead of confessing that his absence would never make her heart grow fonder.

"I knew you would understand. You are a wonderful woman, Lillian. And we will have a wonderful life together. You can take me at my word."

A smile quivered at the corner of her mouth, fighting to overtake the frown she felt inside. How she wanted to agree with great enthusiasm. Instead, she remembered the hand in her dream, struggling for someone to help take hold and pull the victim out of a serious quagmire before it was too late. Longer and longer the arm grew from the depths until a shoulder passed and then a familiar face emerged out of the deep.

The face was hers.

———— •••• ————

Lillian stood shivering at the city port that was active with many ships coming in and out. Anthony's vessel, filled with timber, sat ready to depart for San Francisco. She disliked coming here with the sights and sounds of rough men uttering language that matched the filthy clothes on their backs. Everett was a booming mill town of manufacturing and shipping, filled with a colorful array of people who worked there. Smokestacks belched black tufts of clouds into the air. Lillian nearly coughed as the smoke tickled her throat. If the wind shifted to the west, the smoke would carry into their modest neighborhood, reminding them of the rough-and-tumble parts of the city. The mills and the port served businessmen like Anthony and his fine timber harvested from the thick Washington forests, cut at the lumber mills, and ready for transport to those rebuilding after the terrible earthquake in California. She sighed, knowing she must not be selfish. People needed the lumber Anthony's company would provide.

Lillian could sense men perusing her as she drew the cape closer around her shoulders to shield herself from the biting wind that carried moisture from the sea. Thankfully, the large hat she wore provided some protection from the leers she knew were not fitting. She pushed the thoughts aside to reflect on the fine dinner last evening when Anthony officially proposed on bended knee between the main course and the silky custard for dessert. He promised a large-cut diamond upon his return from California. Glancing out of the corner of her eye at her ringless left hand, she was glad he had chosen to wait. Maybe the diamond would mean more to her when he returned triumphant from his timber enterprise. These past few days had been like a whirlwind—the strange dream, Anthony's visit to tell her of his extended absence—topped off by the engagement.

Mother and Father were happy about the proposal but sad Anthony had to leave so suddenly. But Mother could always cheer a stormy day with optimism—a lesson Lillian ought to follow. "I think it's wonderful how he wants to provide for you," she had cooed. "Look at this fine job he has. And I know just the house he wants for you. We can think about decorations and furnishings. It's very exciting."

Lillian strained to see through the drifting fog to Anthony's tall form, straight and proud among the laborers onboard ship. He then came portside by the rail and waved. She waved back. He disappeared for a few minutes, then reappeared on the gangplank, striding down it and along the wharf to where she stood.

"So you came," he murmured, taking her in his arms. "No one could give me a better send-off."

"I can't believe you're leaving, but I know it's necessary." She sighed.

"I'll send telegrams of my progress. And I expect you'll do the same."

She nodded. "I'll visit Berenice soon and find out how she spends her days with her husband gone." Lillian had very limited talents except in the area of embroidery and teas, which were all so useless when dealing with a restless heart.

"An excellent idea. And decide too how you wish to decorate

the new house." He gathered her in his arms. "It's time for me to depart. Kiss me farewell."

She obliged, her fingers clinging to the rough tweed jacket, and felt tears spring into her eyes. Why…she didn't know. Maybe this meant feelings of love were welling up with the sense that she'd miss him and especially his attention. He'd begun to spoil her, after all, and it felt sweet.

"Please be careful," she said. They broke apart and stood gazing at each other. Just then Anthony took a picture from his pocket, one Mother had taken of Lillian when she graduated from grade school.

"I have this near my heart."

"I'm just a schoolgirl in that picture!" Lillian moaned, staring at the black-and-white image of a young thing with long hair draped about her shoulders, sitting prim and proper in a straight-back chair with hands folded across her lap, unaware of the twists and turns that life would bring. She remembered the picture-taking well. Father wanted a special photograph taken of his only child completing her studies in school—and one of the few in the area to finish. Come to think of it, she had not had a portrait done since accomplishing that educational goal. This must be remedied, she realized, especially given the thought of Anthony carrying a schoolgirl photo in his breast pocket.

"You look sweet and innocent. It will accompany me on these long days and nights. Now I must say goodbye."

They kissed one final time. He offered a debonair grin, whirled, and headed for the ship, only to be stopped by various men along the way seeking his direction. Now her man of interest found his attention drawn elsewhere, and suddenly she felt very much alone. Her shoes scuffed along the walkway in unladylike fashion as she walked to find a streetcar, wondering if his interest in her would linger in his absence.

Chapter 2

"You must be so excited!"

Lillian startled, sending her embroidery needle flying to the rug below. A glint from the nearby lamp revealed where it had landed, and she hastily retrieved it before the family cat came out to explore. Lillian hadn't expected such enthusiasm over the engagement from her friend Berenice—shown in her wide grin and shiny eyes. "I think I will be when he returns."

"How well I understand that."

A shrill cry interrupted their small sewing circle, summoning the new mother to a wooden cradle. Berenice lifted up her daughter and held the baby in her arms. Lillian couldn't help putting down the embroidery to walk over and gaze at the infant. Little Peggy Jane gurgled as she stared up at Lillian with large blue eyes. Lillian wondered if she would have a child as quickly as Berenice, with mere months elapsing before the young wife found herself expecting. She swallowed hard, trying to picture herself a new wife and sudden mother, all alone while her husband floated down the coast with his shipments of timber. "How do you do it?" she finally asked.

Berenice kissed the top of her daughter's head. "You mean mothering?"

"Everything. With Jim gone and you here alone, caring for a baby, wondering when he will return."

"I don't mind it very much. It's the winters I dread most." Berenice gave the maid, Carrie, instructions about the goat's milk already warming on the stove before turning back to Lillian. "This is going to be a difficult winter. I felt a chill in the air just the other day while walking Peggy Jane in the carriage."

"It only rains here," Lillian mused. Snow never proved a difficulty in Everett. Winter brought dreary gray skies and copious amounts of rain, sending rivulets down the windowpanes and making her yearn for pleasant spring weather.

"Once winter comes calling, it's here to stay. Especially where Jim works, way up in the mountains." Berenice stared into the eyes of her daughter and again pecked the babe on the forehead. "Oh little one, if only you could know how handsome and strong your papa is. So many rely on him. We mustn't be selfish and wish him here." She crossed the room and stared out the window at the waters of the distant sound glistening in the sun's rays where, just a few days ago, Lillian and Anthony said their farewells.

Carrie returned with the warm bottle, offering to feed the baby, but Berenice shook her head. She took a seat in a wooden rocker and began feeding little Peggy Jane. Lillian liked the tenacity and determination of the woman only a year older than she and with a strength Lillian hoped to have when she needed it most. "So what exactly does Jim do?" she asked.

"He's the superintendent of the Cascade Rail Division for the Great Northern Railway. The one that runs through the mountains east of here. Last year, I didn't see him for several weeks, especially with all the snow. He takes it upon himself to personally oversee clearing the rail lines. That means using the rotary plows. When things go wrong, he must correct it. People depend on him, both the workers and the passengers. And not just for travel but for everyday needs like the mail. He even stays in his own railcar that runs along the line—he is so devoted to his work."

Lillian could imagine Berenice's dread of a long winter season. She herself dreaded the weeks ahead of her while Anthony sailed off with his timber, though the two of them had fostered precious little of a relationship since they began courting, having only passive encounters, walks, and dining. It must be different for Berenice, a married woman and mother left with an anxious heart, in a large empty house, while the next snowstorm held her husband captive. "It must be difficult."

"I sometimes wish he had never taken the job of superintendent," she admitted. "We had such sweet times in Montana with picnics and celebrations and walks." She put the bottle aside and lifted little Peggy Jane to her shoulder to burp her. "But he got word of the promotion while we were there and took it. I think he did it to impress my father, truthfully. But I was in love. The work became a part of him, so it became a part of me. I followed him here to Washington, and here I am."

Lillian straightened in her chair. "How did you know you were in love?"

Berenice's large oval eyes darted to Lillian, and her tiny pearl lips curved upward into a coy smile. "I wouldn't have left my Montana home if I didn't love him. You just know in your heart. You can't help but think of him day and night. You make plans about what you will say, what you will wear, what you will do when you meet again. And you know also by his love for you." She paused. "And from what you've told me, Mr. Travers is indeed in love with you."

Lillian never doubted Anthony loved her. He had her picture in his pocket after all, even if it was one of her as a schoolgirl. He shared a proclamation of love by way of a proposal and a future engagement ring. But it wasn't enough. Berenice alluded to excitement in her relationship with Jim. A longing to be with the one she loved. Lillian only felt uncertainty about the future.

"What's troubling you?" Berenice asked, surrendering a sleepy Peggy Jane to the maid's care.

"You seemed so certain about Jim. Knowing you were destined to marry. I wish I felt that way about Anthony. But I don't."

Berenice laughed. "It wasn't that simple," she admitted. "Far from it." She sprang to her feet and strode into a back room. When she reappeared, her arms held a large book. She took a seat on the settee and motioned Lillian to join her. Berenice opened the book bit by bit to reveal its contents in thoughtful fashion, as if savoring each page. It contained photos, penciled embellishments, and written remembrances and thoughts, along with ribbons, pressed flowers, and other memorabilia preserved through the years. "This is my book of love," she said with a girlish giggle. "Look at this picture of us back in Montana. It's my favorite. Doesn't Jim look marvelous?"

Lillian gazed with interest at the picture of Berenice holding a cat in her lap. Jim O'Neill stood behind her with his hand resting lightly on her shoulder, seemingly enjoying the beauty of a fine summer day.

"Father wanted me to meet the new railroad man in town," Berenice remembered. "So he invited Jim to dine with us. I wore my best dress, and Florence did a wonder with my hair. Jim couldn't take his eyes off me, even if he did enjoy the meal." She giggled again. "When we took an evening walk together, I knew at that moment we would marry."

Lillian sighed. How confident Berenice sounded after meeting him once—sure and steady, without any doubt to mar the way. And how uncertain Lillian felt, as if she might be making a big mistake if she opened her heart wide enough to embrace Anthony's love. Berenice continued to flip the pages of the scrapbook, sharing a story of the pressed flowers from a bouquet of wildflowers. Jim had picked them on a walk where they had taken a wrong turn in a meadow and gotten lost all afternoon. The letters shared while she still lived in Kalispell were next. They spoke of loyal meetings and love all around. She then traced one penciled notation with her finger. A deep flush colored her thin, pale cheeks. "This is quite private, I must admit." she added with a nervous giggle, "But when one quotes Song of Solomon, at least it's the Lord's Word."

"Oh my." Lillian chuckled along with her. "The reverend would agree, I'm sure."

"No he wouldn't. He would say these verses should remain in the Holy Book and not displayed in the open. A matter of propriety, I suppose. Though our communications are private." She flew to her feet. "And I see I've already said too much."

Lillian adored Berenice's lightheartedness and even shyness in matters of love. Suddenly the young woman floated over to the piano and occupied the bench, rearranging her skirt as she did. "And for that I will play 'Wait Till the Sun Shines, Nellie.'" Her fingers danced over the ivory keys with such a delightful singing voice that Lillian could not help but join in.

Wait till the sun shines, Nellie
When the clouds go drifting by
We will be happy, Nellie
Don't you sigh
Down Lover's Lane we'll wander
Sweethearts you and I
Wait till the sun shines, Nellie
Bye and bye

The song ended in a flourish with them laughing like young girls running in a meadow on a fine summer day. For a moment, Lillian's melancholy vanished. *If only this happiness would last*, she thought. It had for Berenice, who shared letters of two people desperately in love. If such conviction would flood her heart—that Anthony and she were right for each other—peace and confidence would hold them together in this long absence. After all, Anthony had only been congenial and heartfelt in his emotion. Maybe once they exchanged telegrams of love, or something else yet unrevealed, the feelings would be different.

"Now you look thoughtful," Berenice observed. Rising from the piano bench, she scooped up the cat that played with her skirt. "What is it?"

"I want the love you both have," Lillian blurted out, then stepped back, embarrassed by the truth that had launched so boldly from her lips. "I guess I want to be assured of it. . .that Anthony and I are sweethearts. But I don't know. It all seems rather sudden. And now he's gone for only the Lord knows how long."

Berenice smiled as her fingers ruffled the cat's golden fur. "You will know. There will be no mistake. I dearly love the thirty-seventh Psalm." She set down the cat and made for the large Bible sitting prominently on a table. Carefully, she opened the heavy book to the bright red ribbon that already marked the scripture, as if she knew what would unfold. "'Trust in the Lord, and do good; so shalt thou dwell in the land, and verily thou shalt be fed. Delight thyself also in the Lord; and he shall give thee the desires of thine heart.'" She sighed. "I love this passage. Another of my favorites is in my scrapbook that I inscribed when I think of Jim. 'Mark the perfect man, and behold the upright: for the end of that man is peace.'" She turned to face Lillian, her eyebrows drawn together. "When you can do nothing else, dear Lillian, you can always pray for your intended, that he may be guided by peace and God's will in all things. It can't help but work out for the good."

Berenice's words chased Lillian all the way home that afternoon. On the breath of air came the pungent smell of smoke from chimneys and the horns of ships, ready to leave with their wares to distant ports of call. She thought of Anthony standing proud on his ship that carried lumber to the needy. She ought not be selfish. Families needed lumber to rebuild their homes. He had confessed his love for her despite his pending absence. She had nothing to fear and everything to embrace.

Mother awaited her arrival on the porch, waving an envelope, her face beaming. "You have a letter!" she called.

Lillian took the envelope from her outstretched hand and settled herself in a wicker chair.

My dearest Lillian,

All is well. I have made it to San Francisco, and they are happy to have the lumber for the rebuilding effort. There is a great deal of work to be done. I've never seen such sadder streets after such devastation. The quicker the building is finished, the better it will be for all.

For now I must remain here to set up the business. Perhaps you can come visit me. I already miss your beautiful smile and soft voice. Say the word, and I will make whatever arrangements are needed. But know you are in my constant thoughts.

All my affection,
Anthony

Mother looked at her with narrowed eyes as the letter drifted to the porch floor and Lillian snatched it up. "Is everything all right?"

"Mr. Travers wants me to go to San Francisco."

"San Francisco? Whatever for?"

"He misses me, he says. Have we any relations there?"

Mother shook her head. "No, of course not. And it would be unseemly for you to go unattended. Where would you stay? The city has not been the same since the earthquake, you know. From what I've heard it's still in ruins."

Anthony's letter confirmed it as well. Lillian had no interest in traveling to a city that was struggling to come alive after the earthquake and fire that destroyed most of it. Everett was harsh enough. She could not imagine being in the middle of the mayhem. "I think I should wait."

"Thank you, dear. I know it must be hard. But 'absence makes the heart grow fonder,' as the saying goes. Wait here with us and hold on to your promise. He will return soon, I'm certain."

Lillian nodded but knew the simple sentiment would never be enough to overcome the doubts that remained.

———◆◆◆———

A week had passed, and Lillian still hadn't answered Anthony's suggestion of visiting him in San Francisco. Mother inquired a few times if she'd responded, and she said she would. But the empty paper revealed her indecision. It pained her even more when her other good friend, Helen, had announced her engagement several days prior and burst onto the front porch to show off her ring. Lillian sat in the wicker chair, staring at nothing in particular, despite her friend's excited chatter.

"I heard you're getting married too, Lillian. Where's your ring?"

She brought herself out of her melancholy to concentrate on her friend's query. "Anthony is bringing it when he returns from his business trip."

Helen giggled in glee, twisting the ring around her finger as if it were a special prize won by a young girl at the county fair. "Oh, I have so many plans to make. We thought next spring for the wedding, but I don't know if I can wait that long. Where are you having the reception? Here?"

Lillian looked off into the distance. "We still have to decide." Just then a vision came of friends and family pressed around, all offering congratulations, the band striking up the music as she and Anthony took their first waltz as husband and wife. She wanted to smile and thank everyone for coming and bask in the love that welled up for her new husband. But the vision only conjured doubt instead of eagerness for a marriage.

Lillian shook her head and tried to support her friend. Helen went on with more plans, giddy and carefree as only a bride-to-be in unmistakable love could be. And here she sat, the questions riding higher than a kite flown on a summer day. Maybe everything would be different if she simply accepted Anthony's invitation to see him in San Francisco. Surely he would know of a reputable boarding-house for her to stay in. But what would she do except become a fixture when Anthony returned from a day of work? They might share words, perhaps a loving caress or a kiss, or take a walk. Would she be closer to knowing her heart's question: *Is he the right man for me?*

Mother swept into the sitting room where Lillian had yet to pick up the sewing she had planned to do, waving another letter in her hand. For a moment Lillian thought Anthony had re-sent his communication, imploring her mother to convince Lillian to go to San Francisco.

"I've received a letter from Elizabeth." Lillian must have worn a strange expression on her face, because Mother added, "You remember. My niece and your cousin."

"I'm sorry, I don't."

"No, I suppose you wouldn't. You were very young when we had the family reunion at that lovely park one summer. She and her husband live in Wellington. And she's going to have a baby at Christmas. Isn't that a wonderful gift?"

Lillian thought of Berenice tenderly feeding Peggy Jane and realized it wasn't just the idea of marriage alone that concerned her, but everything else too. Home, family, and children—none of which gave her confidence. "That's nice," she said absently, picking up her latest work of embroidery.

"She was hoping my sister could come when the baby is born, but she has the consumption, you know."

Lillian wound the thread around the needle to form a perfect French knot, ready to give the small cardinal she had sewn a dark eye to see. "I'm sorry to hear that, Mother."

"Why don't you visit Cousin Elizabeth? It will occupy your mind and give you something to do. You both are close in age. I think it would help her immensely to have family near."

Lillian had just poked the needle through the fabric to create the knot and poked herself. She winced and put her finger in her mouth, tasting saltiness. "Where does she live again?"

Mother glanced at the letter. "Wellington. I will find one of your father's maps to locate it, but it's in the mountains."

Lillian winced again and not from the needle piercing her finger. The notion of being in a town in the mountains made her wonder about its isolation and wildness. "What am I supposed to do there?"

"Oh heavens. Be a good and kind cousin and keep her company. Her husband, Clyde, works long hours for the railroad. You could be of comfort and learn a great deal about running a household."

Like how to be a wife and mother to a man absent for long periods of time. Like Berenice. She wanted to say it but didn't. "How long would I stay?"

"As long as she needs you, I imagine. And with your Mr. Travers away, it seems the perfect timing."

Lillian felt certain Mother would say this must be God's plan too, but she did not. Instead her mother strode out of the sitting room. Lillian looked down at her sewing project. The embroidered cardinal's lone black eye from the completed French knot smirked with a sideways glance as if to inquire what she would do. To stay would be selfish, with her cousin in a delicate condition. To go would mean entering untested waters. She lay the embroidery aside, stood, and began pacing the rug beneath her feet. She knew nothing about caring for a woman and her baby. She knew even less about a rugged existence in remote places. She wished she could ask Berenice her opinion. With her baby girl cooing in her lap and Berenice's large eyes staring thoughtfully, her friend would say how much having family near when times are difficult means everything. Especially in the absence of a husband. Lillian could understand that too, with Anthony's lengthy sojourn in San Francisco. Right then she realized she'd rather be with her cousin in a far-off place in the mountains than huddled in a boardinghouse in a ruined city street, awaiting Anthony's appearance. Or cooped up here in Everett, listening to Helen expound on wedding plans while Lillian sewed until her fingers bled, waiting for Anthony's return.

Lillian stood and walked off to her desk to write the letters.

Chapter 3

⁓

OCTOBER 1909

WELLINGTON, WASHINGTON

THE CASCADE MOUNTAINS

"Get up, you lazy good-for-nothin'!"

A kick sent a wave of pain racing through Griffin's side, jolting him awake. Squinting his eyes at the window, he could barely see the rays of the new dawn filtering over Windy Mountain, whose tall peak would soon completely obscure the sun from view. Griffin fumbled for his pocket watch—a treasure given to him by his grandfather. He was a kind person, like Griffin's mother, the kindest soul to grace this world.

"Don't bother looking," said a voice. "You're late already."

He struggled to his feet and hunted for his clothing. His bunkmates slowly forced shoes onto their feet and drew worn coats over shirts stained from their labor. Across the way, the mischievous eyes of Oliver McCree glinted in the lantern light. Griffin had no interest in beginning his day tangling with the likes of that man, but nothing ever changed. He knew what was coming. If it didn't come from Oliver, it did from the man's cronies. Not that any of them were learned men, but they still kept on with the jabs.

"He can't read the hour on a clock," sneered Oliver's right-hand man, Beau Crawford. "Don't know why he has that fancy pocket watch of his."

"Griff here is as dumb as a lump of coal," Oliver pronounced, to the chuckles of several bunkmates.

Griffin grimaced when he recalled stumbling to his bunk late one evening, only to find it filled with coal. Black dust covered everything—from the blankets to his clothing, and even himself. For days he struggled to clean it up. Townsfolk stared at his filthy appearance. Mrs. Bailets, the postmistress and wife of the hotel owner in town, proved sympathetic and offered to wash his clothing. He wouldn't hear of it but did accept the use of the big washtub at the hotel and soap flakes to do the job. Meanwhile, the bunkmates elbowed each other, chuckled, and asked when Griffin would ever be decent again.

Griffin tried his best to ignore them as he pulled on a pair of thick wool socks Mama once made him. He grabbed a hunk of bread and some cheese from the larder and opened the door to gaze out at the still, darkened landscape. Behind the town stood the tar-black poles of burnt pine that once stood majestically with large limbs and feathery needles until fire wiped them out. He recalled that time well. The railroad was blamed for the trees catching fire from cinders spewed out of the locomotives. The flames nearly swept into town. Thankfully, the large water tower used to fill the trains saved the structures, but the fire took away all that was pleasing to the eye in mountainsides covered in lush pine. Water now gushed down the mountain with the spring snowmelt, bringing mud and rocks. Before the town in the valley below stood tall pine trees that grew for eons of time, with the sound of the rushing Tye River beyond.

The town of Wellington wasn't much to look at—with its assorted rustic cabins, bunkhouses, a hotel, saloon, general store, and depot—but it served its purpose as a railway stop for trains passing through the Cascade Tunnel or entering it. When time allowed, Griffin would explore the amazing tunnel carved through the mountain that replaced the series of railroad switchbacks around the Windy Mountains where locomotives painstakingly pulled trains up and around. It had all happened before Griffin's arrival here, but he'd heard the stories from the older folks how the tunnel became a blessing and at times an extreme hazard. Even when he did go, Griffin did not stay long exploring the tunnel's damp and dark innards after hearing stories of men dying from the bad air. Electric lines now powered the electric locomotives to push the passenger and mail trains through the tunnel and avoid the deadly gasses from the coal burners. How mankind could come up with such amazing achievements like blasting tunnels through mountains and powering locomotives with electricity fascinated Griffin. And made him jealous that he had no schooling.

"Hey, I got the newspaper from Seattle," exclaimed a young men named Jack McClintock, waving the paper. "Want me to read you the front page?"

Oliver looked over at Griffin, catlike with narrowed eyes and a toothless grin on his rough and prickly face. "Naw. Let Griff read it."

"But he—" Jack began.

Oliver held up his hand to silence the young bunkmate and demanded to see the paper. He then flung it into Griffin's startled hands. "C'mon, Griff. Out with it. We wanna hear the latest news."

Griffin looked at the picture on the front page, recognizing the strange contraption called an airplane that could grace the skies like a bird. Jack once explained it to him, though Griffin did not understand the complexity of the invention or how man could conceive such an idea. He now rattled the paper and began reciting. "Another great thing occurred this day when men took to the skies like birds and flew an airplane high up in the clouds—"

Oliver ripped the paper out of his hands.

"Hey, that's my paper you tore," Jack protested.

"You ain't reading it. You can't, can you?"

Griffin said nothing as he swiped up his cap and made for the door.

Oliver stepped in front of him, blocking his exit. "You know nothing. This is about Orville Wright setting a new record in an airplane over Germany."

Griffin returned the stare unflinchingly, rising to a challenge he knew he could not win in the face of Oliver and his cronies. He brushed by the man and made for the door and freedom. By working hard he could numb the malice of others, who (in his opinion) were as dark and dirty as the lumps of coal they threw in his bed and on his possessions.

A whistle pierced the air, announcing an approaching train. Griffin watched through pinched eyes as the large electric locomotive pulled up, wheels screeching on the tracks. The engineer's head poked out the window and waved. Griffin waved back, recognizing the fellow who often ran the fast mail train that passed through several times a day, delivering large quantities of mail to Seattle. Griffin saw his friend Joe Walters struggling to slide open the heavy door to the mail car. Griffin went over and reached up to give him a helping hand. His other friend on the train, Matt Weiss, the train fireman, worked the coal burners that would now take over the task of pulling the mail cars to their destinations. A sharp odor of coal smoke stung his nostrils, signaling Matt's effort.

"Everything is being stubborn today," Joe Walters complained.

"I told you this car needs a refit," Griffin said. Joe unhooked two bags of mail to toss to Griffin, who would take them to the post office. Griffin transferred a modest bag of mail that Joe promptly stored away.

Matt Weiss now called down a greeting from the open door. "Hey, Griff! Only a few more months and I can buy Dorothy that ring." A grin lit his face streaked with coal dust. "And a good thing too."

"You've been saving a long time for that," Griffin said.

"I can't wait." He took off his hat and scratched his head of dark hair that matched his dirty face from stoking the coal burner.

"I told Dorothy once we get hitched, I'd find another line of work."

"The railroad is good work."

"Yeah, but it's long hours and too much time away from home. Dorothy don't like the train here in the mountains neither. She says it's dangerous. Especially with the winters."

Griffin couldn't argue with that. Winter came early to the Cascades, with the first flakes of snow often seen in September. Once the snows hit, the rotary snowplows had all they could do to keep the tracks open for the trains. But it proved a necessity as the delivery of the fast mail train could not be hampered by weather excuses. "Mail plus time equals money," the bosses said. If the Great Northern Railway couldn't deliver in a timely manner, they would be fined or the contract renegotiated. The potential loss of revenue made the big bosses of the GNR nervous and demanding.

Griffin glanced upward into the crystal-clear blue sky and, except for a wind, could not imagine a finer fall day. "I know winters can get rough," he admitted. He'd worked here in Wellington five years now, and every year the snows reached the windows of the Bailets Hotel. "We do the best we can and let the good Lord do the rest."

"Someone said you had gotten religion, Griffin," Joe remarked, jumping down from the car onto the black ground of coal fragments and sparkling stones reflecting the morning sun.

"I got Jesus, if that's what you mean. Right here." He patted his worn coat over his huge chest.

Joe kicked up the stones. "You know they say it's just a crutch. A man ain't worth his weight if he can't do it on his own. He's got to be able to survive, you know."

"Can't make it without God," Griffin murmured, thinking back to the goings-on in the bunkhouse that morning and realizing how true that statement was, more now than ever. When he felt the world piled on him, he sensed God's peace. It's all he had when the storms came in with a vengeance, both on this mountain and in the scorn of others. Like today.

Matt listened in on the conversation from the train. "My ma

would agree. She made me go to one of those old-time revivals. The ones they have in the woods of Tennessee. I wonder sometimes if I should settle back East, but Dorothy wouldn't have it, being from Seattle and all."

Griffin had visited the city of Seattle a few times, thinking on its position there fronting Elliott Bay. He thought the bustle of the city would provide the antidote for a tedious life on the railway but found it overwhelming in its sounds, the boisterous populace, the smoke, and the filth. He liked seeing the snow-covered peak called Rainier on the horizon, the majestic sight strengthening his resolve to remain in the Cascades and the isolated town of Wellington clinging to the shoulder of Windy Mountain.

Matt continued. "I miss the woods of Tennessee. Here it's difficult. Snow and cold and being all alone. I don't know how you've stayed here as long as you have."

Griffin wondered what drew him specifically to Wellington. Every time he went on errands to Leavenworth or Skykomish or even Scenic, he always felt that Wellington was his home. And with such a decision, he knew finding a good woman to live a life of isolation with would never happen. So living this isolated life might be a fleeting venture after all.

"I'm gonna get me a quick shot of whiskey at the saloon before we skedaddle off," Joe said. "What about you, Matt?"

"Have to keep an eye on the burners."

"Griff?"

Griffin shook his head and told the young man he needed to handle the mail. Griffin heaved the bags and walked the wooden walkway down a ways and up the hill to the tiny town post office. When he arrived, Mrs. Bailets was checking on the mailboxes and tidying up. He marveled how the woman could help her husband oversee the major establishments of town in the hotel, store, and post office and still keep her wits about her. Somehow she did, and he told her so.

"I don't know how I do it either," she agreed in a haggard voice, repinning a bit of dark hair sprinkled with gray back into the knot behind her head. She huffed when he brought in the two bags. "I'll swear on the family Bible that mail is for Scenic."

Griffin looked at the sack in each hand, unsure of what to say.

"Do you really think Wellington is big enough to have two sacks of mail? That's more than I have in a month. Maybe two. Only around a hundred of us live here, you know. Scenic is a much bigger town."

"I don't know, Mrs. Bailets. I just deliver it."

"I'll prove it right now. Open up that bag." She placed her hands on her hips.

Griffin picked up a bag and did so, his thick fingers clumsy and awkward as he untied it. He took out a few letters and gave them to her, only to see her normally somber gray eyes ignite as if a flame had been kindled. "You see? These are for the hotel there in Scenic. Read the addresses for yourself."

Griffin's blackened fingers took an envelope and stared at the writing that made no sense. "I'm sure it is," he told Mrs. Bailets. He felt certain she knew he couldn't read a word but in her consternation had forgotten.

"My land." Her hand flew to her mouth. "I'm sorry, Griffin. I forgot you can't read."

"It's no bother, ma'am."

"Anyway, you'd better get that mail back quick. The mail train's about to leave."

Griffin obliged, taking the sacks of mail and hurrying back down the stairs and walking the tracks to the depot. Up ahead he spied several workers waving their arms at him, shouting for him to get off the tracks. He yelled back about the mail, but they shouted again and pointed to the third track. Griffin obliged, accessing the wooden walkway as the mail train blew the whistle. It took a moment for him to realize the bags he possessed needed to be on the train. He waved his arms, hoping Joe or Matt would see him.

"What in tarnation are you doing, Griff?" Beau Crawford yelled.

Griffin could barely draw a breath. "Mrs. Bailets said these aren't our mailbags. These need to be on the train." He finished the sentence just as the train tooted and left to wind its way around the mountains to Windy Point and eventually Scenic.

"Too late now. You better hope nothing important is in there. Take 'em to the depot so it can go on the next train."

Griffin nodded reluctantly and headed for the depot when several fellows from the bunkhouse, led by Oliver and with grins plastered on their faces, walked out to confront him. "So you took the bags down to Mrs. Bailets, and they were the wrong ones," Oliver said with a sneer. He threw back his head and laughed. "What did I tell you, boys?"

Griffin felt the tension in his arms. "They were taken off the train by the mail clerk. I only hauled 'em down there."

Oliver stepped up to him, too close for comfort. "Did you check to see if they were for Wellington?"

Griffin blinked, ready to respond, when Oliver cut him off.

"You couldn't because you don't even know what the letter W is. And you don't think."

Griffin fought to relax his fist. How he wanted to land one right in the man's jeering face. In all their faces. It wasn't the first time he'd imagined it either. Maybe they could do a contest where he would challenge the wretch of a man to a fistfight and let the swings fall where they may. Perhaps netting two black eyes and a broken tooth on that sneering face would bring momentary satisfaction.

"You oughta hightail it down Old Glory and get those bags to Scenic."

Griffin winced as the man mentioned the treacherous walk over steep terrain to the main station in the town of Scenic.

Turn the other cheek.

I can't. I'm tired of it, he argued to himself.

Out of the corner of his eye, Griffin saw Mrs. Bailets marching up alongside the tracks, not caring in the least that her skirt dragged in the mud. The men watched her approach and began to disperse. How he disliked her having to run to the rescue yet again.

One day he would be the avenger and the rescuer to boot. And it would taste sweet.

"The mail needs to be stored safely at the post office, Griffin," she told him, pointing to the bags. "The rest of you men can go about your business. This is none of your concern." She stood there with her hands on her hips, staring, until Oliver moseyed off.

"You don't have to help me," Griffin mumbled.

"I'm helping the mail delivery. And I don't know a living soul on earth that doesn't need help. We have to help each other. It's how we survive in this place." She winked. "And there's another reason I'm here. Mr. Bailets needs help in the hotel storeroom once you're done. If you don't mind."

Griffin knew she was keeping him out of sight of his enemies once again. But it was only temporary. Darkness would fall with the townspeople shuffling off to their respective homes and bunk rooms. And Oliver would be in the bunk room along with his buddies, armed with plenty of ridicule to go around.

He turned to follow her to the huge establishment sitting on a hillside that catered to travelers when the whistle blew with the arrival of the passenger train from Seattle. From his vantage point he watched two passengers alight from the first-class coach, one of them a fine woman in a stylish coat with gleaming buttons, wearing a fancy hat three times the size of her head. She appeared like one would imagine of a woman in high society: perfectly spotless, bright, and well proportioned, a jewel among the disheveled workers and a dirty rail town framed by the blackened poles of dead trees flanking Windy Mountain.

The fancy woman now headed in his direction. His knees became weak. Thankfully, Mrs. Bailets stood within earshot. "Good day," the visitor said. "I'm here to visit my cousin Elizabeth Hanks. Do you know her?"

Griffin found himself tongue-tied. He'd always kept to himself when passengers came and went in town. Now to find a beautiful woman addressing him, he had no idea what to say. Though he would like to welcome her to their town, at least.

"Welcome to Wellington, miss. I'm Mrs. Bailets."

"Lillian Hartwick. I am inquiring about my cousin, Elizabeth Hanks."

"We know the Hankses well. They live in the cabin there just down the road. Number 103. Her husband Clyde is off to Leavenworth, I believe, inspecting a new rotary snowplow."

"Thank you." Lillian cast a longer glance at Griffin as if expecting him to offer a pleasant greeting also.

He swiped off his cap and cleared his throat. "Excuse me and welcome, ma'am."

She nodded with a slight grin, then turned to make her way down the dirt road, carrying a carpetbag in hand.

"Whatever is a classy lady like her doing in Wellington?" Mrs. Bailets murmured. "I give her three days in this place before she catches the Seattle Express out of here. Mark my words." The pronouncement ended with a short chortle, and Mrs. Bailets lifted her skirt to mount the stairs of the hotel. Griffin considered the pretty woman quickly disappearing among the dark and dreary buildings of Wellington. Despite what Mrs. Bailets said, inwardly he hoped she would stay a good long while.

Chapter 4

⁓

Lillian inhaled a deep breath with her first step off the train into what seemed like a forbidden place. During the ride, she'd wrestled with her decision to come and wished Mother hadn't been so keen on it. The only thing that gave her confidence in her decision was the telegram from Cousin Elizabeth that pounced on the idea of a visit from family, along with her heartfelt plea: *Come when able!* Lillian wondered about the urgency concealed in those words and if she was up to the task. She knew nothing about caring for an expectant mother or a new baby. She also knew nothing about living in this isolated part of the state, where one might as well be on some distant isle in the vast ocean, as she once read in a book.

Hearing the conductor yell *Wellington!* Lillian had gazed out the window at a mountainside of tall, lifeless black poles and assorted rough buildings barely clinging to a ledge above a steep ravine. Tightening the grip on her satchel, she cautiously approached the door, knowing she could easily find her way back to Everett on a return train if she so chose. And then she would be a stranger at Anthony's bequest in the loud city of San Francisco. At least here, surrounded by the beauty of the mountains and in a town that appeared but a dust speck compared to other metropolises, she could hide away for a time.

Lillian stepped down the narrow metal steps with the conductor standing nearby to help. She sensed folks in the town giving her the once-over before going on with their tasks. She inhaled a deep breath, wondering where to find Elizabeth. Just then she caught sight of an older woman standing beside what might be her son, tall and broad-shouldered, taller than any man she could recollect seeing in Everett. Immediately, she went over and inquired about the Hankses' home.

Having received the information on its location, Lillian gazed once more at the massive man, thinking how he must duck in every doorway he came to, before turning about and walking carefully down the slick wooden walkway in the direction pointed out by this Mrs. Bailets. *Dear Lord, I'm not one for much praying, but help me find my cousin.* She spied several other railway men outfitted in dirty trousers and filthy coats and like the gangly man at Mrs. Bailets' side, offered her a greeting by removing their caps. She could imagine the look of downright dismay on Anthony's face with her living in the wilderness among these people, mud soaking the bottom of her skirt, her once gleaming ankle boots caked in black mud and animal droppings. This was a life of hardship—one she never thought she would experience outside her sheltered existence in Everett. She inhaled a deep breath. Too late to turn back now. Her cousin was expecting her.

Lillian came to the edge of town to see the train track disappear around a bend, as well as any buildings. She turned back and suddenly saw him again, coming down the muddy path. The giant. Had he followed her from the depot? The thought disturbed her, and her fingers tightened around the handle of the satchel.

Again he removed his cap. "Excuse me, Miss, but I was wondering if you need help finding the Hanks home. I saw you walk away from the town here, and there's nothing but the tunnel. And

I have your trunk. Left it back there."

Lillian inhaled a sharp breath. How she wanted to tell him she had everything under control and was merely curious about the surroundings. Instead she felt chilled, and her feet ached from wandering around in muddy shoes. "Thank you. Glad you came." They began walking back toward town, but he kept a respectful distance.

"If you were to keep going, you'd reach the Cascade Tunnel."

"My goodness. There's not much here to the town, is there?"

"Only about a hundred of us live here. We help the trains coming up and over the pass. There's the hotel, the post office and store, the depot, the telegraph office, buildings for the rail workers. . ."

"My cousin's husband works for the railroad. Clyde Hanks."

The giant nodded. "I know him. He helps mostly with the snowplow." He stopped before her leather trunk and hefted it up. Above them stood a ramshackle place with a sagging front porch, not much bigger than the gardener's shed back home, clinging to a precarious perch on the side of the mountain. "This is it."

Lillian stared at the shack, trying hard not to allow her emotions to betray what she felt on the inside—that she might have made a mistake coming here to a place she knew nothing about. And then her feelings escaped. "Rather small, isn't it?"

"No room to build on the side of a mountain." He placed the trunk on the porch. "Hope you have a nice visit. If you need anything, just send for me. The Hankses here know me."

"Thank you again." Lillian waited for the giant to move off before knocking on the door. It swung open, and an expectant woman appeared.

"Oh my! Lillian?"

"Yes, yes, it is."

"The train must have been early. Which almost never happens. Please, please come in."

The world of a mountain town became swallowed up by a tiny home of a sitting room with a small settee and several chairs, a tiny kitchen with a small cookstove, and two bedrooms. "I won't get lost here," Lillian quipped.

Elizabeth stared, not quite understanding, before her eyes widened. "I'm so used to this life, I don't even think of how small it is. Why, you must live in a castle!"

"No, not quite. But it is larger."

"I haven't been to Everett in so long. I should really return for a visit. But I won't go anywhere until summertime."

Lillian removed her gaze from the compact surroundings to watch her cousin toddle over to one of the straight-back chairs, supporting her lower back with one hand and easing herself into it. She appeared large under the blouse tied with a ribbon at her throat, overlaying a long skirt, looking quite ready to give birth. "Once it snows here, there's no place to go anyway," she continued. "Clyde is busy all winter with the snowplow to clear the tracks. They call him to go everywhere. It gets very lonely here."

"You sound very much like my friend Berenice. Her husband works for the railroad. In fact, he's one of the big bosses from what she told me. James O'Neill."

At this Elizabeth straightened. "Oh my goodness! You know Superintendent O'Neill?"

"I suppose that's who it is. His wife and I are good friends. I just visited Berenice a few weeks ago, and—"

"He is the boss for the Cascade Rail Division of the railroad." Elizabeth looked frantically about the tiny room, then stood and began rearranging a few books tossed on a table. "So sorry for the mess."

"Is something wrong?"

"Your mother said nothing about it. I mean. . ." She paused. "You knowing the big boss and all. Maybe you would rather stay at a nicer room at the hotel. Or Scenic would be much better."

Oh dear. Now she thinks I'm a prude. That her household is not good enough for me. The mere thought made her uncomfortable. Of course she didn't want others to think they were beneath her just because she knew the O'Neills. "Elizabeth, I'm here to visit with you and assist in any way that I can. As long as you have a place for me, I'd rather stay."

"Your room is not much. Just a bed and table and lamp and..." She hesitated. "There are no maids here. I could see if one of the neighbors..."

"I will be fine." Lillian sighed, wishing Elizabeth would not look on her as some kind of honored guest. She was here to help after all, to fill the lonely days with chatter and projects, of which she mentioned the ideas to Elizabeth.

"Oh yes, there's a great deal to do. I want to make baby clothes. Put away food. And make some candles for the long winter nights."

"Make candles?" Lillian blinked, thinking of days gone by when all this was common practice on the frontier. But this was 1909 after all.

"They are good to have along with oil lamps. Too much wind and snow to rely on electric lamps. One never knows when supplies will become scarce or the lines will go down."

Lillian considered what a sheltered existence she lived in Everett and how much life differed here. And suddenly she saw the visit turning into lessons in housekeeping and motherhood. To prepare her for Anthony, perhaps? Or maybe to teach resilience in difficult circumstances. She inhaled a deep breath, twisting her fingers in her lap, praying she was ready for whatever life dealt her.

"Let's have a cup of tea," Elizabeth suggested, and with that comforting thought, Lillian's worry began to dissipate. Her cousin waddled into the tiny kitchen and peered out the back door to the large rain barrel as Lillian followed. "I washed clothes the other day. My, there isn't much water."

"Where can we get some?"

"Down at the water tank. There's a spring. If you see Griffin around, he can deliver some water."

"Griffin?"

"The man who accompanied you here."

Lillian recalled the man who kept her from disappearing into a tunnel when she walked beyond the town boundary, and the one who carried her trunk. He'd mentioned a willingness to help. Immediately, she went and found her wrap. "I'll go and find him."

"Lillian, you are a darling. I can see now how helpful you will be. Thank you for coming here. I know it was a big sacrifice."

Lillian smiled and stepped out into the blustery day filled with the sights and sounds of an active rail town. Glancing down the tracks, she noticed the water tank and made her way toward it. To her relief, she also spotted this Griffin who towered over everyone, his arms ladened with heavy boxes. He paused when he saw her, and his dry lips turned up on his rugged face that was covered in beard stubble. The face then contorted to one of concern as he placed the burdens down. "Are you all right, Miss? Do you need help?"

"I'm sorry to bother you, but my cousin Elizabeth Hanks is out of water and. . ."

"I can help once I deliver this to the depot." He thought for a moment then shrugged. "These boxes can wait. A mother needs water."

Lillian liked the concern in his voice and the endearing word *mother* that brought visions of cradling an infant, soothing a raging fever with a cool cloth, or offering words of wisdom to a wandering heart. She realized she must send Mother a telegram and tell her she arrived safely.

Lillian looked on as Griffin found several metal buckets and filled them from a large tank. He worked quietly, glancing around at times as if drawing strength from the mountains surrounding them before filling another bucket. Thankfully he did not inquire of her business but only set his sights on the task before him. She couldn't help wondering what kind of life he led here in a mountainous wilderness, far removed from civilization and from comfort. And why he stayed.

Suddenly a voice shouted down the tracks. "Hey, Good-for-nothin'! We need those boxes."

Lillian's hand flew to her mouth as she watched Griffin's face redden. A man with a balding head strode up, only to stop abruptly before her. "Why, excuse me, ma'am. Is this man bothering you?"

"No, of course not. I asked him to fetch some water for Elizabeth Hanks, my cousin."

"Well, I'll gladly bring it to you." The man glared at Griffin "You go on and get those boxes to the depot on the double. Can't do nothin' right, can you?"

Lillian watched the evolving exchange, realizing well the animosity, especially from the smaller but stout man with the balding head addressing the giant. And now there might be a fistfight happening right before her eyes on her first day in Wellington. She inhaled. "He won't take much time to deliver water, and we need it," she said, nodding toward Griffin.

"He's got plenty of other work to do, ma'am," claimed the balding man. "He has errands to run."

"I'm sure. But he was quite courteous when I arrived. It shouldn't take long to deliver some needed water. I could use his strength for these tasks. Unless helping each other—and especially my cousin who's expecting a baby—is not a common activity in Wellington?"

The man stared, first at her then with a fixed glare at Griffin, before moving off, grumbling to himself.

Griffin turned away and busied himself with toting the buckets in a cart.

"I hope you won't get in trouble for delivering the water. I just didn't appreciate what that man said about you. It was rather cruel."

He shrugged and said nothing, only pulled the cart along the muddy path toward Elizabeth's house. She marveled at his strength as he hefted the load up the steep hillside to her cousin's home. "You must do this a great deal."

"It's from carrying mail bags and boxes, ma'am." He then lifted his cap. "What's next? You told Oliver you needed more help."

"That was just a ruse to get him to leave. But maybe you can tell me why you two don't get along?"

Griffin twisted his cap in his hands. "I'm not smart like most here. My father was called an idiot as a youngster, and I suppose I am too."

His words jolted her. "That's nonsense. You are most certainly *not* an idiot!"

"Miss, if you only knew that I can't—"

"I don't care. People can be cruel, and I do not intend to have it around me. No thank you."

"Yes, ma'am. Thank you, ma'am." He nodded once more, tugged the cap back on his head, and turned to leave.

"Please. What is your name again? I'm Lillian Hartwick."

He turned back, slightly startled. "Griffin Jones."

"Thank you again for your help, Mr. Jones." She watched him lumber down the hillside and to the water tank where he had left the boxes. She couldn't recall meeting someone of his stature before. Of course she had heard of different sized people, from dwarfs to giants. Maybe that's why the man called Oliver had no respect for him. He thought Griffin a clumsy performer for others' amusement and not a person of worth.

Elizabeth joined her at the doorway. "Griffin is very giving and helpful. But the men here in Wellington hate him."

"Why? One man nearly tried to start a fight with him. Someone named Oliver."

"Probably because he was helping a pretty lady."

Lillian gave her cousin a sideways glance and couldn't help but drop her head.

"I'm not sure," Elizabeth continued. "Clyde says that Griffin is slow."

"Of course he is. Look how big he is."

"No, in other ways."

Lillian shook her head. "That's a poor excuse for heaping insults. Something needs to change in people's hearts."

Elizabeth laughed. "If you think you can change people's ways, you may find that harder than you think."

Lillian shut the door more loudly than she would have liked. "I won't have folks acting like schoolchildren. Mocking others for their size is child's play."

Just then Elizabeth's hand went to her belly, and she laughed. "The baby agrees. I felt a kick."

Lillian couldn't help but giggle before scooping water out of the barrel for their belated tea. In the distance, Griffin balanced the stack of boxes. For some reason, a prayer for safety filled her lips, not only for him but also for herself.

Chapter 5

NOVEMBER 1909

"You're just like her. You won't amount to a thing."

The man's fist raised before his wide eyes. Every part of him trembled, even his feet clad in cracked shoes held together with rag strips and his lanky arms covered by a ripped jacket to ward off the cold. He turned his face away and shut his eyes, expecting the clenched fist to fall. Instead, the man muttered something unintelligible and groped for the half-full bottle of whiskey. It wouldn't be long before the man emptied it.

Griffin flopped over on his left side to try to catch a few more winks, trying to forget the dream of childhood that mirrored the dark night. How he wanted to escape the roughness of a rail town and start elsewhere. Life for him began on the railway with his father, a fireman on the train, shoveling coal in Leavenworth until Griffin left town and found himself in Wellington. In Leavenworth, Mama worked long hours sewing dresses for the rich women. But like many railway workers, the monotony of it, mixed with boredom, led to drinking and carousing. Griffin recalled his father bringing home some young, giggly thing while Mama worked in the back room of a store with mannequins outfitted in her handiwork, sewing long hours for meager pay. Papa warned Griffin not to say a word about the woman with stringy hair that shared in the bottle of whiskey before they disappeared. When Mama came home, boasting pale skin and dark circles under her eyes yet asking about his day, Griffin couldn't help but blab about the female visitor. She said nothing, as if she expected to hear such depravity, and went to boil the evening potatoes.

One night, despite her fatigue, Mama sat him on her lap even though he was a large squirt for nine years of age. "Promise me, Griffin. No drinking. No rough play or fistfights. Always respect a lady. And trust in the good Lord for everything. The Lord is all that matters, you know. His kingdom." She then reached over and showed him a Bible with torn covers. "You need to learn to read the words here. I don't know a heap myself, but enough. Psalm 23 is my favorite. 'The Lord is my shepherd; I shall not want.' When you got Him leading you, you don't need nothing else."

Griffin murmured these words of scripture often when life felt confusing. Some fifteen years later, he still could not read the words of the Good Book as Mama wanted, but he did know a little of Psalm 23. It gave him a measure of peace even this night, despite the memories that tried to rob him of it.

For some reason, his thoughts turned to the fair Lillian. A month had passed since her arrival, and with her cousin's pending due date with her baby, things were busy for the fair-skinned, brown-haired woman. Not that he should even think of giving her a once-over with Wellington crowded by railmen who all liked seeing and talking to the beauty that had arrived to their tiny town. Thankfully, she kept to herself, occasionally walking about to enjoy some fresh air and sunshine when the sun's golden rays chose to make an infrequent appearance. In Wellington, everyone was readying for another busy snow season that came with life under the rugged eye of Windy Mountain. They moved quickly to finish preparations to hunker down for the season.

Griffin realized after an hour of contemplation that sleep would not be his friend, and he stood to his feet, despite it still being dark. He heard the wind howling and glanced out the frosted windows to see swirls of white. Winter had begun with a vengeance. He wondered if Lillian was ready for life in a frozen world, unlike coastal towns such as Everett that saw mostly rain. For someone new like her, a Cascade Mountain winter could come as a stark surprise.

With the arrival of the snow season, Griffin would be called on to do a variety of other tasks, chief of which was to keep the rail lines clear for the fast mail train—the Great Northern Railway's bread and butter when it came to monetary contracts. He would be tasked with shoveling or helping with the rotary snowplow or other jobs. No one would complain either about his supposed mental slowness when it came to needing strength. The lines must be kept clear so businesses flourished, and with it, the flow of money, no matter what fell from the sky.

Several of the men in the bunkhouse stirred, and the young man Jack McClintock rolled off his bunk to take a look out the window. "It's here," he murmured with a huge yawn.

"Can't keep winter away from these mountains for long," Griffin said.

"Don't you wish you could go somewhere else?" Jack wondered. "Somewhere warm? I keep telling myself I ain't gonna spend another winter in this place."

"Where would you go?"

"Some island out in the ocean there. I've seen the pictures. Big tall palm trees. Coconuts. I've never tasted coconut. Have you?"

Griffin chuckled. "No."

"Every year I think I should go. It's dangerous here anyway."

"No more dangerous than any other town. At least this town is small. Haven't seen a fight in the saloon in a while."

Jack shook his head. "It's dangerous in other ways, let me tell you."

Griffin wondered what he meant as the man sauntered off. Did he mean the winters here? Griffin hastily slipped on thick, oil-coated pants and a wide leather belt. Others had begun to stir. Several cursed when they saw the snow, knowing full well what it meant. Once snow arrived in the Cascades, it was here to stay. Many months would pass before it melted and the greenery of springtime took its place. Meanwhile they would contend with meeting train schedules amid snow piles, snow slides, and other problems.

"So, did you ask your God for a good snow?" Oliver said with a snort.

Griffin ignored him to shrug on a warm shirt and an overcoat. One of the other men had begun frying bacon on the potbelly stove. Griffin only wanted to leave this place before things stirred as they did most mornings. If Oliver couldn't get in his daily ridicule, it was like his very breath was stolen. But Griffin refused to give him the chance today.

When he stepped outside, the wind bit through his clothing, though the swirling snow seemed peaceful enough. Only eight inches had fallen so far, and not much would need to be done on the rail line yet. But he grabbed a shovel anyway and began clearing a path on the wooden boardwalk to some of the buildings under the brightening skies of a new dawn. He glanced down the row of houses to where Lillian lived and caught a lamp in the window and a shadowy figure. He wondered what she thought of Wellington's first big snowstorm of the season, with many more to come. He shifted the shovel to the other shoulder and ventured to the house to scrape off the snow on the wooden boardwalk and the stairs. Not that his shoveling would do much with plenty more snow to take its place, but it was a start.

The door burst opened, and the man of the house, Clyde Hanks, came out. "No sense shoveling here, Griff. Plenty more will fall, I'm sure."

Griffin shrugged. "Gets me warmed up for all the shovel-ing to come."

"You'll be shoveling in your sleep 'fore long," he said with a chor-tle. "Just as well. My missus only has a few weeks until she delivers.

Probably a good idea to stay ahead of it all. Surely by noontime Mr. O'Neill will call out the plow, and then I'm gone."

"Your wife feeling all right?"

He shrugged. "As well as can be expected. Big and clumsy, she says. Glad we have her cousin here."

At this, Griffin looked beyond the man's frame, hoping to catch a glimpse of Lillian.

"Bet you smell the coffee, eh? Want some to warm you up?"

Griffin glanced at the shovel and back toward the eating bunkhouse where he normally ate his meals. A nice home felt inviting on this cold, snowy day. "That would be fine, thank you." He didn't add that the measure of warmth at seeing Lillian's pretty features would do an even better job than the hot coffee. Instead, he wiped the snow off his jacket and stomped his boots before entering the tiny place. He heard female voices coming from the kitchen and smelled the coffee mixed with the aroma of cooking. Shadowy figures passed each other until Lillian appeared with a platter.

"Oh my goodness. I didn't know we had company."

"Found Griff here in a snowbank," Clyde said with a laugh. "Actually, he was clearing a path to our place. Probably a good idea."

"It's November," Elizabeth said with a grimace, gently lowering herself into a chair, her hands clasped over her ever-enlarging belly. "At least Christmas is coming."

"And so's Clyde Junior," her husband said with a laugh.

"Or Miss Rose," she added with a smile, then turned to Griffin. "Clyde's got it in his head we're having a son."

Griffin said nothing except to mouth the words *thank you* to a quiet Lillian who served him a plate of thick flapjacks drowning in syrup. Out of the corner of his eye, he watched her bustle about, noting that after just a few short weeks, she knew her way around the kitchen. The flapjacks were excellent, made with a sourdough starter that rivaled anything the cook at the bunkhouse or even the hotel could muster. When the gracious Lillian floated back into the tiny sitting room to take a seat with her own plate of flapjacks,

Griffin commented on the food. She looked very small this day, despite sitting perfectly straight, her back never touching the chair, maintaining an air of dignity as only a lady of means would.

"Elizabeth made these," Lillian confessed, her gaze focused on her plate. "I burnt the first few I tried to make."

"It will come with time," Elizabeth reassured her. "Trying to cook on a small cookstove with unpredictable heat is difficult."

"I've never done any cooking at my house. I'm not sure how much help I will be."

Griffin could see the tense lines crisscrossing her face and her lower lip taking on a slight tremble as if the culinary difficulty weighed heavy on her. "We all have to start somewhere," he offered. "You don't have a better teacher here than Mrs. Hanks. And I'm sure they're glad to have you here." He couldn't help his eagerness to silence the sadness enshrouding her and find that confident woman once again.

Lillian shrugged. "I feel like I'm more of a burden than anything useful. There is so much to running a house. I never gave it a thought until now. We have a maid in Everett, of course, and she does most everything." She paused suddenly and then lapsed into silence. After eating a few bites, she quickly stood and took everyone's finished plate.

Elizabeth shook her head when Lillian disappeared. "I'm not sure what's ailing her these days. Maybe the baby coming makes her nervous. Dr. Stockwell comes to town today to check on me."

"This is a very different life than city life," Griffin said. "And now we have snow."

"Maybe she misses her family. It's only a few weeks until Christmas. I hope she can find some contentment. I do need her. It's so lonely around here."

Griffin swallowed the rest of the coffee while pondering how one brings contentment and confidence to a young lady used to city life. He would ask the good Lord for an idea. He stood then, thanked them for the fine meal, and returned to tackle the town walkway with his shovel while considering Lillian's somberness.

He watched Mrs. Bailets making her way through snow toward the tiny post office perched on a hillside. The folds of her skirt gathered up fluffy white snowflakes as she walked. He pushed ahead to clear the path with the shovel. When they both arrived at the porch to the post office, he removed his hat. "Morning, Mrs. Bailets."

"Well, good morning to you. And thank you for clearing away the snow." She paused. "I see you were visiting the Hankses." A wry smile formed on her face. "And how is Miss Hartwick?"

"Sad. She thinks she doesn't belong here."

"Humph. I said as much. A soon as the New Year comes and Elizabeth delivers, that young thing will be on the train heading back to Seattle."

"Unless you've got a suggestion that might keep her here."

She pointed her face upward in annoyance. "Young man, what do I care about a woman pining away for her life back home? I have more to deal with here than I can handle. The store is becoming the death of me. Always does during the holidays. The post office is getting busy. And then there's the train passengers who want food and trinkets. And others who want to celebrate or cause a ruckus at the saloon."

"I was thinking. Maybe Miss Hartwick could lend a helping hand. Like watching over the post office here so you can do other things?"

Mrs. Bailets now centered her gaze on him. "You just told me she wants to leave."

"She needs to meet others rather than staying at home all the time. The post office is just the ticket. You're a good teacher. You could show her how to help sort mail, that kind of thing. That should be easy. Better than trying to learn to fry flapjacks, I'd say."

An eyebrow raised on her scowling face. "I'm not certain what you mean by that. But I must admit, an assistant at the post office does sound quite appealing. Then I can spend more time with the store and the hotel. The ordering of supplies is a mess, and if I don't get it sorted out, I'm not sure we'll have what we need. Especially if we end up having a hard winter."

"I can ask Miss Hartwick if she'd be interested."

Mrs. Bailets held out her hand. "I'm concerned though. Elizabeth's about to give birth. That young thing will be busy enough without taking on more."

"Maybe a few days a week then. Something to get her mind off of things. It can get boring here mighty quick."

Mrs. Bailets chuckled. "I have a feeling that with you around, Griffin, she won't have time to be bored. Go ahead and ask her. Even two days a week would help me get out from under the clutter. Make sure Elizabeth doesn't mind, though. I don't want to take away from her helping when the baby arrives."

Griffin removed his cap, sending snowy clumps falling to the ground. Mrs. Bailets snickered before entering the tiny post office. He wanted to rush right back and ask Miss Hartwick outright but decided to wait for the doctor visit to make certain everything was all right. Instead he went down to the depot to assist with the shoveling. He rehearsed what he would say to Lillian just as soon as he got off work. He thought of her downcast face brightening and her cherry-red lips turning up into a smile at the thought of the job. They might even engage in meaningful conversation. And everything would be much better in this snowy world of Wellington. But a relentless storm could put a damper on things if the rotary snowplow saw its first major work of the season. That meant Elizabeth's husband, Clyde, would be gone, and Lillian might need to remain behind to help.

He stood for a moment to see clouds shielding Windy Mountain and the naked black tree trunks of burnt-out forests given a frosting-over of white to ease the damaged scene. Just then a whistle sounded, and the mail train made its usual appearance, with Joe Walters waving at Griffin from the engineer's position.

"No snow in Leavenworth," Joe called down from his perch. "But you always have it here."

Griffin saw the stack of boxes inside the railcar for the hotel. At least Mrs. Bailets did get some ordering of supplies accomplished, despite bemoaning her situation to him. In no time he had the supplies unloaded while Joe told him how he was looking forward to his relations coming to visit for Christmas. Griffin wished he had such a gift of a visit from family, but being an only child with both parents long gone and never learning of other relations in his life, he lived the life of an adult orphan. And the bleak memories of the dream last night rolled back into his thoughts like a stubborn ocean wave.

"Hope it's a fine visit," Griffin said to Joe, trying to think on better things. He turned then, and suddenly she was there, smartly dressed in a coat and hat—and tiny and demure compared to his hulking six-foot-five frame.

Lillian Hartwick.

He heaved a breath. The words he planned to speak became entangled in his throat. *Lord, help me.*

Chapter 6

Griffin Jones stood there gaping at her, despite the friendly encounter just a few hours ago over a plate of steaming flapjacks. Another man swiped off his cap and waved from the train window. "I'm Joe," he called down.

"Lillian Hartwick." She watched the man disappear inside the mail train with a wry grin plastered on his face. What had they been talking about? Why did it appear that everyone had secrets but her? And what secrets could be kept in a place like this anyway, populated by rough-and-tough railway men? Men from all kinds of backgrounds and sizes, including the working Griffin who now decided to slip off his cap in her presence as if taking a cue of politeness from his friend.

"Got something to ask you, Miss Hartwick." Griffin's voice came out in slow, deep syllables.

"Well, please be quick. I'm waiting for the Express train and that doctor. He was supposed to come by horse from Scenic, but the snow is preventing that. Elizabeth told me no one goes up or down Old Glory in the winter. Whatever that means."

Griffin nodded, and she realized he understood what her cousin meant. He then turned and pointed to the foggy mountains beyond. "Old Glory is a trail that leads down to Scenic, the next major rail town heading west. But it's very steep. Some have tried walking down it in the winter and didn't make it." He pointed his fingers sharply downward to show her the terrain, his mouth hanging open as if ready to explain. Instead, he asked if she had been to the town.

"I must have stopped there on my way here, but it made no impression. One town looks about the same as another, except I have to say this one has very little for the common traveler."

"Scenic has a nice hotel set back near the woods. And there's the hot springs."

"Hot springs?"

"Water that comes up from inside the ground. They say it cures different sicknesses."

Water that cures sickness? "How very interesting. I never knew such things existed. I should like to go visit sometime." With that statement, Griffin took a step forward and then just as quickly retreated. "Of course I would never consider such a walk like that now. But maybe I can take the train to Scenic, especially before we get buried by snow. Which I'm sure happens, being way up here in the mountains."

Griffin nodded and looked beyond the town. "Snow is everywhere—except, of course, inside the tunnel. They have electric lines in there with an electric locomotive to help push the trains through. Tunnels are dangerous anyway, even with burning a little coal to keep the trains warm. It puts out smoke that kills."

Her stomach tied into a knot. Her cousin had failed to tell her the dangers existing in a place like this. A hillside where one can fall to their death. A tunnel that can kill. "How awful. Are there any other dangers I should know about?"

He pointed to her laced-up shoes with good-size heels and soles not conducive to icy boardwalks. "Don't want you to fall wearing those and hurt yourself. Maybe get some boots. Mrs. Bailets probably has some around."

"I understand your meaning, Mr. Jones. Thank you for the advice." She turned away until his gravelly voice drew her back.

"If you pardon me, ma'am, I was meaning to ask you something. Mrs. Bailets is looking for an assistant to work at the post office. Even a few days a week would help and. . ."

What? A stranger asking her to consider employment? She cast him what she hoped was a look of shock. "Surely you must be joking." Lillian glanced away, straining to see through the cloud of falling snow, hoping the train bearing the doctor would come soon. Already the cold had begun seeping through her coat. Her toes felt numb. She knew Griffin continued to stare at her, even after his nonsense request, and that made her chills more pronounced. A lady never considered taking up a job like this. Perhaps he thought her less handy in the home as a companion for her cousin and only good for sorting envelopes. She opened her mouth to voice her irritation over his intrusion into her life when she saw this Mrs. Bailets hurrying down the boardwalk toward them. The woman paused midstep and gazed at Lillian with wide eyes and a smile.

"There you are! Wonderful! I was hoping to see you after Griffin told me you could assist a few days a week at the post office. I am so needed at the hotel right now that having someone keep watch on everything here and receiving and sorting the mail during this busy season would be a godsend."

Lillian gaped, looking first at the gratified woman and then at a sheepish Griffin, who averted his gaze. "Thank you, but. . ."

"Oh, and if you're concerned about your cousin, you can help, of course, when her time comes. The baby's not due for several weeks though, correct?"

Lillian nodded, and suddenly Mrs. Bailets was telling her to bring an apron and report tomorrow for work. When she flew off toward the hotel, Lillian had all she could do not to scold Griffin for interfering in her life. What would Mother think if she discovered her only daughter employed as a common laborer? Or Anthony Travers, for that matter? But she couldn't very well refuse the headmistress overseeing most of Wellington's commercial enterprises and potentially darkening her name in this tiny rail town. Maybe she could go tomorrow and see what the duties entailed. It might be nice to make a little money and buy a train fare to see the hot springs at Scenic.

She paused in mid thought. *What on earth am I thinking? Work in a post office?* And all because Griffin had put the strange idea in everyone's mind. She ought to tell him to leave her alone, that she was engaged to the president of a timber company for goodness' sake and it wasn't proper. Despite the rush of words that filled her mind and nearly gripped her vocal cords, she bit her lip. Griffin hurried off to engage in his own labors, as if sensing her quandary. But she had little choice. Mrs. Bailets expected her help, if Elizabeth agreed. And that was that.

———◆◆◆———

"You're looking just fine, Elizabeth." Dr. Stockwell then told a joke about a patient he swore would deliver a healthy baby boy but had triplets. "Any pains?"

"Just some back pain, Doctor. And I better not be having triplets!"

Stockwell laughed. "Not in your case. Looks like Clyde Junior may be making his presence by the due date. I think you have a few weeks yet. A first baby always takes his grand time coming into the world."

Her blue eyes flew open as she exchanged looks with Lillian. "You said Clyde Junior. You think it's a boy?"

"Could be, judging by the way you're carrying so high. But of course, the Lord knows."

She sighed. "Clyde would be so happy. Having a girl growing up in this town could be difficult."

Lillian wondered about that comment.

The doctor chuckled. "You all don't do so bad here. Mrs. Bailets commands quite a presence in this town. I'd say the ladies take charge more than anyone gives them praise for." He tucked the stethoscope back in his bag. "Do you know anything about birthing?" he redirected to Lillian.

Lillian stepped back. She could imagine the look of shock on her face as she felt her cheeks warm. She bit her lip to keep from laughing. "Me? Of course not."

He sighed. "Better make certain the midwife Mrs. Mallory will be on hand to help you, Elizabeth. Can't promise I'll be here when the time comes with the unpredictable weather and all. But I will do my best."

"Mrs. Mallory will do just fine," Elizabeth said. "Thank you for coming, Doctor."

Lillian was still caught up in the doctor's question about whether she knew birthing, along with Mrs. Bailets abruptly hiring her for the post office of which she had no earthly skill. What was it about her that made others think she possessed the skill for such tasks? Could it be the Divine at work? The reverend at church would say these tasks strengthened the fibers of faith. Though when he first said it, she and a few women exchanged glances, wondering what he meant. The reverend was clear that all God's people must work out their faith with fear and trembling. What more fear could there be than working beside Mrs. Bailets at the post office or helping Elizabeth's baby to be born?

"You're awfully quiet," Elizabeth observed, slowly rising from a chair, her hand supporting her back as she winced from the heavy load. "Is everything well?"

"Mrs. Bailets needs help at the post office with the seasonal mail." The words came out so fast, they surprised even her. "I—I told her you were soon due, and. . ."

"But not for several weeks. Do you want to do it?"

"Mrs. Bailets assumes I will, but I'm not sure. Mother would have a fit. It's not proper to be employed as a laborer. And I don't want to leave you. It's why I came here, after all. To help."

Elizabeth chuckled. "It sounds like you want to do it but are thinking of excuses not to. Go and make a little money for yourself. It would be a fine Christmas gift, better than anything I can give you."

Lillian had never felt the need to make money, especially not now on the verge of marrying a wealthy businessman. But she welcomed the thought of extra pocket change. And there were other things about working that could be beneficial to her stay. Like helping her get to know the people of Wellington. "Mrs. Bailets wants me to start tomorrow. It would only be a few days a week for a few hours."

Elizabeth smiled. "That's perfectly fine, Lillian. I'm sure we'll know when I'll need your help here. Please go if you wish."

And that was that. She had a job as a postal assistant, courtesy of Griffin. She didn't know whether to curse him or thank him for intervening in her life. Time would tell.

———◆◆———

Lillian tried to steady her nerves the morning of her first day of work. Never in her wildest dreams would she have imagined herself going off to work with one of Elizabeth's aprons tucked under one arm and a basket with a biscuit hanging off the other. But in a strange way, the opportunity gave her purpose. Since her arrival in October, she'd felt more akin to Elizabeth's lady's maid without any meaningful duties, save the talks with her cousin and running a few errands. Her homemaking skills left much to be desired, except the embroidery—of which she had already completed several projects to Elizabeth's delight, including a few dinner napkins that Elizabeth used the other day. Still she could not take command of the cooking and wondered how they would eat after Elizabeth's delivery.

For now she took a long drink of coffee, ate some bread with flavorful jam, and offered a quick farewell to Elizabeth.

"I pray it goes well," her cousin murmured as she gave her a kiss on the cheek.

Lillian prayed silently too. The other day she'd found Elizabeth reading her Bible and, after Elizabeth had left, picked up the book for the first time in what seemed like forever. The thin pages parted to Psalm 46.

God is our refuge and strength, a very present help in trouble. Therefore will not we fear, though the earth be removed, and though the mountains be carried into the midst of the sea.

Lillian couldn't imagine cleaving to a God she had never seen, let alone during great trial. How did one do such a thing? She'd been obedient in churchgoing, listening to the long-winded messages and the hymns sung by the choir. But it felt superficial and without much meaning. A duty rather than a life.

"You look like you're full of questions," Elizabeth had observed that day. "You're wearing a funny frown on your face."

Lillian's finger lightly tapped the thin page. "The Bible talks about God as an ever-present help. But how can God help? He doesn't have arms and legs. How can He help in times of trouble?"

Elizabeth smiled as she folded her hands over her large belly. "It's hard to imagine an unseen God way up in heaven helping us. But He does, in mysterious ways. I didn't tell you this, but I lost two babies before this one came along."

Lillian froze in her seat. "Oh dear. I'm sorry to hear that. I don't know if Mother ever said—"

"No one knew. Even Clyde only knows about one of them. But I feel certain those two children are waiting for me in heaven. And that is my peace, that they are with God. Of course I want my babies here with me. But I know they are safe where the Father is. He gave me peace even when my life had turned upside-down. He kept me from falling into despair. God lost His Son, you see. He understands."

Lillian never considered that a God in heaven with angels playing harps could understand loss. But then she realized what Elizabeth meant. A Father losing His Son on the cross. A Father who understood pain and trial.

Lillian wondered if God cared about her nerves today over the new position at the post office that created a tight feeling in her stomach. She stepped outside to find new snow had fallen overnight, with a path from the snow already cleared off by some unseen shovel leading from the house and along the boardwalk to the post office. She could venture a guess who had done it. She smiled and ambled on, pausing every so often to shake snow off her skirts from snowbanks bordering the walkway. The sun made a rare appearance, and Windy Mountain lay covered in a fresh blanket of white. It appeared majestic yet mysterious—this mountain peak hovering over their humble town, speckled black by burnt timber. Below the town, the Tye River gushed frigid waters that eventually made their way to the Pacific. In some ways the scenery appeared beautiful, and in other ways unforgiving.

She reached the stairs that climbed to the tiny building perched on a hillside. A figure dressed in a wool coat stood on the porch as if expecting her arrival. "Thank goodness you came," Mrs. Bailets declared. "I thought for sure you wouldn't. We were told you know Mr. O'Neill, the superintendent of the railroad."

Lillian wondered how she found out. "His wife and I are friends is all."

Mrs. Bailets led the way into the tiny post office. Inside stood a bag of mail and other letters spread out across the wooden counter. "I hope you feel well about doing this," she said. "I don't want to be lectured that I forced a young lady to labor on my behalf."

"It's my decision to be here."

"Good. I'm glad."

Lillian took off her wool coat and donned Elizabeth's apron. Mrs. Bailets outlined her duties of sorting the mail into boxes that townsfolk would stop by to receive and gathering any outgoing mail to go out on the mail train when it arrived. She showed her the stamps and postcards, how to calculate postage for packages, and how to make change. Lillian saw nothing extraordinarily difficult with it all and began thinking how fun it might be instead.

"I will be back to check on things. If you need me, send someone to fetch me at the hotel."

Lillian picked up the letters strewn across the counter to see names scrawled on them, some hard to decipher, but the house numbers helped her identify the correct boxes. Soon she had the mail sorted, along with what was in the mail bag. She stacked a few boxes and dusted the counter, all the while wondering what Mrs. Bailets would pay her. She hadn't even asked about her salary, which made her chuckle.

The front bell tinkled, and an elderly woman shuffled in. "Who are you?" she barked. "Where's Susan?"

"I'm helping her. I'm Lillian, her new assistant."

"Humph." She strode over to her box. "Where's my letter from Charlie? Box 38."

"I sorted the mail on the counter here and put in all the letters I found—"

"It's empty! Charlie always writes me. Did you lose it? A fine thing. I walk all this way, and my mail is lost."

Lillian blinked at the accusatory tone. *Oh no.* This is not how she wanted to begin her work here in Wellington, with people thinking she was mismanaging mail. "I'll look around," she offered, wishing Mrs. Bailets hadn't left so hastily. The older woman continued to bark as Lillian looked through the letters in each box but saw nothing for Box 38. "I just don't see anything. I'm sorry."

"I'm going to report you. You lost Charlie's letter. You have no idea how much it means to me. How could you?"

Lillian felt like hiding under the counter. She had just decided the job wasn't for her when Mrs. Bailets burst in. "I forgot to tell you one thing—" she began.

"Susan, it's high time you got here!" the older woman charged. "This young woman lost my letter from Charlie."

"Dear Mrs. Winston. I told you the letter usually comes on Thursday. Remember? Today is Tuesday."

The older woman blinked. She looked at the homemade calendar on the wall that had just turned to the month of December. "Oh dear. I get so mixed up."

"It's perfectly all right. I'll see you Thursday."

Lillian drew in a deep breath as she watched the older woman shuffle out the door. "She told me I had lost her letter. I didn't know what to do."

"She's forgetful. She comes in every day looking for a letter from her son. His letters usually arrive once a week, but she comes in every day looking for it. As far as I know, he's never been here to visit. Quite sad. But at least he writes. I once told her to leave this place and go live with him. But her husband once worked for the railroad, and she refuses to leave. He died about two years ago from a heart ailment."

Lillian looked out the window as the older woman gingerly descended one step at a time. A wave of compassion flowed through her, along with determination to make this work. Maybe with this change of heart, she'd discovered God's ever-present help in times of need.

Chapter 7

~~~~~~

DECEMBER 1909

Lillian could hardly believe how the next few weeks flew by. While the time of her arrival and through November seemed to travel at the pace of a snail, since working at the post office with Mrs. Bailets and readying Elizabeth's home for the pending arrival, the days came and went. She hummed "Joy to the World" as she sorted out small square envelopes of Christmas greetings arriving for the townspeople. One in particular caught her attention with the name of Charles Winston in the return address. Her heart leaped. The elderly Mrs. Winston, who still came daily to check the mail, would find joy today when she received her son's holiday greetings.

"You look happy," a gravelly voice spoke from the doorway. Lillian looked up with a start to see a tall, hulking figure with a small bag slung over one shoulder. Griffin, bearing the daily mail delivery. She saw him most days while she worked, as though he knew her schedule and wanted to pay a visit. Or maybe it was just her imagination.

"Mrs. Winston got a card from her son." Lillian walked over

and slid the revered envelope into the box. "And maybe there will be more happiness for others, I see," she said when Griffin gently tipped the bag onto the counter, keeping the envelopes from falling to the floor. He then reached into his pocket and pulled out a small brown box. Lillian stared, suddenly weak-kneed, wondering what on earth Griffin was doing.

"This was the only package on the mail train," he said quickly as if perceiving her confusion.

Lillian noticed the postmark from San Francisco. Anthony Travers. "Thank you," she said and slipped it into her apron pocket.

"How is Mrs. Hanks feeling?"

"She's worn out. She wants the baby born. The doctor says she's a few days late." Lillian felt the package inside her apron bump against the counter, and her fingers curled around it. What could Anthony possibly have sent her? Surely not the engagement ring?

Griffin continued to stand there expectantly, as if he too wouldn't mind knowing the contents of the package. Though she knew that couldn't be true. Could it? "So, do you have plans for Christmas, Mr. Jones?" she asked absently while scanning the cards that had arrived and then sorting them into the boxes.

"Mr. and Mrs. Bailets usually have a nice dinner at the hotel. We get the day off from the railroad, as there are no trains. So unless it snows again, maybe some of the fellows will want to play cards."

Lillian inhaled a sharp breath. "Playing cards on Christ's birth? Really, Mr. Jones?"

"I never heard it was a sin, Miss Hartwick."

She shook her head, thinking of the rabble-rousers that frequented the saloon, engaging in nightly gambling and poker, and she twisted her lips in disdain. Railmen were known to engage in mischief when they weren't on duty. The stories Mrs. Bailets told her were enough to make a woman blush and turn away. But she never thought the gentle Griffin would be so bored as to engage in such antics.

"But I'll listen to other ideas," he added, looking down on her expectantly. "A visit?"

"It's not my place to offer a visit. And the baby is due any day now."

"Maybe we could take a walk on Christmas Day."

Lillian shook her head and turned her back on him, again hearing the rattle inside the box hidden in her apron. "There's so much to do. And Elizabeth could have given birth by then."

"Well then, I expect you won't begrudge me time with some of the fellows over a deck of cards and some talk about the meaning of Christmas." He placed his cap back on his head. "It does no good to judge before you know what a feller is actually planning, does it?" He turned and hurried out of the office.

Lillian felt the warmth rise in her cheeks, realizing he used opportunities like a game of cards to be a friend to the other men. She closed her eyes and sighed, then flicked them open and went back to the letter sorting.

Just then the door opened, and Mrs. Winston shuffled in. The sight of the elderly woman sent joy surging through her. "There's a card for you!" Lillian announced in glee, rushing over to give her the mail.

For the first time, Mrs. Winston said nothing and only stared at the envelope. Tears pooled in her stark gray eyes, and her face looked even more wrinkled and pale. "I saw Mr. Sherlock at the telegraph office," she said in a low voice.

Lillian stood by expectantly, waiting for news that her son would finally be coming to Wellington for a visit.

"Mr. Sherlock said my Charlie died in his sleep."

At the terrible news given by the telegraph operator, Lillian felt like a plank board had slapped her. "What?" she croaked.

The elderly woman's shaky hands peeled open the envelope Lillian had given her. She then held up the card, a pretty one with cardinals resting on a branch covered in snow, framed in holly and berries. "It's from Charlie. He must've sent this before he died."

Lillian couldn't help the tears that filled her eyes. "I'm so sorry."

Mrs. Winston tucked the card into her coat pocket and turned for the door. Lillian watched her shuffle off. "If there's anything I can do...," she began.

Mrs. Winston paused with her frail hand clasping the door-knob. "Just tell your family you love them. Before it's too late." She shuffled out the door.

Lillian couldn't move after this but found a chair and collapsed, tears speckling her cheeks. Between Griffin's rebuke and now this, she felt as useless as a piece of tar paper flapping in the breeze. What good could come from her being here?

———•••———

When Lillian closed up the post office for the day then walked through snow back to the Hankses', her mind wrestled with mixed emotions. Only when she arrived at the house to see a very pregnant Elizabeth with a mixing bowl in her hands did Lillian snap out of her melancholy to rescue her cousin. "I can do that. You need to rest."

"I'm making gingerbread cookies."

The sweet and spicy scent felt homey and comforting. Lillian considered it as Elizabeth told her to add five cups of flour to the batter. "Do you think there will be enough cookies to give away?"

"Oh, this makes a large amount. There will be plenty."

"I—I think I know of some folks I'd love to give cookies to."

"Of course!"

Her melancholy became replaced by a meaningful task. Elizabeth sang Christmas carols while she and Lillian, with flour smeared on dresses and their faces, cut out cookies with assorted cutters that Clyde had crafted out of metal, including a bird, a heart, and a tree. They both shared tales of holidays gone by and the cake Lillian once tried to bake but forgot to add the leavening. "It turned into a large flapjack," she recalled with a chuckle. "At least it didn't burn like the ones I made here. Mother called it a thick crepe."

On the heels of her previous disaster with making flapjacks,

Lillian urged Elizabeth to do the cookie baking but assisted as much as she could with the rest. In no time, the fragrant aroma of gingerbread filled the air. Lillian removed cookies from the oven and placed them on the table to cool. Seeing the ones in the shape of birds, Lillian told Elizabeth the news about Mrs. Winston's Christmas card and her son.

"How terrible! The poor woman. I can't imagine losing your child and then receiving a card from him!"

"I'd like to bring her a few of these cookies if that's all right. Birds were on the card she received."

"That's a wonderful thought, Lillian. I'm sure it will help her to know others are thinking of her in her time of loss. . ." Her voice faded as her lips pressed tight. Her hands gripped her belly. "That was a good birthing pain."

Lillian ceased rolling the dough. "Are you having pain? Should I summon Mrs. Mallory?"

"I'm fine. The doctor said the first one can take a while. I don't want to bother her until I'm sure it's time. After all, it's nearly Christmas." She bent to take out a small sheet of baked cookies, then let out a groan and gave Lillian the potholders. "You'll have to do it. I'm going to lie down and rest."

Lillian took out the cookies and wondered if the time had come. Elizabeth assured her she was fine, but Lillian made a mental note to let the midwife, Mrs. Mallory, know about Elizabeth's condition when she went out to deliver the cookies. She glanced in the sitting room to see her cousin restless on the settee, even though her eyes were closed. She wondered what it felt like to carry the weight of a babe within and then feel the birthing pangs.

Lillian packaged cookies in some tins she found in the cupboard. She then put on her wool coat, scarf, and hat with a dark blue ribbon and picked up the tins. She considered waking her cousin to tell her of her errand, but watching her with her eyes closed, she decided sleep might be the best thing.

Stepping outdoors to find flakes of snow dancing in the air, she saw that Wellington appeared quiet for it being the advent of Christmas. Lillian thought she heard laughter escaping from the saloon, the only part of the Bailets family enterprise in the town she took exception to. She wondered if, besides the cards, Griffin decided to indulge in a snifter. At least Anthony didn't partake of a stiff drink, and for that she was thankful. And then she remembered she must open the gift he had sent when she returned.

Arriving at Mrs. Winston's residence, she knocked on the door. It opened to reveal Mrs. Bailets and another woman, to her stark surprise.

"Lillian! How nice of you to come by."

"Elizabeth and I baked cookies. I thought Mrs. Winston would like some." She glanced behind Mrs. Bailets to see the elderly woman rocking in her rocker, a picture in her lap, her stark gray eyes staring at nothing in particular.

"I'm sure that will brighten her day." Mrs. Bailets then gestured Lillian to another room. "She is not doing well. Won't eat a thing."

"I'm truly sorry. What terrible news to receive at Christmas." Lillian didn't know what else to say or do but gave Mrs. Bailets the tin of cookies that now seemed like a feeble gesture under the weight of such sadness.

"I see you have other deliveries, so I won't keep you." She gestured to the two tins Lillian had in her possession.

"Before I leave, I have a situation I'm hoping you can help me with. I need Mrs. Mallory's help. Do you know where she may be found? I think Elizabeth might soon deliver. She's very uncomfortable and talks about having birthing pains."

"Oh dear. She's in Scenic, Lillian. She's helping with a delivery there."

"What?" A sudden panic gripped her. "For how long?"

"I don't know. The train will come in the day after tomorrow—if the weather doesn't get worse."

"But that could be too late! Is there anyone else that can help with the birthing?"

Mrs. Bailets blew out a sigh. "I don't know. I'll ask some of my friends. I could come if needed. For comfort. But I'm not a midwife, mind you."

Lillian thanked her and hurried off while murmuring under her breath a prayer that Elizabeth wouldn't deliver this night. Just then she spied a familiar figure walking along the boardwalk, and in an instant her spirits lifted. "Griffin!" she shouted. Then, remembering etiquette, she corrected herself. "Mr. Jones."

The man whirled, and through the haze of snowflakes, a smile broke out on his face. "Miss Hartwick. Happy Christmas."

"Thank you. I—I need help. I don't know what to do. Elizabeth may be ready to deliver, and I've been told the midwife, Mrs. Mallory, is in Scenic. I need her."

"There are no trains until the twenty-sixth," he said gravely.

"Is there any way she can make it here? Without the train?"

Griffin blew out a sigh. "Don't know how well she can walk in snow. And like I once said, Old Glory in snow is dangerous. She'd have to climb that hill. I don't think it's possible. Especially at night and with snow falling. And in women's skirts."

Lillian brushed away a sudden tear from her eye. "I don't know what to do. What if Elizabeth delivers tonight?"

Griffin stepped forward, and for a moment she wondered what he would do. He then bowed his head and closed his eyes. "Dear Lord, we ask You to give us peace this night. We ask You to watch over Mrs. Hanks as she is ready to bring forth her child as Mary did with Your Son. Because of that, we know You will help us and give us peace and know-how. In Jesus' name."

Lillian stepped back when the prayer finished, and he looked down at her. An awkward silence held them frozen for a moment with the snow swirling around them. Her mittened fingers tightened around the tins until she realized she still held them.

"Here. These are for you and the men. Clyde would want his fellow workers to have some Christmas cookies. Elizabeth and I made them this afternoon."

"Well thank you, Miss Hartwick. We'll enjoy them for sure. A happy Christmas to you."

She managed a small smile, turned, and walked back down the road. Even with so many unknowns plaguing her, especially with her cousin on the verge of delivery, Griffin's prayer had fortified her soul. She had never relied on God for much in her life. To her, God was the preacher at the pulpit or the grand stone edifice of a steeple. But Griffin acknowledged God as Someone to trust with anxiety and fear, and he believed God would answer. Though she found it strange, it left her intrigued.

When she arrived back at the tiny house, Elizabeth was pacing the room, lines of distress crisscrossing her face. Lillian winced, and suddenly the prayer Griffin uttered reappeared in her thoughts. *Help me, God!*

The evening wore on, and Elizabeth continued to have pain. Lillian did her best to distract her with stories from childhood. When her cousin finally told her she would need to send for the midwife, Lillian knew the time had come to tell her the news. "She's not here, Elizabeth, but I'll go fetch Mrs. Bailets. She'll know what to do."

Elizabeth only groaned as she clung to the bedpost. "Hurry."

Dear God, what am I going to do? She'd never felt so alone and fearful as she threw on her wraps, still damp from the errand earlier in the afternoon. She hastened for the door and opened it to stare face-to-face with Mrs. Mallory and a snow-covered Griffin standing on the stoop, his fist raised, ready to knock on the door. Her mouth dropped open in astonishment. "Oh my goodness!"

Mrs. Mallory immediately entered to seek out Elizabeth, even as a myriad of questions filled Lillian's mind, along with a simple joy over God's speedy answer to her heart's cry.

"You have friends in high places, Miss Hartwick," Griffin remarked.

"If you mean God in heaven, I am bewildered. I can't believe you brought Mrs. Mallory. Come in, come in. I'll fix you some tea." Curiosity bubbled over as she hastened to set the kettle on the hot stove. She turned to see Griffin standing nearby, his wool hat covered in snow and hair poking out in wet strings, his face worn, his coat wet with melting snow. "Don't tell me you went down that terrible hill you were telling me about. Old Glory?"

He nodded. "I left for Scenic as soon as you told me what was happening. Took me a while. When I got there, the big boss, Mr. O'Neill, was at the hotel and had heard from the telegraph operator that Wellington needed the midwife. When I told Mr. O'Neill it was your cousin, Elizabeth Hanks, he made the decision to send his private car to bring Mrs. Mallory here. Some passengers wanted to leave anyway, and his aide had to report on the condition of the track as well as the tunnel. We arrived a half hour ago."

"I can't believe it. And none too soon." Lillian was thankful Jim O'Neill remembered her friendship with his wife Berenice in Everett. She felt blessed to have such friendships that could help in times of great need. "I will send him a telegram of thanks."

The kettle put out a billow of steam, and she rescued it to pour hot water into the teapot. Mrs. Mallory hurried out and instructed her to boil more water in hopes that the little one would soon enter the world.

"I think I'd better go find Clyde," Griffin said. "I'm sure I know where to look. He's probably checking over the rotary snowplow."

"The tea is nearly ready. . ."

He bowed. A clump of snow fell at his feet. Lillian couldn't help but laugh, adding to the whirlwind of emotion this day. The laughter felt good, like a soothing balm.

"I'll enjoy it when I return," Griffin said. "Oh, and thank you for the cookies. My bunkmates ate them all."

"Already?" She hurried back into the kitchen and retrieved some cookies. "Here. After all you did this day, it's the least we can do."

"Thank you." Again their gaze lingered until Griffin retreated to the door. Lillian watched his departure, thinking of all he had done and the treacherous trip he had made on their behalf. Or had he made it because he cared about her needs? She shook her head as her cheeks warmed, trying not to entertain such a notion.

But the thought did make her feel wanted and even attractive in the midst of this snowbound adventure.

———•••———

Lillian stifled a yawn that felt ready to break her face in two. At least it was a good kind of exhaustion. Just a short time ago the front door had flung open with Griffin bearing yet another gift—Clyde, who came to celebrate with his wife over the birth of their newborn son, Clyde Junior. Everyone now slept peacefully after rejoicing over the birth just before the stroke of midnight that heralded Christmas Day. To see Elizabeth cradling her healthy son after the losses she had endured with her other children moved Lillian to tears of joy. As did the thought of celebrating Christ's birth in the manger, which became all the more real to her. What a beautiful and perfect gift.

Griffin stayed for tea after finding Clyde, again thanking her for the delicious cookies, then departed for the bunkhouse. She thought about him returning to that cold and cheerless place and how lonely it must be for him. But how eager he was to help in any way he could, even risking his life to go down that treacherous hill to Scenic. He was not just a giant but a gentle one, and she hoped a blessing would return to him, somehow, someway.

Just then Lillian remembered the gift Anthony had sent. With all the excitement, she had forgotten about it. Now she retrieved the small package and carefully undid the string that held the brown wrapping to reveal a beautiful cameo pin made of ivory, accompanied by a note in Anthony's fine handwriting.

My dearest Lillian,

This pin reminds me of your beautiful profile, which I miss terribly this Christmas. But I have good news. Come January, I will be returning to Everett, and I hope you will be there to greet me. Wonderful things await us in the dawn of a New Year. Including my love.

With deepest adoration and best wishes for a Happy Christmas, I am yours,

Anthony

Lillian's gaze was still on the words—*January,* and *I hope you will be there. . .*

A sudden pang of sorrow gripped her.

She didn't want to leave her new home of Wellington.

Chapter 8

Not a day went by that Griffin did not think about the beautiful Lillian Hartwick, with her intense blue eyes that reminded him of clear skies over the snow-crusted mountains, her flowing brown hair and pleasant smile. Thoughts of her presented a colorful picture with Wellington encased in blankets of white, ready to stay that way until late spring. He'd heard, of course, of the plan for her to see her fiancé, or rather that she return posthaste to Everett during the holiday so they might be reacquainted. But when Mrs. Bailets told him Lillian decided to remain in Wellington to help her cousin and the new baby, along with working a few days at the post office, hope welled up inside him. The looks of endearment she seemed to give after presenting the Christmas cookies could have signaled something new. But he didn't dare entertain the foolish notion that Lillian chose not to make the trip to Everett on his account. They had barely conversed but greeted each other with simple introductions along the narrow boardwalk or at the post office when he delivered mail from the train or brought coal for the heater. He yearned for meaningful conversation with her if the door ever opened. How or when that would happen, he had no idea. But if it did, he prayed her thoughts would move from this fancy fellow of the city to his direction.

As usual, his bunkmates were their squirrelly selves accompanied by an unending parade of insults. Today Griffin had searched for his Bible but could not locate it anywhere until a sheepish Jack McClintock came out of the shadows and gave it to him. He'd never been more thankful to see the treasured book with its crinkled pages and scratched cover.

"Sorry, Griff. Oliver made me hide it. He said it was just a joke but..." The young man's eyes grew large and his small Adam's apple moved as he swallowed. "I didn't want to go to hell for hiding the Good Book."

Griffin nearly chuckled but instead found compassion well up. "We'll talk about it at midday." The young man nodded, his shoulders hunched over as he walked away. But Griffin had praise on his lips. What Oliver may have been trying to do in the night shadows, God could turn around for good. Especially if it made others consider the words in the Good Book. He sighed and flipped the thin pages with his finger to stare at the writing he wished he could read and understand. A light shown bright as his gaze drifted to the flickering flame of a lit lamp. If only he had a teacher. Someone to help in his time of need. Someone to help him learn how to read and write.

Anticipation lit his feet as he hurried out to face more snow that had fallen. Shouts down the track followed by a loud mechanical rumble alerted him to the men hard at work with the plow to clear the tracks. It became a never-ending job trying to stay ahead of the snow that at times tested patience and determination. Most were accustomed to the war of winter. They had a good team of workers to battle the next snowstorm that came on the horizon. Like Lillian's cousin's husband, Clyde Hanks, who worked the plow with skill.

Griffin bustled over to the coal shed, thanking God under his fog-filled breath that today was coal day. Filling a large steel bucket, he glanced over to see the tiny post office building peering out from behind a wall of white. He knew when Lillian worked and hoped the schedule hadn't changed.

When he arrived, he peered into the frost-covered glass to see her beautiful form sorting mail. "Good morning, Miss Hartwick," he said cheerily as he bumped his way through the door, lugging in the coal for the heater.

She whirled and, to his relief, gave him a smile. "Oh, thank you. We need it."

He filled the modest coal bin and then checked the fire. "We got more snow last night."

"It doesn't seem to stop. I'm not sure now what will happen."

Griffin peered at her to see her blue eyes take on a faraway look. "Is something wrong?"

"My fiancé is supposed to arrive in Scenic this afternoon. I have a ticket to travel there. Now I wonder if the train will run?"

The happy thoughts Griffin had entertained the last hour vanished under the thought of her fiancé and their affections rekindled. He could do nothing about it. After all, in Lillian's eyes he was a simple worker. Nothing more, nothing less. "The trains should be running. The snowplows are making headway."

"Well, I have no plans to go sliding down Old Glory, thank you." She said it with a teasing lilt to her voice. "I still can't believe you went down that mountain to find help for my cousin. Clyde told me how dangerous the walk is, even drawing a map to show the area. It's straight down. He said you could tumble your way to Scenic."

"Some have. And some died crashing into the big trees."

Her warm expression changed to a wide-eyed and open-mouth look of aghast. "My goodness. I guess that makes the trip even more heroic." A reddish hue glazed her cheeks, and she glanced down at the few envelopes before her. "The mail has calmed down tremendously since Christmas," she said, changing the subject. "Likely I won't have a job much longer."

"I'm sure Mrs. Bailets has other things you can do. Or maybe she will let you run this place on your own. You know what to do."

Lillian shrugged. "It's probably better that I'm no longer working here. If Mr. Travers were to find out what I've been doing, working at a post office, he would not be happy. And if word gets back to Mother, she will be horrified."

"I don't think helping others with their mail is a terrible thing to do. You think too little of this and what it means to others, Miss Hartwick."

"Well thank you, Mr. Jones. I don't want to keep you from your work. And thank you for the coal delivery." They exchanged smiles before she returned to her sorting. But none of the previous joy filled his now downtrodden steps, only the sad realization that she might not be here for much longer. He would like to prevent her from leaving but had no idea how. Or if he should even try.

———◆◆◆———

The conversation with Lillian occupied Griffin's thoughts, despite meeting with Jack McClintock for the noonday meal and discussing the Bible. Later at the hotel, when he spilled some coal in the hotel kitchen, leaving a dark imprint on the wood floor, Mrs. Bailets cast him a concerned eye.

"Sorry about that," he mumbled, looking around for the broom to sweep it up.

"You don't seem your cheery self, Griffin. Those measly characters you bunk with after you again?"

"Actually it led to a good talk about the Good Book with Jack."

"I hope you aren't entertaining disagreements about religion. Arguing doesn't do anyone any good."

"No. I only say things when someone is interested. But right now, I—I need to go to Scenic this afternoon. I've got some business of my own…but I need a reason to be there. Do you have any errands I can do?" He bit his lip, wondering why he would confess such a thing to Mrs. Bailets. He could imagine the look of surprise and even disgust from the woman if he told her the real reason—to spy on Lillian and discover all he could about this fiancé of hers. He felt the need to protect her, and yes, to satisfy his curiosity over what kind of fellow had captured her heart. Such knowledge would tell him plenty.

"Why yes, as a matter of fact I do. We got some registered mail for the superintendent. Since it's reported he's in Scenic right now, I'd just as soon have somebody deliver it to him personally and not use those fellows on the fast mail train who drink more than they deliver the mail."

Griffin was certain he wore on his face the astonishment he felt inside and quickly said, "I'll do it."

"Miss Hartwick knows the superintendent personally, so I thought perhaps she could. She told me she was going to meet her fiancé there."

"I can do it for you." He considered for a moment. "This way, Miss Hartwick won't be bothered trying to find Mr. O'Neill. I don't think she would know where to look. She's never been there."

"Then it's settled. Stop by the post office at three to pick up the letter. You can hop on the train after that."

Griffin could not believe his turn of fortune. Not that any of this would influence Lillian or her affections for her mysterious fiancé. But at least he would know what was happening, and hopefully the journey would tell him what to do about his attraction for her that only seemed to grow with time.

———◆●◆———

With the registered letter addressed to Mr. O'Neill concealed in his pocket, Griffin stole away to a seat in third class. Just before he entered the car, he caught a glimpse of the fair Lillian, dressed in a fitted coat and a hat that nearly took up the entryway, appearing rather pale and without a smile on her face as she boarded the plush first-class coach. He thought little of it as everyone looked pale and worn on a winter's day, especially with the holiday season over and the daily matters of life occupying thoughts and actions. But he did hope the color of her face meant she was dreading the meeting to come.

Griffin tried to imagine what the man looked like that had captured Lillian's heart. Nothing like himself or the railmen, for certain. He'd seen the dapper gentlemen that disembarked the train in Wellington to drink whiskey at the saloon or catch a meal at the hotel. He could not see himself in one of those fancy dinner jackets, though he did have the pocket watch that would look nice with it, courtesy of Grandfather. And just then he pulled out the revered piece to check the time. He knew how to read a timepiece, despite Oliver's hate-filled remarks. He knew God wanted him to pray for his enemies. Mrs. Bailets even remarked after unruly drunks tried to damage her hotel that she would pray for their wretched souls. To pray for someone as hateful as Oliver would take more than himself, though. It would take an act of God working on his heart.

Griffin pushed aside these sentiments to concentrate on what was before him, the letter in his pocket and the brown-haired beauty riding in first class. The whistle blew, and the train began to pull away from the depot. Griffin glanced out through the frost of unique patterns on the window to see the steep embankment below with Wellington's precarious foothold on the edge of Windy Mountain. The tall thin pines, weakened by fire, held blackened branches weighted by the snow. Just the other night he heard a crack up on the hillside and knew another tree had succumbed to winter's fury. Occasionally he would see a cloud of snow descend off the mountain in a distant slide under the sheer weight of the growing, snow-laden mountainside. He had to admit as the train chugged to Scenic on a switchback, this area was as beautiful to behold as a Currier and Ives print. But hidden in its beauty lay unspoken hazards that could not be taken lightly.

The trip was brief, and soon the train chugged into the Scenic depot. He felt certain he'd see Lillian soon embraced by the arms of her handsome fiancé, dapper in a fine suit. Instead she stood on the platform, glancing around as if uncertain where to go or what to do. He ducked behind the outline of another passenger, not wishing to cause any questions in her mind if she caught sight of him. He would let God help guide this venture. He had the letter to deliver after all.

Griffin went to make inquiries of Mr. O'Neill's location in the small town. When a porter acknowledged the man's presence at the hotel, Griffin straightened his hat and trudged through a hastily shoveled road toward the pretty log hotel. In an idyllic setting with mountains framing it, the place appeared more pleasing to the eye than the Bailets rough and tumble hotel in Wellington. Griffin opened the solid wood doors to be greeted by the music of a violinist. Chatter and the clinking of silver and crystal came from the dining room as patrons ate and drank while seated in wood furniture with tables covered in white.

Griffin walked into the lobby, which had a fire burning merrily in the stone fireplace and patrons chatting with each other while seated in wooden rockers. He approached the hotel clerk at the corner desk. "I have a registered letter for Mr. O'Neill."

"Certainly." The clerk rang a tiny bell. "Mr. O'Neill is in a meeting right now with his associates. I will see that it's delivered."

"This is to go into his hands alone. If you would direct me, please."

The clerk sighed and ordered the arriving bellboy to show Griffin the room. Instantly he felt out of place in his disheveled clothing stained with the dirt of the railway, but he kept his sights on the matter at hand. He swept off his hat when introduced to a man with deep-set eyes, a boyish face, a prominent nose, and a small chin. Two gentlemen sat with him. Light glinted off china cups filled with coffee.

Griffin gulped and slowly approached. "Excuse me, sir. A registered letter for you was mistakenly delivered to Wellington."

"You personally came here to give it to me?" Mr. O'Neill glanced at his companions who chuckled.

"A registered letter must be important as the postmistress told me, sir. I felt you should see it directly."

"Well, I thank you then." O'Neill took the letter and then sat back to study Griffin. His fingers flicked ash from a cigar over an ashtray. "You work for the GNR in Wellington?"

"Yes, sir."

"My thanks for your hard work." He nodded at the other men. "In my youth, I worked many years in different positions with the railroad. Where I am now comes from that hard work, and a good deal of it unkind."

A small smile quivered in the corner of Griffin's mouth. He felt an instant liking for this important man of the Great Northern Railway. Anyone who could sympathize with the plight of the working man deserved praise.

Mr. O'Neill continued to study him. "You do look familiar. Have we met?"

"Just before Christmas. Here at the hotel, in fact. I came to see about the midwife for a young woman about to give birth in Wellington. You assisted in having her transported, sir. And just in time."

"Ah, yes. I remember. And you must also have made the acquaintance of Miss Hartwick then. She is well known to my wife. Very interesting." Again, he flicked ash from the cigar stub. "Thank you again for intervening on their behalf."

Griffin nodded. He placed the hat back on his head and returned to the lobby. The noise from the dining room again drew him, where he noted a familiar woman sitting by herself in the corner. A bell-boy had just left her table, and her delicate fingers held a telegram. Seeing the stricken look on her face after reading it, he knew right away what the note contained. The fiancé would not be coming to Scenic. Griffin didn't know whether to celebrate or mourn and offer sympathy. *Dear God, direct my thoughts and my conversation.* He waited quietly for an answer before approaching her table.

Chapter 9

Lillian tried to calm her trembling hands. Before her rested the three-day-old telegram, Anthony's latest, in which he announced his intent of taking the train from Seattle to see her. He'd arranged the lodgings and planned a good visit before his departure the following day. She tried not to fidget by counting slowly to ten and thinking about what she might say to Anthony when he arrived. Only a few months had passed since they said farewell at the wharf, but it might as well have been a lifetime. In their conversation though, she must be careful not to alert him to her menial labor at the post office. A young lady ought to be given to works of charity or the like. But what charity could be found in the tiny rail town of Wellington except for the sad day before Christmas when she gave the card from a dead son to his grieving mother, Mrs. Winston. The very act should substantiate her newfound work at the post office, in her opinion. She assisted others in communicating with loved ones. And if questions arose about the meager salary she received, she could donate it to needy railway families. Lillian nodded, confident of her reasoning should word slip out of her position.

Lillian strained to see the wood clock displayed on the fireplace mantel in the dining room. She exhaled rapidly and felt for the placement of her large hat. She opened her small handbag to retrieve a hankie and dab her face. Presently a server arrived with the cup of tea she had ordered and a small envelope on a china plate.

"For you, madam," he said, bowing.

With trembling fingers she used a small knife to cut open the envelope, revealing the Western Union logo and a brief message.

CALLED AWAY UNEXPECTEDLY TO SAN FRANCISCO. WILL CONTACT YOU SOON.

ANTHONY TRAVERS. NORTHWEST TIMBER CORPORATION.

Lillian put the note in her small handbag, picked up the teacup, and took a sip. She'd had a strange feeling when she arrived at Scenic that he wouldn't come. Why, she didn't know. While she did notify Anthony that she would not be returning to Everett at Christmastime due to her cousin's needs, he seemed accepting of it. She had no reason to think him disingenuous. She sighed. At least she didn't have to worry about him finding out about her work. All of it had been laid to an unceremonious rest.

A giggle broke the air. She eyed a fashionably dressed woman lifting her wine glass to sample the potent fruitiness with her beloved sitting across from her. How happy they looked as they enjoyed a marvelous time in each other's company. And how lonely she felt under the announcement that Anthony would not be coming to Scenic.

Just then a shadow of a figure passed before her when she returned to her cup of tea. The shadow persisted, and she glanced around to see a familiar figure towering nearby. He swiped off his hat and bowed slightly. "Miss Hartwick."

Shock rippled through her. "Oh! Mr. Jones! Whatever are you doing here?"

"Delivering a registered letter to Superintendent O'Neill."

Lillian straightened in interest. *Jim O'Neill is here in Scenic?* "Is he with his wife? I would very much like to see her." *Oh, to have the kind presence of Berenice to talk with.*

Griffin Jones shook his head. "No. He's with two other men. I believe it's a business meeting." He paused. "But he did say kind things about railway workers. He seems to know our duties well, having once been a railway worker himself."

"He does. His wife told me how he began his work on the railway as a waterboy in the Dakotas of all places and worked his way up." She then nodded at the empty place setting opposite her. "Please sit down. I'm straining my neck trying to look up at you." She chuckled but then saw him shift his stance and tighten his grip around his hat.

"I'm not dressed, and—" he began.

"Since my fiancé was called away to San Francisco and we both work with Mrs. Bailets in Wellington, we will call this an impromptu business meeting." She pointed again to the chair while waving the server over to ask for another menu.

Griffin sheepishly pulled out a rustic oak chair that lent itself to the fine wood interiors of the place. "I'm not dressed for this. . ." he said again. "I should not have come over to greet you. I will cause you embarrassment."

"I agree you aren't dressed for this place. But everyone can just look the other way."

The server returned with the menu, looking down his nose at Griffin. "Is this man bothering you, miss?"

"Of course not. He's my guest. But thank you for your concern." She smiled at Griffin, who appeared as if he'd rather be stacking wood in the lumberyard under her Anthony's strict observation rather than be here. For the first time, she felt remorse for those in other situations. All were God's children. Money did not make one better than the other, nor did a nice set of clothes or anything else. But these were the times they lived in, and now female patrons nearby shifted in discomfort, staring at them.

Griffin noticed and now stood. "I must leave, Miss Hartwick. I won't cause you trouble."

Lillian sat ready to offer another rebuke when three finely dressed men approached their table. To her delight, she recognized in an instant Berenice's dear husband and the head of the Cascade line, Jim O'Neill. All three nodded, even as Griffin stood there stiffly, appearing like a black sheep among the well-to-do. "It's so wonderful to see you, Mr. O'Neill."

"And you, Miss Hartwick. I see you and the railway man here have run into each other."

"I was hoping to have him enjoy a meal after all he's done for my cousin. But as you know, railway workers do not possess nice clothing for dinner out."

Jim O'Neill turned to his friend. "Arthur, you must have something that would work for this man. You always travel with a wardrobe."

"But, Jim, I—" He paused when he saw Jim's raised eyebrow. "Of course." He nodded to Griffin. "If you would follow me."

Lillian saw the look of shock written in Griffin's wide eyes, but to her delight, he followed the man out of the dining room, albeit with slow steps.

"Berenice would be happy to know we saw each other," she told Jim O'Neill with a laugh. "She misses you greatly. She shared the picture of you both in Montana with her cat before I left to come here."

He chuckled. "Please do not force me to say anything to the contrary of dear old Marmalade. I would certainly land in a boiler for it. But only for a moment." Suddenly his gaze took on a faraway look. "I miss her and our little girl dreadfully. But with the unpredictable weather, I wonder if I dare see her. She knows winter is difficult, and it pains me to delay."

"Unpredictability is our lot in life. My intended was called away on business. That's why I'm here. We were to have our first encounter since he left for San Francisco several months ago. But he was called away on business."

"I understand delays all too well. If a rotary plow has mechanical issues, I must either find a replacement or fix it immediately. Any delay will then delay the clearing of snow from the tracks and delay transportation needs. Like the important mail train for which we have quite a healthy monetary contract." He paused as if ready to say more, then shook his head.

"It's still difficult for those who wait. But I know Berenice understands your great responsibilities that keep you occupied."

"So, since your fiancé cannot attend, you now feel at ease inviting a railroad worker to dine?"

Lillian shrugged and took up a glass of water to sip it. "It's better than eating alone. And we have plenty to discuss about Wellington." She then straightened as an idea crossed her mind. "I'm sure inquiring into details about rail status and life in an important rail town can't help but also be informative should there be any issues. And I could relay those issues by telegraph to you if need be."

"Ah, I see. It would be beneficial to know, especially in bad weather and with the electrics and the wires. Without them, the trains cannot pass through the tunnel." He paused. "You could be of great help."

Lillian smiled. "Of course."

Just then she heard a rustling, and two men approached the table. To her amazement she stared at a tall man wearing a tweed jacket too short for his lanky arms, trousers, and a white shirt. His hair was slicked back and the rough face freshly shaven. Griffin Jones might have been a dapper fellow from any afternoon function in Everett, and a handsome one at that. "Why Mr. Jones, is it really you?" From the way his head hung low and his finger tried to loosen the upper button of the tight collar constricting his throat, she knew who he was. Though he did look magnificent.

"I feel like I'm someone else," he admitted.

"You are," proclaimed Jim O'Neill. "But only for a brief time, you understand. Wellington needs good workers, as does the GNR up and down the line. There is always room for advancement though, for a job well done. Such as a dispatcher." O'Neill now took some money from his breast pocket and gave it to the awaiting server. "For now, enjoy a nice meal with my compliments."

"Why, thank you!" Lillian stared in awe and gratefulness for the man's generosity. If only she could remove the look of discomfort from Griffin's pinched face.

He slowly pulled out the chair and sat opposite her, staring at his untouched place setting filled with crystal and silverware. Jim O'Neill and his associates bid them farewell and left. "I don't belong here," he muttered.

"Is that really for you to decide? We have a nice meal paid for by the superintendent of the railroad, and if you are able to dine like a prince, why not enjoy it? This is probably the first time you ever have, am I correct?"

"I've never eaten in a place like this," he confessed. "I've been to the hotel in Wellington, but it's not like this." He glanced about the room with Lillian sharing in his perusal of the place. A few couples and businessmen talked quietly with light reflecting in their faces, enjoying the fine bounty.

Lillian gestured to the menu. "I'm sure this looks foreign to you as well."

Griffin stared at it blankly then glanced around. "I wonder if the hotel has some good beef."

"Didn't you see it on the menu?" She watched Griffin look at the menu with uncertainty, then push it toward her, encouraging her to order for them. When the server came strolling by, Lillian gave their orders, selecting a beef stew for Griffin and poached salmon for herself. She then studied the man seated before her. It amazed her what nice clothes could do to a dusty railroad worker more accustomed to a coal bin than to a hotel dining room. But the discomfort on his face set in wrinkles, and his bent head showed a humility that spoke to her heart. "Where did you live before coming to Wellington?" Lillian inquired.

Griffin talked for a time about his hard life in Leavenworth. Lillian tried to picture life in the streets with a mother as a seamstress, barely eking out a living in some shabby room in the corner, sewing dresses for the well-to-do. Lillian knew such dressmakers in Everett, as Mother commissioned them to make her frocks for special occasions. One such dress of pure silk with a soft rose-colored velvet jacket and lined skirt, complete with a large hat, seemed to catch the eye of every eligible bachelor at the dance. She wondered then what Griffin would have looked like at such an event and if he would be able to lead a waltz.

"Are you all right?" Griffin asked.

Lillian felt the warmth in her cheeks. "Have you ever attended a social dance, Mr. Jones?"

"I went to a few. But nothing like you're used to. It was more like storytelling and dancing a jig."

The server arrived with their early evening supper. Griffin's wide-eyed gaze took in the monstrous helping of stew, while Lillian calmly indulged in salmon bathed in a creamy dill sauce.

"This is the best stew I've ever had," Griffin said between bites. "Don't tell Mrs. Bailets." He winked, and Lillian couldn't help but laugh.

"I'm sure she realizes there are far better establishments than her hotel in Wellington."

They ate for a time until Griffin broke the silence by inquiring about her past. The description of it seemed quite mundane and privileged. Schooled by tutors. Learning sewing and embroidery. And disastrous piano playing. "But my friend Berenice paints and plays the piano like a concert pianist. We sang the most endearing song too." And suddenly the words to "Wait Till the Sun Shines, Nellie" burst from her lips in singsong fashion.

When the song ended , Griffin stared, his spoon loaded with food poised in midair. "That was good. Have you ever had singing lessons?"

Lillian chuckled. She wondered if she possessed any gifts of value. "Heavens, no."

"You should. I always thought my mama a good singer. But I would say you do it very well." He rested his fork on his half-eaten meal. "There's only one talent I wish I had."

"What's that?"

"Reading." He motioned to the table next to them and the patrons perusing their menus. "I couldn't read a word of the menu tonight."

Lillian stared, wondering if that's what he meant weeks ago when he'd labeled himself an idiot. Just the mere mention of such a hate-filled word ignited her indignation. "So you can't read. There's no shame in that. I'm sure many in these parts have not had a formal education. You live in the wilderness, after all."

"There is shame if your mama gave you a Bible and you couldn't read a single word of it. Like that psalm. I think twenty-three. The one about the Lord is my shepherd."

"Then we will read Psalm 23." She raised her hand for a server as Griffin stared at her with his mouth open.

"Madam."

"Please bring me a Bible."

The servant blinked. "A Bible?"

"I know it isn't a food or drink request, but surely you know where one is kept for the hotel guests."

The server bowed and quickly returned with the book, for which Lillian gave him a coin. She then flipped it open to the psalm and handed the book to Griffin. "Can you read any of it?"

"The LORD is my shepherd; I shall not want. He maketh me to lie down in green pastures: he leadeth me beside the still waters. He restoreth my soul."

Lillian smiled. "Now turn to Psalm 37. It's a favorite of my friend Berenice."

Griffin was able to find the numbers three and seven. But when Lillian asked him to read the verses, he shook his head. "I was only reciting Psalm 23 from memory," he admitted.

"So I gathered. You need to be able to read so you can commit more of it to memory." She held out her hand for the book, which he gave to her. The lesson began with reading the opening verse. "Fret not thyself because of evildoers. . ."

"These are very difficult words to sound out," Lillian realized. "I will see if Mrs. Bailets has some children's books. I can teach you."

"Thank you. But. . .don't tell my bunkmates until I know more and can surprise everyone."

"I think that's an excellent goal." With that statement, the tense muscles in his face relaxed and he once more picked up his fork to finish his hearty meal. "You're smart, Mr. Jones. I see no reason why you couldn't be reading the Bible very soon."

"That would be a true gift, Miss Hartwick. More than I can say. Mama would be proud. One of the last things she told me before she went to heaven was to read the Bible and learn it."

"Then we will fulfill her wish."

Griffin's lingering gaze and the slight smile on his face spoke more than one of thanks. Suddenly Lillian felt her emotions beginning to slide into areas she never thought would happen—and on a slope as slippery as Old Glory if she wasn't careful.

Chapter 10

⌒⌒

FEBRUARY

For the first time in his life, Griffin felt happiness. He should have felt it on previous occasions when the Lord moved in his life. Those times before arriving to Wellington five years ago had been stressful beyond measure, with the drudgery of his existence in Leavenworth. There, he'd caught some kind of sickness that left him with a hacking cough. Some thought it was consumption. For weeks he'd struggled with it, living in a tiny shack on the edge of town with barely any bread and meat to strengthen him. He'd worked odd jobs when he could, but the illness hampered his efforts and made others leery of hiring him. Until he met Barney Love, a traveling minister, as he was delivering coal one day. His life changed for the better when the man named Love—an appropriate last name for such a high call—ministered the love of Christ and found him medicine and sustenance to recover.

Happiness filled Griffin's heart when he trusted in the Lord to help him make decisions that eventually led him to Wellington. After the move to the mountains, the breathing issues disappeared and life began afresh. Though two years later, Oliver McCree came and life grew rough around the edges. Griffin prayed often for him, but the man proved relentless. It made little sense. If jealousy was in play, he wondered why. Unless something deeper irked the man.

But at this moment, none of that could steal his happiness over the meeting with Lillian that now spawned her interest in tutoring him. After her work was done at the post office, they gathered for reading lessons, staying warm and dry from the freezing, snowy weather to learn his ABCs. From all accounts, this year was looking to be one of the snowiest on record. The men had a difficult time keeping the rotary snowplows doing their jobs. On more than one occasion, Griffin was obliged to pick up a shovel and whittle away the snow from several accumulating storms so the plows could work. Cleared tracks meant dollars, for the passenger trains and particularly the mail train that paid hefty money to have mail safely delivered to points west. In a heavy winter like this one, the work proved never-ending.

Today Griffin worked the snow away with gusto. Soon it would be three o'clock and time for another reading lesson with the beautiful Lillian Hartwick. For the last few weeks, he'd thought of nothing but the meal they shared at the hotel in Scenic. He couldn't believe he'd actually worn nice clothes and eaten in rich surroundings with Lillian. He sensed the man who had lent him the clothes wasn't pleased with the situation, but the associate dared not argue with the superintendent of the Cascade Rail Division, Mr. O'Neill. Though while Griffin was trying on the jacket, the man called Arthur talked about his thirteen years working for the railroad and his position as trainmaster overseeing the trains and promoting safety. Griffin said little, still numb at the thought of borrowing the man's clothes but happy they shared a common interest in the railroad and in assisting others.

Griffin walked with his head held high, even as the buildings of Wellington began sinking under the rapidly accumulating snow-drifts. More flakes fell on his face and stuck to his eyelashes as he made his way up the hill to the post office where a light from within beckoned to him with its warmth. Pausing at the door, he stamped his feet to remove the excess snow and walked in. His cold hands welcomed the heat from the coal stove while Lillian scurried about with a bag of mail.

"I don't understand how an office this small can be so busy sometimes." She paused to swipe back a tendril of brown hair that fell across her cheek.

"I can return another time," Griffin offered.

Lillian stacked the remaining pieces of mail in a basket, then removed her apron to reveal a formfitting brown short coat over a cream-colored blouse with ruffles at the throat and a full-length brown skirt. Her picture of beauty could brighten the darkest winter day. "No, we will not delay." She promptly sat on the bench with a children's reader in hand. "Let's begin."

Griffin sounded out the letters of the story that Lillian presented, and in no time he'd finished reading the picture book.

"Excellent! For that, you earn a reward." Griffin watched her scurry to the back room and return with a basket. "Sadly they are cold now, but I'm sure they will be fine. Elizabeth's apple muffins."

"That's nice of you, Miss Hartwick. Just you teaching me to read is reward enough, though." He said it sincerely but couldn't help grabbing a muffin and eating it in four bites. Lunch had long since worn off.

"It's not easy to admit a weakness and then try to strengthen it. But I think if you continue to practice, you could be reading the Bible by spring."

Spring. How nice the word sounded, prompting an image of the cold and the snow giving way to sparkling streams, lush meadows, and plenty of wildflowers. And he would very much like to gather a fine bouquet for Lillian and savor the look of utter delight on her face.

Oh Griffin, these are the most beautiful flowers I've ever seen! May I kiss you?

He blushed at the thought that pleased him greatly, then glanced up to see Lillian staring at him with narrowed eyes, her forehead furrowed.

"Are you all right?"

"Uh. . .it's hard to think about spring with all this snow," he managed to say, glad for once that people could not read minds.

Lillian nodded. "Clyde has hardly been home. I'm glad I'm with Elizabeth. He's working that big snowplow night and day and still can't get ahead." She sighed. "But spring has to come sometime."

And maybe love. Though he knew better than to entertain such thoughts of bouquets and kisses with a woman of high society—and one already betrothed. But even with their lessons over the last few weeks, he'd heard nothing about her fiancé. The silence puzzled him. If Griffin was betrothed to the love of his life, he'd be shouting it from the rooftops. Why did Lillian appear mute about it? "I'm sure you are looking forward to returning to Everett when the weather gets better," he hedged.

She shrugged and glanced out the snow-dusted window. "I have too much work to do here. I can't leave Elizabeth and Mrs. Bailets and you, Griffin. People are relying on me. Mother doesn't need me anyway, and Anthony is doing what he does best—his timber business."

Griffin's thoughts were on that one part of the heartfelt explanation. *I can't leave you, Griffin.* If only that feeling would last. If only he could give her a good reason to leave this important fiancé of hers and consider him. But what did he have to offer? Coal dust and a book about ducks and a dirty bunk room shared with miscreants for a home. Hardly the ingredients for a recipe of love and success.

"You seem a little distant today," she said. "I hope you aren't getting discouraged about your reading. These things take time."

"I understand. We'll just keep thinking about spring that's coming. And continue with the lessons, if you can help me."

"Of course." With this statement, Lillian produced yet another book that Mrs. Bailets had lent her. They opened it to the first page, and the lesson began anew. When the time ended, Lillian urged him to take the book. "You are a pupil, after all, and should study," she said with a high-pitched laugh. When he looked at her in what he hoped showed his amusement at her comment, her laughter dimmed, and she stole away behind the counter. "I must close up."

"Yes, thank you. Until next time." He lifted his hat in a parting farewell and made for the exit. Out of the corner of his eye he caught Lillian staring after him. Or was it just wishful thinking?

———◆◆◆———

"Lookie what we got here, boys!"

Two days had passed since the reading lesson with Lillian, and so far, so good on Griffin's ability to sound out the sentences with Jack McClintock's help on the more difficult words. Until Oliver burst into the bunk room, snow-covered from yet another storm, and whisked the book from the chair next to Griffin's bunk.

"A lad's reader." He laughed long and loud. "You really think you're gonna learn any of that, Griff?"

"Give it back," Griffin said in a low voice.

"Or what?" Oliver's dark eyes stared in a challenge as he held the book high. A mischievous grin broke across his face. He strode over to the woodburning stove in the back corner of the room.

"The book isn't mine. It belongs to Mrs. Bailets."

Oliver opened the door to the stove and held out the book.

Griffin wasted no time lunging for Oliver. The book flew out of the man's hand and dropped into the firebox where it burst into flame.

"No!" He tried rescuing it with metal tongs, succeeding in pulling out burning embers that tumbled to the wood floor. Men shouted that Griffin was about to burn down the bunkhouse. Beau Crawford and Jack McClintock used a metal scoop to toss the embers out into the snow, but a black hole remained in the floor of the bunk room.

"Now look what you did," Oliver shouted. "You tried to burn

us out. Didn't he, boys? Look at the floor!"

Several men nodded, though a few looked as if they wished they were somewhere else.

Griffin clenched his fists, ready to deal with the man once and for all. At the last moment he grabbed his coat, whirled, and marched out. Anger burned hot like the embers of the burning book. If he hadn't left, he knew he would have picked up a chair and thrown it in Oliver's sneering face. Pandemonium would have broken out, with Oliver hurling accusations of assault. Maybe even a brawl. And he could have been thrown out.

But Oliver was the least of his worries when he thought of the burned book, now a pile of black rubbish in a snowdrift. How would he tell Lillian? Their reading lesson was tomorrow. If he told her another man had destroyed it, it would make him look weak, like he could not be relied on to protect an item of value. If he said he burned it by accident, it would make him look irresponsible. No matter what he did, his goose was cooked.

Griffin trudged about in the dark, scuffing up snow, wondering where he would go. He couldn't return to the bunkhouse, that much was certain. Finally, he came to the depot and found a back room to rest in for the night. If ever he needed God's intervention, now would be a good time. He tried to get a bit of shut-eye, but the floor was cold and hard, and his thoughts marched in an endless parade. If he could, he would write a letter to Lillian and tell her what happened, to soften the blow. But he couldn't write. After all she had done, he had let her down.

Griffin sat up and looked out a window into the darkness. A part of him stirred to action, one that overcame the depression of the night. He refused to let Oliver ruin his life and use this sad, sick scenario to possibly have him thrown out of his job or out of town. He would confess to both Lillian and Mrs. Bailets what happened. He would offer to pay for the book out of his meager salary and let God handle his enemy—if he could let go of his anger.

The next morning, Griffin awoke groggily to a new day, his back aching from the hard floor with an aching spirit to match. Stomach pains from hunger were fierce, but he had work to do—both practical and spiritual—to set things right. He stepped out to see the skies had cleared but noticed a small group of men walking toward him, flanking a strange man dressed in a dark coat and wearing some kind of badge.

Oliver was there, trying to contain a gleeful smile, along with Beau Crawford and several others as the thickset man in the dark coat stepped forward. "Griffin Jones?"

"What's this all about?"

"You're under arrest for theft and arson." The man produced a set of steel cuffs.

Griffin stepped back as rage began to build. "Arrest him instead!" he said, pointing to Oliver. "He stole the book belonging to Lillian Hartwick and then threatened to burn it. I was trying to—"

"You will have plenty of opportunity to state your case. But for now you may stay in the depot here until the hearing at noon today."

Griffin wanted to resist but, seeing the group arrayed before him, knew he had little choice. Oliver snickered as the man with the badge put the handcuffs on Griffin, then pushed him back into the room of the depot where he'd already spent a long, uncomfortable night. He wouldn't put it past Oliver to leave him here for days but for the sheriff talking about some trial at noon today. If only he could tell Lillian what was afoot. She would vouch for him, as would Mrs. Bailets. Unless they believed the others and blamed carelessness on his part.

Griffin closed his eyes and began to pray. He was very tired of life. If only God would choose not to submerse him in another trial when every day of his existence seemed a lesson in adversity. He blew out a sigh. Maybe he ought to return to Leavenworth and start over. No more hate-filled men like Oliver. And no Lillian to pine over. No more of anything, really.

He blinked his eyes that burned from exhaustion yet with determination still set in his heart. Giving up was not in his nature.

He would not raise the white flag of surrender. He would not leave but remain steadfast until this crude moment vanished as swiftly as it came.

———— ••• ————

Griffin stared at the small entourage that had gathered for the makeshift trial, held in another bunk room that had been cleared but for a few tables and chairs. At the head table sat the judge, who was outfitted in too tight a robe and had shiny hair sticking out everywhere. Griffin thought he recognized the man, but he kept his sights on the matter at hand. He noted several railroad workers he knew and other assorted fellows he didn't. Griffin would have thought this a fabulous ruse of misfits that they would laugh about later, except for the fact they all wore grim expressions on their faces. They meant business.

An unidentified man pointed to the defendant's chair, which Griffin occupied. The manacles around his wrists began to dig into his flesh. Presently, another man at the prosecutor's table stood and weightily delivered a summary of the events in question, finishing with the charges of robbery, assault, and arson.

"What is your plea?" the judge asked Griffin.

Griffin stared at him as he stood. "Before I say anything, show me your right to lead this trial."

The prosecutor jumped to his feet. "He's trying to railroad this proceeding!"

Snickers rose up among the men at the word *railroad*.

"I have no intention of producing credentials to satisfy a criminal," the judge said. "As you won't enter a plea, it's determined then you stand guilty as charged."

"We bring no charges," a female voice suddenly shouted from the rear of the room. Griffin spun about to see Lillian Hartwick march forward, dressed splendidly in a smart suit, her large hat creating a breeze. "I gave Griffin Jones the book in question, and he was saving stolen property."

Griffin stared at her, and to his astonishment, she gave him a quiver of a smile.

Just then Mrs. Bailets entered the room. "Johnnie Meath," she said in a loud voice with her hands on her hips, "you get out of that ridiculous costume this minute. And we all know how bald you are. That mop you're wearing does nothing."

Griffin felt his mouth drop open at the identity of the judge—a locomotive engineer he'd met several times. The man stood and sheepishly removed his fake hairpiece. "Aw, we were only having a bit of fun, Mrs. Bailets."

"It's hardly fun when a book has been destroyed and our bunk room nearly burnt out," Oliver shouted. "It's a crime."

"Fine," said Mrs. Bailets. "Let's have ourselves a real trial then and find out what happened. There's a witness here who saw the whole thing the other night." She glanced behind her to Jack McClintock who stood there clutching his hat. "And if you or anyone else does anything to young Jack here, I'll make sure you never get another drop of liquor at the saloon."

After that pronouncement, several men left their posts and walked out, claiming they were done with the whole charade. Johnnie Meath relinquished his judgeship and joined the men abandoning the fake hearing. After some grumbling, Oliver left too.

Lillian turned to Griffin. "Well, Mr. Jones, as the Bible says, is there no one left here to accuse you?"

Griffin glanced about. "No, Miss Hartwick."

"Then we don't either. Case dismissed."

Jack helped unlock the handcuffs with the key Johnnie had left behind on the table. "This doesn't solve the problem though," Griffin said grimly. "The book is still burned up."

"Don't worry about that now, Griffin," Mrs. Bailets said. "I think we've had enough of these games. I already told my husband to stop with his silly pranks too, like that turkey raffle that turned into a brawl. It just eggs the men on into all kinds of mischief. With the way this winter is shaping up to be, we're gonna need each other, sooner rather than later." She nodded and turned to exit the bunkhouse.

"Thank you," Griffin whispered to Lillian.

"Thank that man Jack. He came looking for us after it happened. I've never seen such a thing in my life. A fake trial, indeed. People in this town are not in their right minds. Don't they have better things to do?"

"No. These fake courts have happened before—but usually with strangers who come to town. The men get bored and decide to have fun. But this could have turned bad. A building almost burnt down."

Lillian patted his arm. "I'm happy you're all right." She withdrew her hand and looked away. But for Griffin, the touch was like one of those ruby-red embers on the bunkroom floor. Only it did not scorch his heart black but made it feel more alive than ever before.

Chapter 11

~~~~~

WEDNESDAY, FEBRUARY 23

Lillian tried hard not to fidget as she drew a needle through the fabric. Over the past few weeks, when not engaged in post office duties or helping Elizabeth with the baby, she worked hard to create the embroidered flowers on a long piece of white cotton that would become a tablecloth. At first, she often thought of the cloth gracing the fine table at her and Anthony's new house in Everett. But as time ticked by, the thoughts became less of that and more of Griffin's smile and even laughter. He had progressed well with the readers and had begun to read a bit of scripture. The joy in his face proved infectious. Sometimes Lillian would sit primly in the chair with the large family Bible belonging to her cousin, opening it to see what caused such joy in Griffin. Elizabeth also shared some of her favorite scriptures. And she read Berenice's favorite one as well: Psalm 37.

But today Lillian found herself quite bored, even with reading and embroidery. The baby napped, and Elizabeth busied herself with baking. Despite the snow falling from another storm, Lillian decided a venture to the hotel to find out the latest news from Mrs. Bailets might lift her spirits.

"Yes, please do," Elizabeth said when Lillian offered the suggestion. "With all this snow, I would like to know when Clyde might be home. He likes his bread good and hot." Lillian could sense the worry in Elizabeth's voice, even as she hoped the freshly baked bread would lure her husband back to his family. It wasn't in her ability to try to locate him in this storm, but Mrs. Bailets might have news. The chief proprietor's wife in all of Wellington seemed to know everything about everybody.

Lillian drew on a pair of Elizabeth's boots, her long wool coat, mittens, and a muffler. She hoped it wouldn't be too cumbersome to walk as she exited the home. Thankfully, someone had shoveled a path to the main thoroughfare, which amounted to a narrow lane beside the empty train track and ran along the slippery boardwalk. She wondered if Griffin had risen early to do the task, as he sometimes did. The thought left her with a warm feeling on this snowy day.

Lillian climbed the bank of stairs and entered the hotel to find a few people loitering about but the place relatively quiet without the train activity. She inquired about Mrs. Bailets and found her carrying an armload of towels.

"I'm not opening the post office today," she said in a hurried voice. "What's the use? The mail train is stuck at the Cascade Tunnel Station. They can't get the rail lines cleared."

"Elizabeth wanted to know what is happening. She's worried about Clyde. Have you heard anything?"

"Just look outside. This is the worst storm we've had in years. I have rooms upstairs with snow in them, for heaven's sake. There's no way anyone can even stay in them. We have to get a new roof on this place."

Lillian could see Mrs. Bailets was beside herself with duties and nodded as the woman hurried off, muttering to herself. She sighed and glanced out the window, realizing it might be better for her to return to the house rather than get caught in the relentless snow. Just as she was about to leave, two men came in, stamping snow off their shoes. Her gaze settled on the taller of the two. She would recognize Griffin in an instant, even with the snow-covered muffler and hat. The other man was his friendly sidekick, as she thought of Jack McClintock.

"Miss Hartwick," Griffin acknowledged. "What are you doing out on a day like today?"

"Trying to escape the needle and thread," she admitted. "I wanted to find out about this storm and when Clyde might be home."

Griffin accepted the mug of coffee given to him by a hotel employee. "I'm sure he's working the snowplow hard. Me and Jack here are going over to the Cascade Station where the trains are stuck. Most everyone else is west of here, helping dig out a snow slide and a stuck rotary plow. They need men at the station to shovel out the trains so they're ready to move through the tunnel when the tracks are cleared."

Lillian had heard of the tunnel running through Windy Mountain, in what Elizabeth called a black hole in the earth. But on a day where white seemed the only color around, a place free of snow seemed appealing. "I would like to see the tunnel sometime—when it's safe, of course." She never forgot how Griffin told her the place could be dangerous.

"Maybe at a better time. On the other side of the tunnel is a great deal of snow."

"Ain't no time like now though," Jack said, running the sleeve of his shirt over his runny nose. "Nothing on the tracks is running because of the slide at Windy Point and the trains stuck at the Cascade Station. Good time to see the tunnel on the rail cart."

Griffin's eyebrows drew together as he pondered that fact. "Well, that's true. You gotta walk for about a mile, though. Then ride the rail cart. And I don't know when you can get back."

"Once the train moves, she can hop on board," Jack said. "They're heading here anyway."

Lillian inwardly thanked Jack for his encouragement as she nearly begged off the foolish idea, especially in such stormy conditions. "It can't be too difficult to follow railroad tracks, can it? I've walked in snow and, yes, in skirts. I'm wearing Elizabeth's boots."

Griffin finished his coffee, then waved his hand. "Could get slippery before the tunnel, with ice from melting snow." He looked down. "Glad you're wearing the overshoes at least."

Lillian snickered. "I learned my lesson after the first snow here." She liked to think she was growing stronger and more capable with life here in the mountains. An adventure in a tunnel would add a lively addition to her activity list that had grown mundane, being snowbound at the house day and night.

But as they started out, with the men rapidly moving ahead, Lillian decided this might not have been the wisest decision. She walked gingerly on the uneven tracks, the only thing plowed, with snow rising up in hills on either side. Her skirt caught mounds of the wet snow, slowing her progress. She nearly turned back at the growing foolhardiness of this venture, until she saw the opening to the tunnel drilled through the shoulder of Windy Mountain. A burst of courage ignited her steps as she continued on until Griffin returned to her side.

"I'll have Jack walk you back," he said.

"Nonsense. I'm fine." She shook the snow off her skirts. "The tunnel is right there."

"Inside there isn't fit for a woman like you," Griffin said. "It smells, it's dark, and—"

"Berenice would be proud that I did this in honor of her husband's work." Lillian inhaled a deep breath, trying to steady the jitters that looked to overwhelm her courage. "At least there's no snow inside. That would be a pleasant relief." She pulled back her shoulders and marched on.

Griffin walked alongside to assist if needed. Cold wind exhaled from the tunnel entrance, as if the place were the gaping mouth of some stony creature. On that breath of wind came strong odors—coal dust and burnt cinders and something rotting within. Just then there came a rumble, and a sheet of snow began falling from above the entrance. Griffin pushed Lillian inside the tunnel, just before the mountain of snow buried her. He looked at this newest slide to obstruct the tracks and scratched his head under his cap. "That will have to be cleared before the trains come through," he noted grimly. "Guess we better keep going, since we can't go back. I sure hope the other side of the tunnel isn't blocked."

Jack lit the lanterns he carried. Inside the tunnel, the rail cart sat on the tracks. Griffin helped Lillian aboard where she stood on the deck. He and Jack positioned themselves at the levers to pump the cart along the tracks. Lillian had never been inside such a dark place in her life. Seeing the white light of freedom slowly fade, she wondered what she had gotten herself into. But she refused to let fear get the better of her. She hung on with the cold wind buffeting her. "At—at least there's no snow," she shouted above the squeal of the metal wheels running along the tracks, the inky blackness broken by orange sparks made by the wheels and the mad flickering of the lanterns. Soon she began to tremble from the raw cold and the dampness.

"The tunnel is a dangerous place," Griffin said loudly. "If trains were running like they used to, you could get sick and die from the fumes. Now they use electric locomotives or electrics to push the trains."

Lillian wondered about that and fought to contain a mounting fear. "You're certain the trains aren't running? I—I don't want to be in here if they are." She strained to see ahead.

Jack laughed. "We'd be goners if that were true," he joked before Griffin jostled his arm to shush him. "Sorry, ma'am. Didn't mean to scare you none." He laughed as he and Griffin pumped up and down.

Lillian focused her attention on a circle of brightness now appearing before her. She shivered, her feet growing painful, her fingers numb. She hoped to find a place to get warm. In the next moment, she could make out the faded image of a train in the distance and her heart began to pound. "Is—is that train coming toward us?"

"No, they're on the spur track," Jack said. "The mail train and passenger train are stuck right now. And getting more stuck the longer they sit there."

"A lot of snow here, and no one's shoveled," Griffin acknowledged as they emerged out of the tunnel into a blanket of white. "What a mess." Jack agreed with a whistle.

All Lillian could think of was how cold she was, so she asked about shelter. "I must go somewhere and get warm."

"It will be warm at the beanery," Griffin suggested, pointing to a small building up on a hill across from the two sets of trains standing fast on the snow-covered tracks. "You could get something hot to eat there."

A cup of hot tea would help immensely. Glancing behind her, she wondered how she would return to Wellington with the way blocked. She had agreed to come, as foolish as it all seemed now. But it couldn't be helped.

Griffin assisted her off the cart. She plodded through deep snow toward the beanery, passing several snow-clad figures returning to the warmth and safety of the train cars. She hoped she could get a ride back to town once the tracks were cleared and the trains moved again.

Inhaling a breath, Lillian headed into the beanery, walking in puddles of muddy water on the floor to see men gathered around tables, shoveling food into their mouths like ravenous animals. The tables where they ate were no better than the floor, and at once Lillian scolded herself for doing this on such a stormy day. She glanced around, hugging her arms around herself, when she caught sight of an elderly woman at the far end of a long table, waving her hand.

"You look lost," the woman said and gestured to the empty seat across from her.

"Just cold. I need something hot. My feet are so cold."

"You poor thing." The woman waved down the haggard server and asked him for a cup of coffee. "They are so busy here," she observed with a chuckle. "I don't think the poor fellows knew they would have to serve two trains of passengers several meals." She nodded at her half-eaten plate of eggs and flapjacks from the morning's fare, now quite cold. "They are serving a good hot soup now. Breakfast is over."

"I—I just need something hot. I—I came from Wellington."

The woman's eyes grew large. "Wellington! How can that be? We haven't been there yet, I don't believe. Are you a passenger on the Express?"

"Oh no. I live in Wellington with my cousin. She just had a baby in December. A Christmas baby."

"How wonderful." She sighed. "I just came from caring for family in Spokane. I'm heading home to my husband just in time for our anniversary." She sighed. "Babies are the sweetest little miracles. Being a grandmother is a precious thing." She nodded at a table in the distance and a young woman trying her best to help her children—a boy and young girl—while coaxing the baby to stop his frantic wailing. "Poor Ida Starrett has her hands full. Traveling with three children on the train, just after burying her dear husband. At least her parents are traveling with her to lend a helping hand." The woman smiled as the server appeared with a cup of steaming coffee for Lillian. "You get to know people when you are snowbound. I'm Sarah Covington."

"Lillian Hartwick. Do you know when the train might be leaving? I was hoping to get a ride back to town."

She shook her head. "We only hear rumors. A fine young man on the train, Ned, tells me the news. He talks quite often with Mr. Pettit, the conductor. We're praying they can clear the tracks so we might leave tonight. Ned said they are bringing up a rotary plow from a place called Scenic."

Lillian perked up at the name of the town that began a change in her heart in ways she never expected. "I know it. There's a fine hotel there. I had the most wonderful dinner." Her voice trailed away under the pleasant memory.

Sarah Covington sighed. "I just hope we can make it there at least. How I would love a real bed to sleep in."

Lillian took a sip of the coffee while eyeing the rough customers nearby. At the tables, the mail train workers played cards and talked boisterously, their speech mixed with soiled words. "My mother would be mortified to find me in such an unscrupulous place. But then again, she would be horrified that I came with two railroad workers to this station on a cart through a dark tunnel."

Sarah Covington stared and shook her head. "I was wondering how you got here. That is indeed a strange thing to do—and in a snowstorm no less. My, you're brave."

"The trains weren't running, so it made for an interesting journey through the tunnel. But it was so cold. I only hope I can get back to Wellington once the train leaves. I have no intention of going back the way I came."

"They are saying we may be here overnight."

Lillian stared. "Oh no!"

Sarah Covington rested her hand on Lillian's. "Now, don't you fret. There's plenty of room in the Winnipeg, dear. And nice little beds, though small. You are most welcome. I'm certain the conductor would allow it, considering the storm. The train isn't full."

Lillian smiled her thanks before hearing another cry. She looked on as another elderly woman took the baby from Ida Starrett to cuddle him. Sarah Covington had told her the woman was Ida's mother, and together they watched the sweet interplay between grandmother and grandson. Lillian wondered what might lie in store for her with motherhood, and as a wife as well. But all that seemed in a much distant future.

Sarah Covington conversed about her family and nursing her ill son. "I never knew a scratch on the arm can make someone so sick." She shook her head. "Simply terrible."

"I'm sorry." She thought of the simple cuts she had endured

in life, wincing at the thought of having a swollen arm and lying feverish in bed as the older woman described. "Maybe I should have my foot looked at. I rubbed the back of the heel raw from walking to the tunnel. I wore my cousin's boots."

"Indeed you should." She stood to her feet. "We have a nurse aboard the train who could look at it, I'm sure. She's traveling with another gentleman who also has a wicked sore. I'm certain she will know what to do."

With that, the older woman put on her wraps and gestured for Lillian to follow. Just as she was exiting the beanery, she caught sight of Griffin, a shovel in hand, talking with several men. Seeing her, he stepped away from the group and offered a good day to both her and Sarah Covington as heavy snow continued to fall from above.

"I will not be going back to Wellington tonight," Griffin told her. "The snow's still falling, as you can see. They're hoping to get the trains moving soon, but I don't know when. I'm sorry."

"No matter. Mrs. Covington here says the train is quite comfortable. And I have a sore on my foot a nurse will look at."

Griffin stared, a bit taken aback by all this, but nodded.

"However, I am concerned that Elizabeth will worry. I need to find some way to tell my cousin where I am."

"The telegraph line is down right now."

Lillian had not anticipated this, nor had she done right in not alerting her cousin to this impromptu journey. "Oh dear. I don't want her worrying about me. I never told her my plans. I only said I would find out news about Clyde at the hotel."

"If someone is returning to Wellington on the rail cart, I'll give them the message. They need to start digging out that slide on the other end anyway." He nodded his snowy head before trudging off to find the workers busy chipping away at the ice and snow around a huge locomotive.

"A very polite young man," Sarah Covington said with a chuckle. "He appears quite interested in your welfare. Which seems a bit out of place for a railroad worker."

"He cares about everyone," Lillian said hastily. She stumbled her way with the older woman through the snowdrifts to the Pullman as she described Griffin's heroic deeds on more than one occasion, even walking down the dreadful slide to Scenic to locate the midwife for her cousin. But soon her thoughts turned to the coach and the warmth generated by coal heaters that felt like a cozy blanket and the chatter of passengers occupying the seats who greeted Sarah Covington as if they were long-lost chums.

"When you get stranded together, you learn to know everyone," Sarah Covington said with a laugh. Then her voice turned serious. "I do hope we leave soon though. I miss my dear friends and, of course, my husband."

Lillian hoped so too. But now she removed her shoe and stocking as Sarah sent for the nurse to look at the red mark on her heel. The nurse recommended rest. Lillian realized if she must be caught in a blizzard with a sore foot, there was nothing better than being with new friends—and especially near Griffin, shoveling out the very train she occupied.

— ◆ ◆ ◆ —

THURSDAY, FEBRUARY 24

"We're moving, we're moving!" Seven-year-old Raymond, the son of Ida Starrett, ran through the car, shouting the news.

Lillian glanced out the frozen windowpane. A terrific squeal, accompanied by crunching, pierced the air as the wheels of their coach loosened from their icy stranglehold and began moving down the tracks. She scraped away the frost to make out the outline of several figures, one standing taller than the rest—who she knew must be Griffin, watching to make sure the train moved safely toward the tunnel.

All was not without issues though. Thankfully Conductor Pettit had allowed Lillian to remain overnight in the Pullman—but in a passenger seat, where she spent a fitful time trying to catch some sleep. Her fingers massaged the crick in her neck, her body overcome with fatigue, and vowed never to do this again. She hated to think of the worry she had caused Elizabeth. But then she received word from the conductor that some men had used the rail cart to return and dig out the slide and that the message of her whereabouts had been sent. But there would be lingering questions, no doubt.

Ned Topping, a rather handsome man with bushy brown hair and a lean face, glanced out the window near Lillian. "They have no electricity because of the downed wires," he reminded her and Sarah Covington as the train moved into the tunnel. "A locomotive is pushing us through. We will pick up speed soon, though, as it's downhill to the next station."

The train rattled through the blackness of the tunnel in only minutes under the power of gravity and a heavy locomotive. When the train emerged, eager faces looked out the windows into the gathering twilight and lights gleaming from the windows of the Bailets Hotel. Excitement radiated throughout the Pullman. Lillian couldn't help but smile to see the glimmers of home. The train groaned, passing by the humble, rough-hewed buildings, until the brakes squealed, bringing the train to a stop on the passing tracks near the coal and water towers and directly beside the fast mail train.

While Lillian was grateful to be back in town, concerns circulated among the passengers. They wished they could depart the train for better lodging, but news came of the rooms uninhabitable at the Bailets Hotel due to water issues and a few rooms filled with snow. Some believed it wouldn't matter—the train would no doubt leave at dawn. Others remained unsure of anything at the moment. The only facts they had were the words from Conductor Pettit stating they would remain in Wellington until the storm abated and the tracks were functional again. For how long, no one knew.

Chapter 12

~~~

Griffin stomped his feet to try to remove the snow and ice caked on his boots. For certain, the precipitation was living up to its name in the form of Cascade Cement that froze everything in its place. Having lived here five years, he'd seen his share of snowstorms infiltrate these rugged mountains, turning everything white until early May. But here in late February, it appeared the heavens had unleashed all the snow of the season in one fell swoop rather than dispersing it in a more manageable amount. He and the other rail workers were worn out from the never-ending battle between snow and shovel. Already, he felt the pain in his back and arms from trying to shovel out snow mixed with ice. Several of the fellows complained of back pain, and one had to be taken off the work line after feeling pain in his chest. The big boss, O'Neill, was obliged to find other workers to maintain at least an equal status over conquering the house-tall drifts. Rumors circulated that even he was at his wit's end. And no one would believe Mr. O'Neill could raise a white flag before anything, least of all snow.

Griffin climbed a few steps and entered the narrow passenger doorway to the mail train where his friends Joe Walters and Matt Weiss were playing cards. "Pull up a carton and join us," Joe said.

"I'll watch." Griffin eyed the coffeepot resting on the small stove heating the car, and finding an old cup to use, poured out the tar-black brew. It did well to warm his insides, even if it tasted like a rusty pipe. "Not sure how much more digging I can do," he said soberly, rejoining the men just as Joe triumphantly laid down a full house to Matt's two pair.

"Were you part of the team working on that new slide?" Joe asked.

Griffin nodded. "As soon as we clear one slide, we get another. The warming temperatures melt it, then the nighttime cold turns it to ice. Have to use those chippers to make blocks of it. No way can the rotary plows cut through that."

"So much for getting out of here," Matt said. "We're getting short on coal too. I was told they'll only have enough to warm the car at night. Though we just have small stoves in the mail car. The passenger cars on that Express take much more."

"Feels good in here now," Griffin commented, downing his coffee.

"Well, enjoy the coffee while you have it. Need to go to the bunkhouse for it after this. And supposedly Mr. Bailets isn't happy about the situation with the Express. He said he can't keep up trying to feed all the passengers three squares a day without supplies."

Griffin hadn't considered that with the trains stalled, so too were the supplies also stymied. "Are we running out of food?" he wondered aloud.

"Soon will be getting down to bacon and potatoes from what I hear."

He wondered then if Lillian and her family had enough to eat and made a mental note to check on them. After watching two more hands of poker, Griffin decided to brave the snow and visit the Hankses. He knew Clyde was still wrestling with the rotary plow while the women tended the house and cared for a baby.

Exiting the mail train, Griffin could see the telltale sights and hear the sounds of the plow revving up once more, trying to dig the tracks out from under another slide. He and the others had begun the process early with hand-shoveling to a depth the plows could handle, but it seemed a never-ending battle.

As he walked the narrow tracks toward the Hankses' house, a man came from the opposite direction, dressed in a fine coat. "Do you work here?"

Griffin stopped. "I work for the railroad, sir."

"Any idea when the train is getting out of here? I have an important case I'm working on, and my associate and I need to get to Seattle as soon as possible."

"I'm sorry, but I don't know. If the snow would stop, we'd have a chance."

The man acknowledged the snowy peaks all around them. "We've heard about the slides and all. Any chance of a slide happening here in town?"

"I never heard of that, sir."

He nodded, digging his hands deeper into the pockets of his wool coat. "Well, I hope there's a way out of here soon. Or else I may have to walk to a train that's moving. I hear the trains are coming into Scenic."

"I wouldn't chance Old Glory in these conditions," Griffin said. "Too dangerous."

The man turned. "Old Glory? What's that?"

"A path down to the town of Scenic that bypasses the rail tracks. But men have died walking it. You slip on the snow, you could end up sliding right into those big trees. It's a thousand-foot drop."

Undaunted by the hair-raising description, the lawyer pressed Griffin for more details. "But if I can get there, I'll be on my way to Seattle. It can't be as bad as you say."

"I wouldn't suggest it, sir. I've done it, and in this kind of weather with it snowing, you probably wouldn't make it."

"I could die in some avalanche too, waiting around here. Which is the lesser of two evils?" He grumbled some more before heading toward the passenger train, nestled between O'Neill's official cars and the fast mail train. Griffin wondered on the remark, not aware of anyone he knew succumbing to a mountainous slide. Though he did hear stories in other areas of the Cascades. But the danger seemed so rare, he gave it little thought to concentrate on more important things. Like Lillian's welfare and checking in with the Hankses.

He trudged through the thick snow that continued to accumulate even as the residents tried to clear around homes rapidly turning into igloos. At last he came to the Hanks home and heard a baby whimpering within. Elizabeth greeted him at the door, with the fussy baby cradled in her arms. "Oh, Mr. Jones."

"Hello. I just wanted to see how you're doing and if you need anything."

"We're low on coal for the bedroom heater," she admitted. "And I could use a load of wood for the cookstove."

"I'll see what I can do. I can bring in some wood at least. You may need to use the cookstove for heating and cooking. Coal is being rationed because of the trains."

Elizabeth nodded. "Clyde was here yesterday and brought us some provisions. Lillian is on the train helping the passengers stuck here."

Griffin stepped back when he heard this. Why would Lillian be on the train of all places? Unless she had plans to leave when the train moved on? The mere thought sent chills rippling through him. His frenzy spilled out. "Why would she be there? Is she leaving? What's wrong?"

"Calm yourself," Elizabeth said with a chuckle. "No, she isn't leaving. It seems she's made some nice friends, and she helps take care of the children. Can you imagine a little child being stuck in a railcar for days? These shacks are difficult enough, but it's my home after all. Trains are so dirty. I told Lillian she could help however it best suits everyone, and she can return here to rest."

Elizabeth nodded toward the window where, if Griffin peered

out, he'd see the faint image of the trapped trains through the blowing snow. At least he felt better knowing Lillian hadn't planned to make a surprise exit. "All right then. Please let me know if you need anything else. I'll check on the coal and bring in the wood." He immediately fetched several armloads from the snow-covered pile beside the house. Elizabeth thanked him by offering some coffee, but he said he must be getting back.

As Griffin returned to the depot, he thought about the Seattle Express, wondering what it was about the train that drew Lillian's attention. Could it be as simple as lending a helping hand? Then he remembered the dapper lawyer on the tracks that he had met, and his imagination got the better of him. Of course engaging with learned minds among the passengers would be far more interesting to Lillian than listening to his simplistic thoughts. After all, he had only just learned to read, and he dealt in coal and mail bags and snow. Hardly a suitable man for a lady with a quick mind. His steps slowed at the picture of her surrounded by folks of her social class, laughing in fond camaraderie and sentiment. It made him feel lonely.

During the rest of the afternoon, Griffin tried to keep his attention on his work but found himself distracted by thoughts of Lillian on the train. Not that he mattered in her life. She was engaged after all. But he still relished the encounters they had, at the hotel and now with their reading lessons. He had gazed steadfastly into her eyes and felt the attraction. Their relationship appeared on a clear track, rolling along with nice speed to a hopeful destination . . .until the relentless snows came. If only this storm would abate and life could return to normal. The trains would depart, and he and Lillian could resume their lessons. But the snow continued, the trains remained stuck on the tracks, and his doubts rose higher than the snowcapped Windy Mountain.

A figure came walking swiftly toward him—more a blur in the heavy snow until he drew close. Griffin recognized him as his fellow rail worker, Jack McClintock. "Did you hear the news, Griffin? I can't believe it. A slide took out the beanery at the Cascade Tunnel Station early this morning!"

Griffin stopped hacking away at the snow and ice at the track near the depot, wiping away snowflakes accumulating on his eyebrows and eyelashes. "What? Was anyone hurt?"

Jack stood mute at first, then nodded. "Two were killed. The cook and a server."

Griffin froze at the news. What had only been a rare occurrence on the railroad, a deadly avalanche, had now happened right here at Windy Mountain. "That's terrible." Griffin glanced over at the buildings of Wellington barely peeking out of the mounting snowdrifts, with the steep face of the mountain towering over them. Could such a thing happen here? An avalanche in town had never once been considered a threat. But gazing at the relentless snowfall and varying temperatures that made the Cascade Cement a household name—where it held train wheels fast to the tracks, buried the rest of the tracks, and coated the mountains all around—he wondered if this year might prove them all wrong. Especially now, when a slide at the rail town east of them claimed men's lives.

Now Lillian's welfare became his main concern. He left the depot and walked back to the trains still standing on the passing tracks overlooking a ravine and the Tye River. At the mail train, he caught sight of his buddies, Joe Walters and Matt Weiss, trying to knock the Cascade Cement off the train wheels.

"It just melts again and freezes them tight," Griffin told them grimly. "Until it stops snowing, we won't get ahead of this."

"Gotta try." Joe gave several more poundings with a long-handled steel scraper to break the ice, then wiped his runny nose on the snowy sleeve of his jacket. "If we don't get the mail train out of here soon, the mail bosses are putting out rumors they'll renegotiate the fees with the railroad."

"Maybe that means you'll get more money for your work," Griffin said with a smirk.

"Ha!" Joe now elbowed the fireman, Matt. "Hear that? We'll get paid extra if we stay stuck here long enough. Fine by me."

"No money is worth this delay, even if my Dorothy would love that ring." Matt rubbed his hands together while staring up at the foggy mountains surrounding them. "This place gives you bad feelings. Look what happened to the beanery at the Cascade Station."

"So you heard," Griffin said in a low voice. "We were just there a few days ago." He recalled sending Lillian up to the small restaurant to warm herself after the cold ride on the rail cart. He thought of the place where she had just dined being suddenly destroyed, and he shivered.

"I just ate there," Joe recalled. "Nice fellers working there. One minute you're alive. Next minute you're not. Makes you think about what's important and what isn't."

Silence overcame them. Griffin turned to see a few passengers from the Express loitering nearby, their eyes wide and faces drawn. They now whirled and headed for the passenger train before Griffin could say anymore. "See you later," he told his friends and then tried to catch up to them. The group suddenly burst into the observation car and told everyone about the avalanche at the Cascade Station. When the anxious passengers saw Griffin standing near the door to the coach, they immediately pounced on him and demanded details.

"We don't know everything," Griffin began. "It's only rumors. We need to wait for all the facts."

"We just had a meal there," one of the men noted, shaking his head.

"Are we safe here?" another asked.

"Of course, sir," Griffin said. But the words seemed hollow in light of what had happened. Yet what else could he do? They were all stuck like paste with nowhere to go until the tracks could be cleared.

Just then he caught sight of Lillian cuddling a baby. What a beautiful picture she made. She then surrendered the infant into the arms of another woman and came forward to greet him. "Griffin! Is it true? About the beanery? Mrs. Covington thought she heard a rumor. . ."

"Yes. It was struck by a major slide. Jack said it happened early this morning. The server and the cook were lost."

Lillian's face dropped as a mist of memory fell over her eyes in watery tears. "The server was so polite. He brought me coffee just the other day." She wiped the escaping tear from her face.

"Are we safe here?" a woman snapped at Griffin, jostling the fussy baby Lillian once held. Lillian introduced her as Mrs. Starrett.

"Yes, ma'am. We've never had anything like that happen here in town."

One of the men scorned his pronouncement. "I'm sure it never happened back there at the beanery either. And now it did."

Another woman began to shriek. "We've got to get out of here! Now!"

"That's Mrs. Lemman," Lillian murmured to Griffin. "Several say she is not right in her mind. I don't know what to do."

"You're doing everything you can," he answered in a soft voice. Her rosy-colored lips, upturned into a small smile, eased the drawn, wide-eyed look of concern. She didn't deserve to be living in this wild, unpredictable place. She ought to be clothed in fine lace and pearls, sitting straight in an ornate chair, gabbing with friends, or sitting opposite a fine gentleman like her intended and eating fine food. But watching Lillian go to Mrs. Lemman in an attempt to comfort her, he knew she was exactly where God wanted her to be. But even with her effort, the woman continued to rage on and then charged Conductor Pettit when he entered the coach.

"We must get out of here now!" Mrs. Lemman demanded. "Before it's too late."

Another young man pushed forward. "I must agree. Can't the train find refuge back in the tunnel, at least until the storm is over?"

"You can't go in there, Mr. . . . ?" Griffin paused.

"Mr. Topping. Ned Topping. And why not? It seems the safest place with the mountains crumbling all around."

"You can't burn coal in there to keep warm," Griffin said. "The smoke from it kills."

Another shriek erupted from Mrs. Lemman's lips. "We're doomed!" she wailed.

"Just push us back in using the electrics," Ned Topping said. "We can go without the coal heaters and wear coats."

"Yes, yes," others chimed in.

"You're forgetting one thing," Lillian charged, stepping forward. "The children. The babies. How do you expect to keep them warm with no heat? They'll get sick."

"The man here is correct about the danger," Conductor Pettit said, acknowledging Griffin. "It's far too dangerous to return to the tunnel. Not to mention there's water building up and thick, black mud. Plus slides on either end. If you go in there, you can't get out if you need anything from town. It's very unsanitary to wander about, and dangerous. You'll be stuck in a dark tunnel inside the coaches."

The men grumbled. Several talked of leaving the train for good and walking to the next town. Others were too distraught to speak about it any further. Griffin wished he had an answer of comfort for them as he looked at the wave of anxiety crisscrossing their faces, like the lines drawn on Lillian's face. He offered a quick "Excuse me" and wandered back to the open door. The only thing he could do was try to change their circumstances and get back to work. At least he did the shoveling well, or tried to, in the midst of a storm that refused to leave.

Just then he felt a tap on his arm and turned to see Lillian. She stared at him with a set of wide blue eyes. "Are we in trouble?" she asked in a soft voice. "Tell me the truth."

"This is the truth. We don't know. But the railroad is working day and night. God is our refuge and strength, Lillian. Our help in trouble." He jammed his cap onto his head and buttoned his already-soaked wool coat. "I read that today. Trust Him."

Lillian's tender lips broke into another smile, and her taut face relaxed. How he dearly wanted to succumb to the attraction of kissing her cherry red lips. "I'm so glad you're keeping up with the reading. Maybe once this storm is over and the trains move on, we

WHEN THE AVALANCHE ROARED

can have some more lessons."

"I'm praying it will be soon. I miss our lessons." He nodded again, reached out to touch her hand, and then quickly withdrew and returned to the snow.

121

Chapter 13

"I wish I could go with them," Sarah Covington said wistfully. "But they all think I'm too old, and I guess I am."

Lillian watched along with her and several women as a few of the men, bundled up in coats and mufflers, headed out into the elements, determined to walk to Scenic despite the warnings not to leave. Two women Lillian's age began murmuring among themselves, considering walking out too. Others continued to insist they find safety in the tunnel, that it couldn't be as bad as the conductor said. Lillian heard the desperation in the voices all around. Every hour, it seemed, the passengers would ask her for updates. They knew Lillian lived here and was acquainted with a few of the railway workers—courtesy of Sarah Covington, who told them of her friendship with Griffin. But she had no news to give, and the train deteriorated into a frantic mess.

Now a new argument arose among the youngest of the passengers.

"Daddy, I want my dolly!" cried three-year-old Thelma Davis. A loud wail erupted in the car as Lillian looked on in dismay. Over the past few days, she had exchanged the assistant-postmistress apron and the care of her cousin for helping on the passenger train with the fretful children and nervous adults. Now little Thelma confronted her doting father when Raymond Starrett took the doll to examine her little patent leather shoes fastened with tiny brass buckles. The father promptly went over to tell the young boy to give it back.

"It's just an old doll anyway," Raymond grumbled, handing it over. "But she better not play with my toy train."

Lillian sighed, wondering what to do to amuse them and keep them out of mischief. Finally she suggested the children all play together in a dream land. And just like that, she whisked them to a place where trains took the Queen (Thelma's doll) on a fantastic trip around the world. Several seats within the Pullman served as special places the Queen would visit. And the children joined in with great enthusiasm, looking for other toys to outfit the make-believe lands. One child had a stuffed bear, and it became the kingdom of the bears. Another decided to make a dress shop with some of her mother's fine accessories.

Sarah Covington appeared in the doorway. "Oh, how I hate to interrupt such a sweet scene, Lillian. But I have good news. We're having a church service this morning! Isn't that wonderful? The reverend here on the train is going to share scriptures. And there will be singing."

Lillian could not have been more delighted by this news that boosted everyone's spirits. Even the children left their make-believe lands to join in. They needed the good news from the Good Book. Besides the children's early morning rambunctiousness, the adults learned the disappointing report of rotary plows jammed in both directions and small slides coming down the mountain faster than they could be cleared. The evening before, the men on the train demanded a meeting with Superintendent O'Neill to discuss the situation and what their options might be. When he failed to appear as they requested, the anger escalated. For Lillian, she saw no way out of this predicament. Griffin had already mentioned that finding refuge in the tunnel was too danger-ous. Except for walking to Scenic, the passengers had little choice but to wait for the tracks to be cleared.

Along with Lillian, most of the passengers entered the day coach where the pastor stood, an open Bible in his hands, before a congregation eager to hear a message from on high. Even the train workers crowded in for the sermon—including Conductor Pettit, porters, firemen, brakemen, and engineers, mail train personnel, and the Express passengers, all standing shoulder to shoulder to seek the Lord for deliverance. The reverend read Psalm 27, finishing with the last verse: "Wait on the LORD: be of good courage, and he shall strengthen thine heart: wait, I say, on the LORD."

Lillian looked around at eyes transfixed on the reverend as he spoke words of hope. All of them had been waiting days in the snow and wind, and now with rains coming and snow solidifying and encasing them in ice much like a tomb, the reading brought comfort. How they needed courage in these times. And the reverend shared words of courage, of holding fast, of not giving in to fear but lifting their eyes unto the Lord who held them all in the palm of His hand. Creases of concern on faces began to relax. A few lips turned up into faint smiles, which grew broader when a hulking man stepped forward and began singing "The Holy City" in a rich, baritone voice. Watching the man, Lillian thought of Griffin—who possessed a similar set of broad shoulders but contained a spirit of peace on him. And suddenly she wished he were here by her side, reciting a psalm of strength, singing an old-time hymn that spoke of a New Jerusalem without fear or pain or death.

At the conclusion of the service, the small crowd wound its way through to the other coaches. Lillian began making her way toward the ladies' car when she heard a familiar voice. Griffin had stood farther back in the thick crowd and now moved forward.

"It's good to see you," Lillian said a bit breathlessly. She didn't care if her voice betrayed her interest. A strong and solid presence is what she needed in uncertain times, which Griffin provided. How anyone could call this gentle giant of a man an idiot, even going so far as to call him a criminal at one time, raised her ire and strengthened her determination to be his outspoken advocate. When all this was over, maybe she would have a few words with his archenemy, Oliver—in the company of Mrs. Bailets, of course—and set things straight once and for all.

"Quite a good service, wasn't it?" Griffin commented. "There's no formal church here in Wellington, so a traveling minister on the train offering a sermon is a fine treat."

"I only wish the words would last. Everyone is so nervous. And angry. They've heard nothing from the higher-ups. Like from Mr. O'Neill, the superintendent." She paused. "I wonder if I dare try to intervene."

"What do you mean?"

"I know the superintendent, remember? He treated us to that fine meal at the Scenic Hotel. His wife and I are good friends. I wonder if I dare send him a telegram about the conditions here…"

Griffin shook his head. "He has a lot to do, Lillian. And the situation is bad. He puts a new plow out to work, then the Cascade Cement breaks it. Or it gets jammed up by a tree taken down by a slide. The snowfall won't let up. It's the worst anyone has ever seen."

"I heard from my cousin about the plows breaking. She says Clyde is beside himself. There seems no end to this. Mrs. Covington told me she thinks we'll be here till spring and is writing her son to tell him so. And right now, I think I believe her."

"But I did hear the telegraph is up and working again," Griffin said. "Maybe since you know him, sending a message to Mr. O'Neill might give him some new ideas. Though I don't know what else he can do."

Lillian brightened at the suggestion. "I will go at once to the telegraph office. Maybe it will uplift some spirits. If he can just meet with the passengers, it would reassure many. They need it desperately." She fumbled for her coat and followed Griffin out into a rainy mist. Fog obscured much of the area, but an occasional break in the low-lying clouds revealed a steep bank of snow like a large hand holding the summit of Windy Mountain in its grasp. She thought little of it, remembering Conductor Pettit had said the area had never witnessed a slide. Instead she trudged through heavy slush to the telegraph office.

Inside the office, Basil Sherlock sat at his desk, nodding to Griffin when they entered. "Some kind of weather we're having, eh?" he remarked.

"I hear at least the telegraph is working," Griffin said.

"Who knows for how long, but yes, it is."

"I must send a message at once to Jim O'Neill at Scenic," Lillian declared. "He must know how bad the situation is here with the trains in the snow."

The man's eyes widened. "Did you say O'Neill? If that's who I think it is, I heard in a recent telegram he's been ill or something. Anyway, no one can move a mountain of snow, missy. Nothing's gonna happen until the weather changes."

Lillian felt her agitation rising. "The longer we wait, the worse this situation becomes."

"I already sent out a grievance by some highfalutin lawyers from that passenger train, all talking lawsuits and what have you. I don't get paid enough to be the go-between here in a disagreement."

Griffin stepped up. "Basil, you don't understand. The assistant postmistress here is good friends with O'Neill's wife. A message from her may help him do something more for the trains or at least talk to the passengers. It's worth a try. Please."

Basil blinked, then shrugged. "I better not get in trouble for sending something like this," he mumbled. "A fellow can only do so much, you know."

Griffin towered over the man who began slinking down in his rolling chair. "Please send it."

"Fine, fine. What's the message?"

Lillian grabbed a pencil and a piece of paper and scribbled out a note.

Mr. James O'Neill, Superintendent,
Cascade Rail Division, GNR
> *Situation on trains dire.*
> *Poor sanitation, food and coal nearly gone.*
> *Passengers near revolt.*
> *Request meeting with you.*
> > *Lillian Hartwick, Everett WA*

Basil read it and shook his head, even as he began sending it. "The boss is up to his ears in issues," he continued to grumble. "There are problems up and down the line. Wellington isn't the only station, you know."

"But here it's the worst," Griffin pressed. "I was in the coaches. They smell like the town privy. The children need food and warmth. There are babies."

"All right, all right. I'll let you know what I hear."

Griffin exchanged glances with Lillian and then escorted her out of the office. She gazed up the street to the hotel, recalling a conversation among the ladies last night—how they were desperate to have something clean and nice for the children to wear. They wondered if a sewing circle might help while away the monotonous hours. Lillian headed for the hotel, certain Mrs. Bailets could find some material and notions. When they arrived, Griffin said he must leave and return to the line to help break up the ice. Lillian nodded, not wanting him to abandon his work of digging them out of the snow, even if his presence gave her courage. "Please take care of yourself."

Griffin stood unmoving. "Lillian—I—" He paused as if ready to say something profound. She wondered what the words might be when he shook his head and said instead, "I'll check back with Basil and let you know if there's an answer."

Even as the drops of rain mixed with large snowflakes, she stood there quietly until a whisper of thanks drifted from her lips. She then entered the hotel, trying not to consider her feelings for Griffin that grew with each passing day. Once the trains were moving again, no doubt both Anthony and Mother would order her to return to Everett. But her former world seemed very unimportant and even prudish compared to what was unfolding on the lower banks of Windy Mountain in twenty feet of snow. Here she felt useful and needed.

The visit to the hotel went better than she ever anticipated. Mrs. Bailets found some old dresses of hers that could be altered into suitable children's clothing, and she supplied the needles and thread. Then a jolly man sitting at one of the checkered cloth tables, indulging in a smoke, stood and ventured over.

"Looks like some fine dresses you got there for a snowy day," he remarked with a chuckle.

"And why is that your business, Mr. Horton?" Mrs. Bailets inquired. "They are not for us anyway. Miss Hartwick needs material to make the children on the train some clothes."

His eyes widened. "Well, that's a fine thing you're doing." He rummaged in his coat and pulled out a bag of colorful gumdrops. "Here. For those children. Can't get them to my boy anyway, being stuck here. Don't want them to go to waste."

Lillian smiled. "Thank you so much."

"Well, I'll be," Mrs. Bailets remarked. "I shouldn't have been so hasty in my reply, should I?"

"No offense taken." He sauntered back to his smoking cigar as Lillian looked on in astonishment.

"Now there's a good lesson," Mrs. Bailets murmured under her breath. "Have you everything you need?"

"This is wonderful. I only wish we had more food."

"Sorry it's only bacon and potatoes," she confessed. "Supposedly Basil got a message out to Scenic today, asking for food supplies. We'll see what happens."

"This is a difficult situation, isn't it?" Lillian hedged, fearful of what she might say.

"We do the best we can to meet each day with our heads held

high, prayer on our lips, and a song in our hearts..."Then she added, pointing to the bag of gumdrops, "and not be so easily offended."

"I'll drink to that," exclaimed the giver of the gumdrops, who was in earshot of the conversation and was now lifting his glass of potent amber liquid in a toast before throwing it down his throat.

Lillian couldn't help but chuckle as she thanked Mrs. Bailets again before returning to winter's blast. A tall, thin man now made his way toward her—Ned Topping, who offered to carry her packages. "I sent a message to the boss, Mr. O'Neill," she told him.

"Very good. Between the message the other gents sent earlier today and yours, maybe we'll finally see something happen. Or at least a meeting."

They walked along, chatting about the passengers and then the church service earlier that day. Ned sighed. "The service was fine this morning, but the good humor didn't last long. There's still bad feelings. Several more are planning to leave this afternoon and walk on foot to Scenic."

"Are you going with them?"

Ned shook his head. "I don't much fancy walking eight miles in this kind of weather. But if we don't move soon, I'll have no choice. My little boy back home needs me."

Lillian considered all the families in the cities, waiting for their loved ones to arrive from out of the snowy mountains. The husband of Sarah Covington, who planned to celebrate their wedding anniversary in just a few days. Good friends of Ida Starrett and her children, including the rambunctious Raymond, who anticipated their arrival after the death of Ida's husband. The mother of three-year-old Thelma, looking to be reunited with her daughter. And now Ned's little boy. She learned from Sarah Covington that Ned had only recently buried his wife and unborn child and now wanted to be home with his son. So much depended on the train leaving this place. She prayed Jim O'Neill would see her message and send the help they needed.

Back inside the stranded train, the women pounced on the dry goods while Lillian gave out gumdrops to the shining faces of the children gathered around her. Raymond Starrett plucked several drops out of her hand and raced off while Lillian distributed the rest to the children, including Raymond's quiet sister, also named Lillian, who waited patiently for some candy. The older Lillian slipped in extra for the girl for having the best name and mannerism of them all, to which the younger Lillian giggled in glee. Seeing them all with smiles cheered the parents and made Lillian feel that the tide might be turning. Hopefully soon, these dear folks would be on their way to their important destinations. The fact of an imminent departure saddened her. Buried in feet of snow, the most difficult of circumstances had turned strangers into friends. But they would soon need to move on, even if the future appeared as murky as a fog-riddled Windy Mountain.

———————◆●◆———————

The phonograph soothed everyone as Lillian sat companionably with several women, attempting to shorten the skirt of a dress to fit little Lillian. Just then a couple began to waltz down the aisle of the coach in time to the music, which prompted smiles from those around them.

"It looks better in here already," a voice commented.

Lillian looked up from her sewing to see a snow-covered and grubby Griffin towering over her with a grin on his rugged face. She couldn't care in the least that he looked like a vagabond on the street in need of a bath and fresh clothes. His presence radiated warmth, steadfastness, strength, and stability. "Any news?" she asked hopefully.

He shook his head. "No answer yet. Sorry."

Lillian sighed and returned to her sewing, trying to fight off the tears glazing her eyes. She would have thought her friendship with Berenice and then the encounter with Jim O'Neill at the Scenic Hotel might have spurred the superintendent to action upon receiving the telegram. But the silence fueled her restlessness. What else could she do for her newfound friends?

Lillian cast the sewing aside and bolted to her feet. "I'm going to see Conductor Pettit. This is totally unacceptable."

"I think all that can be done is being done," Griffin said in a low voice.

"No. There must be something more. Something we have overlooked." She hated to think she was turning into a version of Ada Lemman, with a frantic lilt to her demeanor that bordered on desperation. But these were desperate times, and waiting didn't seem an adequate option.

She wandered through the cars until she found the conductor talking with a fireman about the quantity of coal remaining to heat the coaches. "I'm sorry to disturb you, Mr. Pettit, but something must be done. The conditions in the train are deplorable, and there is only bacon and potatoes. What of the children? They can't be expected to live like this."

"I understand the situation, Miss." Pettit blew out a sigh. "I've made requests through the telegraph office, but I don't know if the messages are getting through. That's why I plan to walk to Scenic myself and personally check on the supply situation. We cannot allow this to continue." He then added under his breath, "I have five children. I understand."

Lillian breathed a sigh of relief and thanked the man. She returned to the main coach, where the giggly children had begun their own dance among the seats in time to the scratchy music playing on the phonograph. "Conductor Pettit is going for food and supplies early tomorrow," she announced to the sewing circle.

"It's high time!" exclaimed Mrs. Lemman.

Others nodded in approval.

"If he goes, then I'm going too," said a young woman named Libby.

Sarah Covington shook her head. "You can't. They won't allow women and children to make the journey."

Libby crossed her arms and held her head high. "I won't be told what I can and can't do. I will go if I must, and I won't let my being a woman stand in my way. Or my dress for that matter. Surely there are men's trousers for me to use. Even if I have to ask a railway man."

Several of the married women gasped. Sarah Covington now pressed a roughly sewn garment into Libby's hands. "Stitch this part of the sleeve, will you, Libby? We don't have enough hands here to make the clothes for the children, and they could use some frocks."

Lillian watched the older woman display calm among the others who sat on the verge of despair. It wouldn't take much for everything to come crashing down around them. She pushed the thought aside and sewed steadily for another hour. The camaraderie of women working on a common goal mattered more than anything. Together they would outwit this storm, one way or the other.

Lillian picked up the dress for the younger Lillian, ready to tackle another pleat, when she saw Griffin approach. She'd forgotten he still stood there in the coach, waiting. "Lillian, it's getting dark. Shouldn't you be getting on to your cousin's? She says you like to go home evenings. I would be happy to walk you. I have a lantern."

Lillian looked around the circle. "We'll be working late. There is so much sewing to do. And Mrs. Covington has assured me there's an unoccupied berth where I can rest tonight. If you could, please let my cousin know that my sewing skills are being put to good use. I will see her tomorrow. I promise."

Griffin's lips parted, ready to say more, but then he left. At that moment she felt a hand jostle her arm, and Sarah Covington looked at her with a knowing gleam in her eye.

"I think that man has fallen head over heels for you, dear. I've seen it plenty of times in my life. He stared at the Beck couple dancing away earlier before setting his sights on you."

Lillian looked away, even as warmth filled her face. "I cannot accept such a thing," she said before adding in a low voice, "I'm engaged, after all."

A hush fell over the sewing circle with heads bent over their work, though the eyes of the women occasionally gazed at her in curiosity. The looks were filled with likely the same questions that bothered Lillian: *How can you leave the man you are promised to? What kind of a woman are you, flirting with another man—and a railway man at that? What does that say about your virtue?*

She knew then what she must do.

I must stop seeing Griffin Jones.

Chapter 14

$\sim\!\!\curvearrowleft\!\!\sim$

MONDAY, FEBRUARY 28

A loud crack startled Lillian awake. She rolled over on the narrow berth, careful not to fall off, and squinted at the still-dark scene out a nearby window. Then she heard it again, a strange sound like the earth falling, and realized it must be yet another snow slide that happened far too frequently to give anyone a semblance of peace. More large trees with full needles had succumbed to the snow's weight and came crashing down. More delays as the trees must be dug out and cut or risk damaging the snowplows. More waiting.

Lillian fought a yawn that came calling. The ladies had sewed well into the night before finally surrendering to exhaustion. But in the end, they finished a dress for nine-year-old Lillian Starrett, to the delight of the girl's mother, Ida. Lillian herself was pleased to have accomplished a big part of the sewing and couldn't wait for the little girl to try it on.

She yawned again and dragged a blanket closer around her, feeling a distinct chill in the air. The coal heater in the coach must have gone out. Thank goodness she'd left on her wool dress, despite the others wearing nightgowns for sleep. Sarah Covington had offered one of her night dresses, but being so cold, Lillian had decided against it. And now she was glad she had. She only prayed that today would be the day of deliverance, that despite the foreboding noises, the train would move west. Sighs of relief, as well as thanks to God, would radiate throughout the cars. But hearing the distant sounds and seeing white in the windows from snow piles that nearly crested the roof of the coach in places, she realized today would be another hard day for her cousin's husband Clyde and the crew working day and night to clear the tracks. More days of snow and slides and downed trees and despair. It had to end soon.

Slowly the light of dawn came filtering through a window not buried in snow, and for the first time, she saw no whirl of white falling from the sky. Lillian didn't realize how much she missed seeing the first rays of morning sunlight stream into a room until going nearly a week without it. She slid off the berth to the cold floor below. A groggy Sarah Covington stirred in her lower berth and greeted her.

"Good morning. At least the snow has stopped." Lillian gestured to the window. "Just to see a clear sky would be a gift." Next to the passenger train, flickers of light danced inside the mail train from the men stirring to greet another day. They had no doubt recounted and sorted mail in the bags at least fifty times while waiting to move on from this place. More than likely, the men whiled away the hours playing long hands of poker.

"Well, that's a bit of good news on the weather," Sarah said in a tired voice. "I feel in my heart we will leave soon."

Lillian hoped so. She dearly wanted an update from Griffin on the rail line happenings, until she recalled the decision to cease communicating with him. Which might prove more difficult than she imagined, considering the rapport they had garnered with the reading lessons that morphed into friendship. But the observation made by Sarah Covington over Griffin's obvious attraction for her proved she tread dangerous waters. For the sake of her commitment to Anthony Travers and the stake of her family in society, she had no choice but to let the man go. Though her mind decided on the plan, inwardly her heart spoke differently. And that heart condition must somehow be corrected—if it could be at all.

After combing her snarled hair and fashioning it into a bun at the back of her head, Lillian wandered to the observation car where several passengers had gathered. To her dismay, Griffin was there, bringing what meager food rations for breakfast he could procure from the hotel in the form of biscuits and bacon. At least there was plenty of hot coffee as she fought to avoid his steady gaze while pouring out a cup from a coffeepot.

"I hope you had a good night here on the train," he said.

"It was fine, thank you." Lillian gave a half nod and turned aside, noting the looks of interest from several women of the evening sewing circle. Her face grew warm.

Ned Topping arrived as well as a few other gentlemen and now moved forward to ask Griffin about the train's departure.

"There are still problems clearing the last slide. Another plow is out, and that hasn't helped."

The men threw up their hands and began to pace.

"How long must we endure this?" one of them snapped. "I have clients waiting."

A second one clamored, "That's it. I'm getting out of here today." He turned and conversed with his friend who agreed.

"Yes, we are leaving."

"Have you thought about this?" Griffin asked. "It's not an easy journey to the next station. Nearly eight miles and down a steep mountain."

Lillian looked on as the men told Griffin they had no choice and would leave anyway, come what may. Conductor Pettit had already announced he was going to obtain needed supplies from Scenic, which spurred the men to join him. All of them wished they had communications to know what was ahead of them and maybe even get assistance from Scenic. But with the telegraph lines down again, they must use sensibility and determination to make their decision. Since the incident with the slide destroying the beanery at the Cascade Station, no one wanted to gamble anymore on the safety of stalled railway coaches beneath the unpredictable eye of Windy Mountain. Time was running out.

After breakfast, Sarah Covington offered prayers for the small group that assembled in the observation car. Griffin stood among them, and Lillian wondered if he also planned to journey down Old Glory to Scenic. He only gazed at her momentarily before the group left the train and headed into a cold, fog-driven morning. Lillian gazed out the window, watching them struggle in the snow. Libby looked on along with her at the men who disappeared down the track. "I'm leaving tomorrow," she declared. "This is my last night on the train. Enough is enough. Though I did give them a letter to post to my employer, I must return to my job. It's not just the men that need to leave. Others of us have to get on with our lives too."

Lillian wished she had something to offer the frenzied woman, but in a way, she agreed. There seemed no reason women couldn't attempt the journey, though the thought of tumbling down Old Glory did leave her anxious. But for a time they conversed about the Scenic Hotel as a place of refuge. Several talked of warming their chilled feet in the famous hot springs or enjoying hot tea in nicer surroundings. All the women listened to Lillian's recounting of the meal she had there, though she left out the detail of Griffin's company. But the memory of him in the fine jacket, gazing at her from across the table, sent a strange surge of excitement racing through her.

Lillian forced the feeling aside when the women gathered in another sewing circle to make clothes. The fretful children clamored to be set free from the prison of the coaches. Seeing little Lillian's drawn face and Raymond's eagerness to throw a snowball, Lillian offered to take the children outside for some fresh air. She put on her coat before helping Raymond Starrett, Harriet Beck, and Lillian Starrett with theirs. Stepping out from the narrow confines of the coaches, they raced about, packed snow into snowballs, and tossed them at each other or assisted Lillian in constructing a family of snowmen. Despite the youthful cheer, the town appeared as despondent as the adult passengers on the train, with folks shuffling through snow and no one engaging in much worthwhile activity. From afar, she recognized Griffin's nemesis Oliver and other men in a heated argument that included Griffin. She worried the enemy was up to more dirty tricks. After a while, she gestured the children back inside the coach to warm themselves before making her way to within earshot of the group of laborers with their shovels tossed into the snowbank.

"I say we leave then," one of the men argued. "We've been breaking our backs out here, and for what? We ain't getting nothing for it."

"You agreed to the pay," Griffin reminded him. "We all did."

"For a day's work. Not shoveling day and night for a mere pittance while O'Neill rests easy at the Scenic Hotel."

Several men muttered an agreement. They left the shovels and walked back to the bunk room. Griffin and the younger man named Jack stood there, shaking their heads. Lillian could not help but move forward to inquire of the situation.

"Some of the men are walking off the job," Griffin said somberly. "They're tired, and they want more pay. The boss won't talk to them. He's too busy with the mess of the snow up and down the lines."

"But they can't leave. We need them. There are children on the train. They can't stop shoveling, not now."

Griffin sighed. "Something needs to be done, and soon." His gaze now lifted to center on the snowy mass of Windy Mountain where even the blackened trees from the wildfires stood like white sentinels. "Very soon." He exhaled a loud breath. "We need to move the trains out of here."

"How? Where? You said it was too dangerous to move into the tunnel. Where else can they go?"

Griffin did not respond but strode back to O'Neill's private coach, parked alongside the passenger train. Lillian watched from afar with appreciation for all he was doing. It made no sense at this critical time to beg off the idea of not associating with Griffin while they were working together to help in this situation. She refused to be concerned about opinions or her betrothal to Anthony Travers. Some things were too important to worry over mere appearances.

Now with new snow showers falling in earnest from the gray clouds, Lillian returned to the train. She didn't want to tell the ladies that the snow shovelers had abandoned their posts and the situation remained bleak. But Sarah Covington sensed it anyway, as she did with most things.

"You don't look happy, dear. What's the matter?"

Lillian shook her head. "The weather will not ease. The laborers are scarce. And again you all must wait."

Sarah Covington only smiled in a stroke of faith that moved Lillian. "Don't you know? They that wait on the Lord renew their strength and will mount up with wings like eagles. I just wrote in my diary today that we are trusting in God to save us. It's all we can do now."

Lillian wished she had her faith. She knew little about relying on an unseen God in the heavens. She made a feeble gesture of it, here and there, with some Bible reading and singing a hymn in church. She felt particularly religious teaching Griffin to read the Good Book. But it was still a book written by men. She did not understand it any more than that, even if Sarah Covington and Griffin Jones appeared to live and breathe its pages. The words of the Book nurtured them, like a good meal. In the Word they found their strength. And how that was possible remained a mystery.

———◆◆◆———

By afternoon, despite the blowing snow, a representative from the GNR arrived at the train to talk over details of the situation with the passengers. Lillian could not help but wonder if Griffin had anything to do with this new action on behalf of the railroad company. The representative, trainmaster Arthur Blackburn, Lillian recalled meeting at the dinner in Scenic. The man lent Griffin the jacket at the request of Jim O'Neill. Now he appeared worn and frazzled. The weight of concerns from the passengers and their list of demands bore heavily on him. Several times he wiped his forehead with a handkerchief, pleading with them to be patient just a little while longer.

"Time has run out," Ned Topping informed the man. "We are leaving tomorrow. The women and children who want to leave as well will need assistance.'"

"Yes!" shouted another. "We need able-bodied men to assist with their travel to this town of Scenic and down off the mountain."

"You don't know what you're asking," Blackburn said, wiping his forehead again. "For one thing, I can't spare personnel to be guides. They are trying to unbury the tracks and get you all out of here." He went on, talking of the great danger in such travel and telling them that if they insisted on leaving by foot, they would have to sign waivers to not involve the railway should anything happen.

The men grew angry, and even Libby could not hold back. "Decent human beings would see that a barn is less filthy than this place," she shouted. "How can you not offer us help? As it is, we have to melt snow over the stoves for fresh water. Are there no sources at all around here?"

The arguing escalated, with Blackburn getting more frustrated as it went on. Even when the tunnel was again suggested as solid protection from the mounting hazards clearly seen all around, Blackburn refused. He again cited the same dangers of poison and asphyxiation as Griffin once mentioned. At least in this argument, when one of the men said he would split firewood himself to heat the cars instead of using caustic coal, Lillian saw the trainmaster waver.

"I will confer with my superiors as soon as possible about the feasibility," Blackburn said. And then to Libby, "And we will immediately see to cleaning the trains and providing fresh water from the town spring."

Lillian wished she had realized the passengers did not have access to the town water, and chastised herself for not thinking of it. But the passengers sported smiles and words of encouragement as if pleased by the outcome of the trainmaster's visit.

"At least we have better news this night," Sarah Covington said, sharing an embrace with Ada Lemman and Ida Starrett. "I believe we are seeing faith move mountains."

The spirit of the train lifted immensely, especially when Mr. Bailets arrived from the hotel with a surprise of roast chicken for dinner. Cheers over the change from bacon and potatoes sent relief pouring over Lillian. The passengers agreed for now to put aside their difficulties and have some fun and frolic. Despite the nasty weather that persisted, they would entertain with their own acts of vaudeville and enjoy some merrymaking. A few offered to do a skit and hastily retreated to separate corners of the coaches to plan its execution. Sarah Covington offered to sing her favorite hymn. The girls dressed up for the occasion, with young Lillian wearing the dress the ladies had sewn and little Thelma Davis sporting a flouncy party dress that her father had in a trunk. The Seattle Express of Despair had changed into one of optimism, and it gladdened Lillian's heart.

At that moment Conductor Pettit burst into the cars, windblown and exhausted, arriving from Scenic carrying treats for the children and news for the passengers. "For anyone who wants to leave for Scenic tomorrow, the way is difficult but should be passable for the young and hardy. But the railroad agrees that the trains are still the safest place for everyone."

"Never mind about that," Libby said. "I, for one, am glad to hear this and will walk out of here tomorrow into freedom. Now to find me that pair of britches. . ." She glanced around the coach at Ned, busily scratching out news to his parents in the form of a letter. "How about it, Mr. Topping? Got anything I can use?"

The young man's face reddened along with a lopsided smile. "As much as I would like to, Miss Latsch, I fear it wouldn't be of help. But I'm sure any of the robust railway men would be honored." Ned

141

smiled from ear to ear, even as Libby waved her hand, pretending to be perturbed. He chuckled softly. "While this has been an interesting adventure, I hope I never see the likes of it again."

"Think of the stories you can share with your little son," Sarah Covington said with a smile. "How his papa was stranded on the side of a mountain in a weeklong blizzard."

He showed off the letter. "Like you, I am writing this all down for posterity's sake, Mrs. Covington. But I'm more than done with living it. If they don't move this barge tomorrow, like Miss Latsch says, I'm walking out of here. And since we now have a plan, let's have some fun tonight."

Lillian could not be happier for the passengers' mood and decided to stay for the revelry. The children gathered in a group and sang "Twinkle, Twinkle Little Star" with their cherub faces all smiles. The young adults put on a skit to laughter and rousing applause. Sarah Covington sang a hymn, and Lillian realized then what a truly gifted singer she was. "You have a wonderful voice," she told the older woman.

"We hold many secrets, dear, until God sees fit to bring them to light." She paused. "Will you stay with us again tonight?"

"Not tonight. I'm sure you will be leaving soon, and if I'm on the train and not helping my cousin, I'll be in trouble." She realized then with all the merrymaking, she had forgotten her real duties to help Elizabeth, who had been alone for nearly two days with the baby. Lillian stood now and put on her coat. "This has been wonderful, but I must go check on my cousin." She waved farewell to the women of the sewing circle, offered a prayer of safety for Libby (who planned to leave at first light), and then gave Sarah Covington a hug. "I will see you tomorrow."

"I believe this is our last day here, dear. As sweet as you all are, I must go home. It will soon be my fiftieth wedding anniversary, you know."

"I'm praying tomorrow is a new day for everyone. Your husband will be waiting for you with open arms."

"Yes, indeed. If he isn't sick with worry. Goodbye."

Lillian could not argue with that as she stepped off the train. A few laborers were still at work at this late hour, chipping away at the Cascade Cement around the train wheels, working to ready the cars to move either forward or backward, whatever the new day might bring. Thankfully the weather seemed to be calming down after the all-day snow, to allow the work by the glow of the lanterns. Maybe as Sarah Covington said, this would be their final night.

Lillian refused to look for Griffin's tall stature among the workers and trudged through the huge drifts toward Elizabeth's tiny dwelling, trying to keep the heavy snows from sucking off her boots. She glanced behind a few times but did not see Griffin following, and for that she was grateful. Things were on the verge of change, she felt, and she must change with it. The old must pass away. The new had to come. And that meant surrendering what she knew for a future yet to be written.

———— •• ————

TUESDAY, MARCH 1

Lillian pulled the quilt to her chin, snuggling closer as wind buffeted the small house. Just then she saw a brilliant flash of light and wondered if it was her imagination. A rumble of thunder followed, and she realized it must be a thunderstorm. *A thunderstorm at this time of year? It's still winter!* She flung the quilt over her head to block the piercing light flashing in the window followed by a loud *boom*. Rain splattered on the windows. The winds shifted the shanty to and fro. She ought to rise and make certain everything was all right with Elizabeth and baby Clyde but felt weary from the evening before with little sleep on the cold train. And a thunderstorm now kept her awake. Yet she couldn't help smiling at the way the day ended, with the sight of the children standing there singing their little song. And then the sweet, melodious voice of Mrs. Covington singing, "His Eye Is on the Sparrow."

Why should I feel discouraged
Why should the shadows come?
Why should my heart be lonely
And long for heav'n and home
When Jesus is my portion?
My constant friend is He.
His eye is on the sparrow,
And I know He watches me.

Lillian drew strength from those words when another bolt of bright light, followed by a crash, sent her sliding downward into the bed for protection. A new sound came like a distant rumble from above, growing louder in intensity, as if something monstrous was coming from all around. Lillian flung away the quilt and came to the west-facing window. A flash of lightning illuminated a cloud of white, roaring, folding over, and crashing into town. The house shook to its foundation.

Elizabeth rushed out of her room, clutching the baby. The corner of the house sagged from some unknown weight. "What was that terrible sound?" she asked, her voice cracking. "It's not even two in the morning. Just the storm?"

"I don't know. I saw something white. And I heard crashing." Lillian began to shake. Whatever it was, it churned up fear. "Maybe—maybe a large tree fell nearby. But it sounded like something much bigger."

Then came a strange quiet, as if the storm had given up, leaving only the rain beating on the windows in earnest. Somehow, someway, she knew something terrible had happened.

Chapter 15

A boom of thunder woke Griffin with a start. He stood up from his bunk. The brightness of the lightning bolts and loudness of the claps of thunder made sleep difficult. He struggled for his pants, tucking in the limp nightshirt, and found his still damp wool coat. His first thought was for Lillian, hoping she wasn't frightened by the storm's intensity. He'd seen her earlier as she was making her way back to her cousin's. He'd wanted to be with her, but he lingered on to shovel a few more hours, helping make up for the lack of man-power due to many workers still upset over the grueling work and little pay. Despite all the trouble and torment with Oliver McCree in the past, Griffin was grateful in his heart toward the man for his effort, along with his pal Beau Crawford—for neither left their posts but also stayed to shovel and get the trains moving come daybreak.

A strange sound filled the inner bunk room, like a throaty rumble that instantly turned into an open roar. Griffin opened the door and stepped out into the driving rain to see what looked like the entire mountain giving way under the bright intensity of the lightning, crumbling in one massive rush of snow down the mountainside.

To his horror, the white wave stormed directly for the three sets of trains parked on the tracks. "Oh God, help!" he cried and rushed back inside. "Get up! Get up!"

The bunkmates stirred. One man told him to shut up.

"What's the matter, Griff?" asked a sleepy Jack McClintock.

"Everybody up now!" Griffin shouted. "Quick!"

The men jumped. Some began to swear. Others asked if this was a prank. Griffin began searching for the oil lanterns and then thanked the Lord above that he found them full.

"What in tarnation—" Oliver began.

Griffin shoved a lantern in his hands. "We just had a huge slide right here in Wellington. It looks like it hit the trains. There's no time to waste. C'mon." He rushed out of the bunk room into the driving rain that pelted him. Rivulets of water ran into his eyes. He stumbled in the thick snow, now a slushy mess, trying his best to determine what was before him. But all he could see were hills of white. Others began to spill out of cabins, the Bailets Hotel, and other places, each talking loudly above the heavy rain.

Griffin spotted a man rushing toward him, barely keeping to his feet as he ran in a zigzag pattern, waving his arms. "Oh Master of heaven, help us please!" the man cried. "They're gone! All of them are gone!"

Griffin stopped him. "What's gone? What's happened?"

"The trains are gone. I saw it. The snow just came down off the mountain and pushed the trains right off the tracks into the ravine. It even took the locomotives. I never saw anything like it in my life! Oh God, help us, please!"

Griffin pushed his way forward with a small contingency of men joining him. The tracks where the trains had stood just a bit ago sat covered in tall piles of snow. The big boss O'Neill's private coach. . . the Wellington rotary snowplow. . .the mail train. . .and finally the Seattle Express passenger train. . . all had vanished.

Griffin watched a few men attempt to make their way down the steep embankment, and he followed after them as best he could. To his horror, the departing lightning storm lit up the deadly work of the avalanche, revealing huge felled trees and splintered cars everywhere. Steam from a locomotive spiraled upward as it rested on its side. He knew well that anyone under all that was alive no more. He wiped a hand over his face to clear his sight. The magnitude of what he was witnessing could have been a nightmare from hell itself.

A few passengers in their nightclothes walked about in a daze. A voice crying for help knocked the sense back into him. Halfway down the ravine, Griffin and others saw two hands poking out of the snow pile and clawed their way through to rescue a man caught within its icy grip. They dragged him out with great force, even as the snow tried to suck the poor soul back in. He lay there shivering, gasping for air, wearing a thin shirt and pants. Griffin realized quickly that time was their enemy. The people could be gravely injured, slowly smothering from lack of oxygen, or freezing in the snow. They had to dig—and dig quickly—if lives were to be saved.

But the magnitude of the destruction quickly overwhelmed him. He had no idea where to begin looking for survivors. The trains were so mangled and spread over such a vast area, it would take a miracle to find anyone alive. But somehow in the midst of unimaginable tragedy, miracles were happening. People were being found one by one, though far too slowly as time ticked by. Some were fellow railway workers with head wounds and upper body fractures. Griffin thought of his mail buddies, Joe Walters and Matt Weiss, and knew they must have been on the mail train when the avalanche hit. And now they lay under all this destruction. Just the other day they'd played a nice game of cards as they sat near the warmth of the small coal heater, waiting for something to change with the trains. They joked about the mail they had re-counted ten times. Matt talked about Dorothy again and the soon-to-be-announced engagement.

Griffin held the lantern high, scanning the debris field, begging God for help in locating his pals. He found what looked like debris of the mail train with bags, boxes, and mail scattered in the snow.

He began to dig with the thought of seeing Joe Walters smiling at him, thanking him for getting him out of this mess, and saying jokingly, *Guess there won't be any mail delivery today, Griff.*

Instead he uncovered the face of his friend, wide-eyed in surprise with his mouth open, staring back at him. And then Matt Weiss was found not far away, his eyes shut, eternity meeting him in his sleep. Dorothy would never see the ring he promised to give her when next they met. The two friends Griffin talked to nearly every day when the mail train pulled into town were dead.

Griffin wanted to shout in rage at the beast called Windy Mountain. Instead he slapped a soiled hand over his mouth to stifle the emotion and continued to look for any signs of survivors in a whimper or a hand waving or some other plea. He could do no more for his friends. He only hoped the meager words he once shared about Jesus meant something to them before death came calling. No one knew the day or the hour. This death had come like a thief, when none of them expected it, in the dark of night while they lay sleeping.

Turning his weary gaze uphill, he saw glimmers of light from the town of Wellington break through the foggy dawn, illuminating the evil mountain rising up behind the town. Some of these people on the train had a premonition of impending doom. Only a short time ago they begged for something to be done. To move them to safety, whether by foot or in the tunnel. But the higher-ups said they were in the safest place. At first Griffin thought so too. But recently, something inside pressed him, a danger he could not pinpoint but in actuality witnessed every day—the danger of a mountain piled high in heavy snow. Despite the many slides up and down the rail line, like the one that took out the beanery on one end and the tracks on the other, those in authority still said the trains were the safest place to be. But in the end, the fury of Windy Mountain won.

Griffin pushed the heart-wrenching knowledge aside to continue the work of finding survivors. Several of the mail personnel had been thrown from the cars into piles of snow and survived. But so many others were missing and likely buried beneath the rubble. Every minute that ticked by meant someone could succumb to lack of air or their wounds or the terrible cold. Theirs was a fight to lose. And it sickened him with the slow work of trying to find the living.

"Gotta find my buddy. Gotta find him," moaned a voice. Oliver McCree struggled past Griffin in snow up to his thighs, with Beau Crawford following behind. Griffin wondered if the cold was affecting the man's mind. Oliver dropped to his knees and began digging frantically. Nearby, the sideways locomotive belched and groaned. "He's gotta be here somewhere. Fred! Hey, Fred! C'mon."

Suddenly the snowpack where he knelt gave way, sending Oliver and Beau into a deep abyss with loud cries, their hands waving wildly. Griffin waded through snow up to his chest in spots, trying desperately to reach the area where they had fallen. In an instant he realized the cause of the collapse—snow that had melted from a locomotive steam vent nearby. Panic seized him. If the steamer gave way and exploded, they would all be goners in a mass of burnt flesh. "Oh God, help me!"

He reached the area and knew he had to be careful not to join the other two men in the open crevasse. Finding a chunk of metal lying on the snowpack to anchor himself, Griffin began digging where he had seen their hands flail. At least the men were still alive. He tried digging with his hands, but the rain had solidified the snow. He reached for the shovel he had brought, supported himself, and began chipping and clawing away the snow. At last, he uncovered Oliver's face, heaving for air. Grasping his hand, Griffin pulled, encouraging the man to try to twist his way out. With great effort Oliver finally slid free. The man gasped and coughed, his limbs shaking like tree branches in the wind, then moaned in pain. Griffin had no time to think but now worked to save Beau. He saw Beau's hand and asked the man for help but received no answer. As he wrestled with him, the snow below gave way and the man slipped farther from Griffin's grasp.

"Beau!" Griffin shouted. The area groaned and began cracking.

He grabbed Oliver and rolled him away from the area, just as it all collapsed. Griffin wiped his tired face with a grubby hand and looked back at Oliver who moaned, cradling his injured arm. "He's gone," he whispered.

Two men came with a stretcher and bore Oliver up to take him out of the ravine. Griffin sat for a time on a piece of metal torn off a crushed train, unable to move. He knew he hadn't the time or the strength to think about the man he'd helped—the very one that had made his life miserable from the moment he arrived in Wellington. Nothing mattered now. Not money or status, not age or imperfection. They were all caught up in a living nightmare as men tried to heave out the living and the dead from snow more akin to frozen quicksand.

Griffin shook his head, trying to clear his mind of the fog from the sights and sounds he witnessed. Several men straggled up, carrying their shovels. "It's like we're in some big ocean diving for drowning people," one man muttered. He breathed heavily and plunked down near Griffin to try to regain his strength. "I've never seen anything like this."

"Nobody has." *Oh, God. Help us.*

———◆•◆———

Morning arrived in Wellington—cold, gray, and deadly. Griffin struggled to fight his way among the rescuers in the massive snowpack, trying to find more survivors. How he wanted to walk on through the woods, away from this living nightmare, to pleasant warmth, green trees, laughing people, a vision of heaven. Instead he plodded along, stepping over debris, searching for something, or rather someone. Farther into the woods, he came upon several men talking to each other. When they saw Griffin, they took a stray blanket and threw it over something in the snow. Griffin did not have to ask the men what it was as they stood, visibly shaken.

"Don't look," one of them told him. "It's a little girl all torn up.

And I—I gotta have a drink."The man whirled and struggled back toward the hillside, with Wellington looking down from above.

Pain gripped Griffin's sides as he turned away from the tiny mass beneath the blanket. Sickness rose up in his throat. He struggled away in the thick snow before dry heaves overtook him. *Oh God, why?* The little girl. . .his friends Joe and Matt. . .and others yet to be uncovered in their graves of snow and ice. They had been so close to getting the trains out. The avalanche had not hit the town except the electrician house and some wires. It would have been fine in a few more hours, he felt certain. Could God not have tarried His wrath until the trains were out of harm's way?

After a time, commotion filled the air. A sign of hope had broken through the night of terror when a few fellows found the living. His agony, amassed in questions and doubt, eased somewhat after a mother, father, and baby were uncovered in the snow, bleeding from severe wounds but alive. The child cried so loudly it seemed the entire area shook with the plea to heaven above. But there was no time to question why. The family needed to be carried to the safety of Wellington, where a hospital had been hastily established in a bunkhouse. Griffin helped on one end of the litter bearing the injured father who moaned from his fractured leg. In front, the wife was carried with the crying child serenading the procession, their faces streaked in red from bleeding wounds on their heads.

When they crested the steep hillside, a man pointed to the enginemen's bunkhouse where the injured were being brought in. At the doorway stood a woman in a coat, gesturing them inside. Lillian. Their gazes met, and Griffin saw her eyes widen as he helped put the injured man in one of the beds. The sight of her safe and well gave him both strength and relief. He knew she had stayed on the train overnight in recent days and breathed a quick thanks to God she had not been on it when the slide struck.

But the brief moment of relief quickly surrendered to their present circumstances. Her voice stopped him short. "Is—is it bad, Griffin? It must be bad. I—I heard all the trains were thrown down the hill."

"Yes. It's very bad. Worse than anyone could imagine."

She looked over at the injured woman with an eighteen-month-old on her breast while the only nurse in town wrapped the baby's wounds in a small tuft of white linen. "Have—have you heard anything of Sarah Covington? Or Ida Starrett? Or—or Ida's daughter, little Lillian? Or the other children?"

He shook his head. "I only know of one who passed away. A little girl. But I don't know who she was."

Lillian nodded, though her eyes stared fixedly as if in shock. And then he heard her whisper, "Elizabeth's husband Clyde didn't come home last night. We don't know where he is. Please find them, Griffin. Please." Her hand reached out to him.

"I'll do everything I can." He looked into her eyes shiny with tears. It took every ounce of fortitude in him not to gather her sad form in his arms and comfort her. But he had a mission of life or death, and he grabbed more tools from the stack outside the bunkhouse before heading down into the ravine. He went with hope and prayer on his lips to bring back good news to Lillian concerning her friends and family. If any good could be found on a day like today.

<hr />

The men worked tirelessly to locate more survivors. Griffin and others followed blotches of red in the snow that might alert them to a possible survivor. For the last hour there had only been the dead, laid out on top of the cold snow with checkered blankets covering them. It hurt his heart to think if they had only moved more swiftly, the less injured might have been spared. But to even think on it proved too heavy a burden as tears stung his tired eyes, turning the landscape and his work into one gigantic blur.

Just then he heard a whoop, and his heart began to race. Several men emerged from behind some trees. Mr. Bailets, who had joined in the rescue, carried a young boy with a long spike of wood jutting out of his forehead. Griffin couldn't help but stare when he saw the grievous injury. Remarkably, the whimpering young boy appeared all right except for the wound. Despite the scenes of destruction, this miracle gave him the hope he desperately needed.

But the long morning turned to noontime with no other signs of survivors. Griffin remained in the area where the boy was discovered, praying for another miracle. It seemed unbelievable to imagine life could be found, with railcars broken open as if a beast had stepped on them. Among the wreckage lay huge trees knocked over by the force of the snow and the heavy locomotives. Griffin stood amazed anyone had survived the accident at all. Like the little boy, most survivors had been thrown clear through openings made in the crushed shells of the coaches. Others were pulled from beneath the snow, tree limbs, or wreckage. But with time passing away at a rapid pace, hope of finding life faded.

Fellow bunkmate Jack McClintock now stumbled up to Griffin, a shovel in his hands, looking as if he might collapse from sheer exhaustion. "The men are saying there can't be any more living, Griff. Too much time has passed. We should go back up there to town for something to eat. I can't do much more without something in my belly."

Griffin nodded, even as he again surveyed the wreckage, his heart falling. "You're probably right," he said reluctantly. The rescue had come to an end with only a few dozen survivors at best. It tore his heart.

Then he heard a strange noise. A pause. Then he heard it again, like the mewing of a cat. He shook his head and rubbed his ears. "Did you hear something?"

Jack paused to listen. The sound came again.

"Oh God in heaven! Someone's alive!" He whirled and looked behind him, scouring the snow. "Keep calling, keep calling!" he shouted to the unseen voice. Several other men joined in the search and at last pinpointed the sound of a weak cry for help. With frantic digging they found a thick tree and, beneath the tree, a woman pinned in an icy pocket with wreckage below. Griffin never felt such determination surge through him, renewing his strength. Someone brought a saw and others axes, which they used to chip and saw away at the tree. Whoever this was had been buried nearly eleven hours, and there was no telling how close to death she might be. But Griffin was determined not to have another person succumb to Windy Mountain's wrath. Not today.

At last they reached a point where they could pull her out. She could not stand, from exposure and frostbite, but whimpered and asked for Frank, Raymond, and Lillian.

"There must be more children!" Griffin told the men, remembering his Lillian had wanted to find the girl bearing her name. "She's calling for them." He began to dig again until he looked up and saw Jack with a tiny bundle in his arms, covered by a blanket.

"Her—Her baby is gone, Griff." Jack could barely choke out the words.

He looked back at the injured woman shivering under a blanket. Her face was pinched, eyes closed, calling for her infant son and for her other children. And Griffin nearly collapsed under the weight of that mournful voice that echoed in his mind.

Chapter 16

⸻⟳

"My hands. My hands are frozen."

Lillian took up a roll of white cloth to wrap the survivor's frostbitten hands from his snowy encounter. He was about her age, still clad in his nightclothes, his eyes bugging out of his head as if he had lived through the most dreadful of nightmares. His hand disappeared under the tuft of white, reminding her of the dream on the advent of Anthony's marriage proposal. The vision of a hand belonging to one crying for help when none could be found. Lillian wiped a tear that escaped out the corner of her eye, drew a breath, and tried to wrap the other injured hand. She glanced around at a few other women tending to head wounds, with several men moaning in pain from fractures. Until Dr. Stockwell and others could arrive from Scenic, little medically could be done for the injured except to bind up wounds, coax down whiskey to ease the pain, and warm them with blankets and hot bricks.

Lillian gazed around at the bunk room hastily converted into a makeshift hospital, mixed with the intensity of what she had seen. She remembered the storm, of course, and had thought it strange to see lightning and hear the boom of thunder in late winter. The baby had woken from the crash that followed, and Elizabeth had fetched him. Lillian had seen something through the window, so she mentioned the sounds to a worried Elizabeth and then threw on her coat and ventured out onto the porch. Rain fell heavily from the still blackened skies. She had peered westward and seen in the departing lightning of the storm a heavy wall of snow over the tracks with no trains that had stood there for many days. *Did the trains leave during the night?* she had wondered. No one had given any indication of some midnight departure. Maybe they had.

But then a frantic commotion had erupted in Wellington. People had come streaming out of their homes in the dead of night. A man slipped and slid on the boardwalk below their dwelling, and Lillian had called down to him. "What happened?"

"A huge slide knocked the trains clean off the tracks!"

"What? No!" It couldn't be. He must be mistaken. Just last night, a joyous celebration filled the Seattle Express. Sarah Covington sang that sweet hymn. There were recitations by the older children. The younger ones sang a song. A rambunctious skit was put on by those who were Lillian's age. Hope sprung anew after the meeting with an associate of the boss, and many had spoken of the possibility of the trains leaving Wellington at dawn.

The clamoring of the townspeople and the scattering of lit lanterns told the terrible tale. The trains had been pushed into the ravine by a huge wall of snow. The early morning had heralded a tragedy she never could have fathomed.

Lillian had informed Elizabeth what she heard, then quickly lit a lamp to find her dress and wraps in the still-dark house. Rain continued to fall from the departing storm that water-logged the walkways. Even as she tried to make her way toward the scene of the accident, the road running alongside the tracks was flooded. Lanterns flickered as news of the horrific accident woke every part of the tiny rail town. Men armed with shovels began making their way down the steep embankment toward the wreck. Lillian had paused to watch, trying at first to make out the scene in the darkness. But inwardly, she couldn't bear the thought of the devastation with railcars that she had occupied only hours ago, and she quickly moved on.

She'd caught sight of Mrs. Bailets waving frantically in her direction as she stood near the enginemen's bunkhouse. "Thank goodness you're here," she said in a trembling voice. "We need to be ready to help the injured in the bunkhouse. Go over to the hotel and find linens, anything to make bandages. And as many blankets as you can. The one nurse we have in town gave me a quick list of what we'll need. And make sure to get some bottles of whiskey."

"So it's true what happened. With the trains. It's all true."

"Our merciful God, I wish it wasn't. But it looks terrible."

Lillian had headed for the hotel, shivering from her drenched wraps and the unfolding stress all around. As she worked with other women to bring over what they could to the bunkhouse now converted into a makeshift hospital, all she could think of was the condition of her friends on the Seattle Express. Sarah Covington. Ida Starrett and her family. Ned Topping. Little Thelma. The outspoken Libby, who was to leave this day for Scenic, as was Ned. With her recollections of the past few hours so fresh, the fate of those friends remained. As time slipped by and fewer passengers were brought into their makeshift hospital, the reality of finding survivors dimmed. She tried to remain hopeful and threw every ounce of her being into making sure those found alive remained in the land of the living.

Lillian returned to her recent recollection of the early morning events with an answer to a heartful prayer for the passengers. A caravan of stretchers appeared, bearing up an injured family. The eighteen-month-old child suffered a terrible cut with dark patches of blood matting his brown curly hair. Seeing the family, and then Griffin's thoughtful gaze, gave Lillian hope that others might be found. Even though he said the situation appeared bleak. And then he told her about the death of a young child earlier that morning.

Her emotions swung like a pendulum after that—from fear for the dead to hope for the living and then back again.

A loud groan returned her to the current situation in the bunkhouse. "I need some whiskey!" a man moaned, thrashing back and forth in the bed. "My arm is killing me. Can't you do something?"

Lillian poured out some whiskey into a small glass and approached him. She could see the distorted upper arm of an obviously broken bone. They needed a doctor to put it safely back in place.

The man's eyes flicked wide open and stared at her. "I never saw anything like it. The snow gave way. My friends are dead. They're all dead."

"I'm sorry." Lillian offered the whiskey. "This should help with the pain. We're praying the doctor can get here soon."

He took a large gulp then stared at her. "I—I know you, don't I? I'm Oliver."

Lillian blinked, recalling the name but uncertain where. "I work at the post office, helping Mrs. Bailets—" she began.

"I know you from somewhere else." He drank down another glass. "You—you stuck up for Griffin at that pretend trial we had. And I. . ." He paused, his face grimacing in pain. "Griffin saved me. I'd be dead like—like Beau if he didn't pull me away when it caved in." His voice drifted off, and then Lillian heard a noise she'd never thought she'd hear. The sound of weeping from a humbled and hurting soul.

"I'm sure he was glad to help—" Lillian began.

"No. You don't understand. I did him wrong. Real wrong. Every day. I hated him. I hated his God." He closed his eyes, the tears rolling down his cheeks.

Lillian only adjusted the blanket a bit and moved off. She wished she had the words to say, but surrounded by all that was happening, she could barely think. Still, it gladdened her a bit to see humility sprout in the man who so disliked Griffin. He would be relieved.

Others needed her help and the whiskey that she dispensed to the injured to ease their pain. She overheard Mrs. Bailets tell a few other women that they were unable to get any messages of help to Scenic with the wires disrupted. "No one even knows what happened here, for all we know," Mrs. Bailets fussed. "We need Dr. Stockwell. We need supplies. We need helpers for the dig down there. We have no one but ourselves. We don't even know if Mr. Mackey made it to Scenic to warn them of the slide. This is dreadful."

Lillian thought of Griffin working in the deep ravine, helping to find victims. He had once gone that treacherous route to Scenic in search of the midwife. He had been there in every situation it seemed. She needed his strength to find her missing friends. She needed him as a likely messenger to tell others of the tragedy that had unfolded and plead for help. She needed his reassurance to keep her sanity, to be a symbol of peace in the midst of darkness. She needed him for everything in life.

Lillian put on her still-damp wraps in the hopes of finding him. Maybe they had enough workers in the ravine and he could go to Scenic and raise the alarm. At the very least, she wanted to tell him how his hated enemy now wept at the thought of his merciful heart helping in a time of great need. But just thinking on that collapse that Oliver described. . .what if Griffin was caught in a similar collapse? She fought to cast the thought aside. Now was not the time for new fears. Griffin was strong, and he had a knowledge of God in everything. That would protect him, she hoped and prayed.

At least the rain had stopped after the deluge in the wee hours of the morning that hardened the once fluffy snow to heavy rock. The activity strengthened in the ravine area with practically every adult soul in Wellington helping in one form or another in the search. A group of men now struggled up to the top of the steep incline, one of them carrying a crying child wrapped in a blanket. Hope sprang alive in Lillian that children were being saved, despite Griffin's mournful news hours earlier of a child who had died. She hurried over to see Mrs. Bailets' husband carrying Raymond Starrett, and to her shock, a huge wood splinter sticking out of his forehead, held in place by another man. Lillian slapped a mittened hand across her mouth to keep from gasping aloud over the ghastly wound. Instead she led the way to the makeshift hospital.

"Not there," said Mr. Bailets. "We need more room with this thing. And we don't want to scare others."

They entered the hotel, and Lillian ran to fetch Mrs. Bailets, who was conversing with the telegraph operator, Basil Sherlock. "Come quick to the dining room! Your husband just brought in Raymond. He—he has a huge stick in his forehead!"

"My land!" Mrs. Bailets declared.

"What are we going to do?" her husband asked. "We need a doctor now."

"There is no doctor!" Mrs. Bailets snapped at him. "Be careful now. Put him on the big table there. And watch out for that—that thing in his head."

Lillian stared at the scene, too overcome to move until Mrs. Bailets ordered her to fetch some checkered tablecloths and rip them into strips. "We must anchor this in place until we can get help," she said, her voice suddenly calm. Lillian fetched whatever tablecloths and towels she could find as several men entered the room and stared at the injured lad.

"That's got to be taken out as soon as possible," announced a gruff voice. Lillian looked over to see the telegraph operator, Basil Sherlock, shaking his head. "We're not gonna get a doctor anytime soon, and he could get blood poisoning, leaving it in there. And that's not gonna happen on our watch." He removed his coat and rolled up his sleeves. "All right now. Get me something with a blade. Like a straight razor. Gotta be new and sharp. And some whiskey." He thought for a moment. "He can't move during this. Gotta tie him down."

Mrs. Bailets did as he requested, even as the boy turned this way and that in pain, crying all the while. Strips of ripped tablecloths were tied around his ankles and arms to keep him still.

Basil's wife joined in to assist her husband with the makeshift surgery on the hotel dining room table. Lillian tried to feed the boy some whiskey to calm him, telling him it was magic potion that would send him to a sweet land. Mrs. Sherlock poured alcohol on her husband's hands to clean them. Several others used the cloth ties to hold the boy down, and the makeshift surgery began. Lillian whispered prayers as she stroked Raymond's stringy hair. He cried and called for his mother. After painstaking effort, the huge splinter was removed, and Mrs. Sherlock bandaged the boy's head.

"Splendid job, Dr. Sherlock," Mrs. Bailets said with a smile.

"Never thought I'd do such a thing in all my born days," Basil confessed. "I'm a telegraph operator, not a doctor. But we do what we have to do."

"I don't think any of us imagined we'd be doing these things," Mrs. Bailets agreed. "Or witness such a terrible calamity in our town."

"Do you know if anyone has gone for help?" Lillian asked, thinking of her original plan to find Griffin. "We must have help."

"Mr. Mackey, a train engineer, left for Scenic a while ago to tell them what happened."

"Do we know if he made it?"

Mrs. Bailets shrugged while Basil said, "He's a solid old codger. I know him. If anyone can make it, he can."

Lillian felt the same way about Griffin, but he was young and strong and had proven himself a match for the arduous journey when Elizabeth had been ready to deliver her baby. He knew what it entailed. He had plowed through terrible snows, down the fateful hill, and burst in on Mr. O'Neill who, on the urging of Griffin who would not take no for an answer, sent his private car with the midwife. Decisiveness and determination is what they needed. They needed Griffin's qualities.

She shivered then, uncertain if it was cold or raw emotion sweeping over her. The pot of coffee she found in the lobby where several had congregated for some food and drink failed to lessen the rattling of her teeth. She never felt so cold in her life.

"You look cold, dear, and you're wearing that wet coat," said Mrs. Bailets. "Go on home for now. Get some rest."

Lillian shook her head. "N–n–no. I can't. Too many need help and I—I need to find Griffin."

"We can't have you getting sick. Drink some more hot coffee then and head back to the hospital. It's warmer there. We are fine here, and I'm sure they need the help."

Lillian did as she suggested. She felt numb walking along, trying to awaken from this nightmare with the hope that all would be set right. But the distant shouts rising up from the ravine while men continued to search for the living and the dead told a different story. Strange clouds rose from the still-burning coal heaters and even the locomotives in the ravine, all of which had gone tumbling down the hill. The mere thought made her tremble again.

Just then she caught sight of a threesome making their way toward her, bearing a stretcher. In the lead was Griffin, his head bent so she could not read his face. "Griffin?" she called out.

He looked around, and to her surprise, his lips turned up into a faint smile. "She is a miracle," he said, nodding at the injured woman on the stretcher. "But we need help, Lillian. She's nearly frozen to death."

No longer did Lillian consider the cold or emotions as she hurried to the hospital to alert everyone of a severely injured woman. She gathered what blankets she could and began warming bricks atop the hot stove, knowing severe cold could be life threatening. She came to the woman's side, recognizing her gray face and thin, bluish-gray lips as she mumbled soft words. Raymond's mother, Ida Starrett. Hours had passed since the avalanche struck. To be buried in snow like that and still be alive—her heart echoed Griffin's words. Ida was a miracle.

Once they had Ida well wrapped with wool blankets and warming with the bricks, Lillian looked around to see Griffin standing by the stove. His gaze caught hers. His usual sparkling eyes were dull, his clothing in disarray, melting snow from his clothing forming cold puddles on the floor. He looked exhausted.

"I can't believe you found Ida after all this time," Lillian said.

"There is hope, isn't there? For the others. . ."

Griffin shook his head. "I don't know if there will be any more. It's been over thirteen hours now. But we won't stop looking, Lillian. As long as it takes."

Lillian's gaze swept the empty beds neatly made up but without patients to fill them. Like Sarah Covington. The young woman Libby, who had planned to hike out in men's trousers today and escape the snow once and for all. Ned Topping, the handsome man who also planned to leave. Little Thelma in her frilly party dress. The Lemmans. Her namesake, little Lillian. They had all been so joyful the night she left them. They had drifted off to sleep with expectation in their hearts and anticipation of newfound freedom after being imprisoned in snow for days. But their hope had been in vain. Deliverance never came, at least in the way they all expected.

Chapter 17

Griffin so wished he could take Lillian in his arms and soothe away her distress over the fate of her newfound friends. He couldn't give her hope, though with God there was always hope. The men still dug, but the chance of survival faded with each passing moment. Now a slow and terrible recovery of the dead remained, leaving everyone on the work detail depressed.

One of the women poured a cup of coffee from the red-hot stove in the hospital bunkhouse, which Griffin took with gratitude.

"I should have gotten you that," Lillian said faintly. "You must be half frozen yourself."

"I am pretty cold," he acknowledged as his gaze encompassed the room. "But you all have done well. I see you got that massive splinter out of the little boy."

"Mr. Sherlock did it with a razor, on a dining table in the hotel. So many have helped. I just wish the doctor would get here, but Mr. Sherlock says the telegraph lines are a mess."

"I wonder if anyone has made it down to Scenic for help."

"I'm so glad you mentioned it. I was on my way to find you

when Raymond came in with the splinter. Mrs. Bailets claimed a Mr. Mackey had gone to fetch help. And maybe others. But we don't know if any of them made it."

"The boss, Mr. O'Neill, needs to know what's happening. We need help. There are so many dead, and—" He saw Lillian cover her mouth in distress and wished he had used better words to convey the sad truth. Griffin gave his cup to Lillian and began buttoning up his soggy coat. "I'd better get going. It's eight miles to Scenic. We can't wait any longer. We need more diggers, supplies, and a doctor. And we have no way of knowing if anyone knows about the slide."

At once, Lillian was by his side, touching the drenched sleeve of his coat. Even if he could not feel it on his skin, just the sight of her hand on his coat sleeve sent strength surging through him. "Please check to see if Clyde is there and if he's safe. And please be careful. I can't—I can't take any more loss."

"I will. I was thinking about that nice meal we had at the hotel. Remember?"

She stepped back, and suddenly Griffin prayed it hadn't been foolish words spoken this day. Instead, she nodded and said softly, "It was a beautiful dinner." She paused. "Wait just a moment." She left him, then returned with a note. "Give this to the telegraph office in Scenic. If you could send my mother a message telling her I'm all right. Her name is Claire Hartwick, in Everett."

He nodded and tugged down his cap. With a final farewell, he returned to the damp, cold, miserable conditions. A few men with sleds had begun the sad task of dragging up the fallen from the slide area to a makeshift morgue set up in the baggage room of the depot. He asked about their identities, but they shrugged.

"Some men. One young woman."

He winced. "Any sign of Clyde Hanks?"

They shook their heads and said the snowplow where Clyde usually worked had not yet been recovered. Nor had the mail car where he likely spent the night, which still lay beneath the passenger train. Griffin had found Joe Walters and Matt Weiss in another mail car and knew it must be somewhere close. But that was the horror of this scene. Some of the cars were thrown clear and its passengers likewise. Others were smashed to bits under other cars or the locomotives and met a terrible end.

With each step he took in the thick snow, Griffin pushed away the horror of finding his dead friends, setting his sights instead on the town of Scenic. Just the thought of seeing the living, with folks ready to help, spurred him onward. At least the rain had stopped, though the skies remained gray to match the somber mood. Never in his worst nightmare could he have predicted a day like today. He'd heard of slides that came and some that did kill a few. Like the one that hit the beanery at the Cascade Tunnel station just a few days before the Wellington avalanche—and a small taste of the disaster to come. But to have entire trains thrown over the bank like toys with men, women, and children inside trying to muster some well-deserved sleep despite the thunderstorm, seemed unconscionable. It left him with a pain that refused to dissipate. No reasoning could ease his troubling thoughts. Only the strength of God could. He offered thanks right then that he knew enough ABCs to read parts of the Good Book. Especially the revered scripture his mama taught him. Psalm 23.

Yea, though I walk through the valley of the shadow of death, I will fear no evil: for Thou art with me.

God was with them all this night. With the children who died. With the others who were crushed or lost. God was with them. And for those who knew Him and trusted Him, even in death, nothing could separate them from His love. Not even an avalanche.

Tears marred Griffin's view, making the snow waver like water. He wiped the tears away and trudged on. Maybe when he returned from Scenic, he'd discover that more survivors had been rescued. More miracles unearthed. More reason to somehow be thankful. He prayed.

A ray of sunlight poked through the bank of dark clouds. Griffin knew his prayer had been answered, though he remained uncertain how. He soon arrived atop the mountainside with a near vertical descent of a thousand feet into Scenic—the notorious path known as Old Glory—and highly dangerous. He could see the footprints of those who had made the trek. Other strange impressions in the snow told him some had fallen and slid uncontrollably into one of the thick pines dotting the landscape. He winced, trying not to dwell on that fate-filled scenario, and stepped onto the snowy pathway others had trod before him. His feet slipped on snow that had turned to ice after the rains, and he realized the trek was foolhardy, even if the sight of a safe haven below beckoned to him.

Griffin felt for the knot of wire in his pocket he found useful in icy conditions. He slipped the chunky wire over the soles of his shoes, praying they would give him better traction, then began the descent step by step, walking in penguin-like fashion, using a large stick for support. He disliked the achingly long progress but did what he needed to do to fulfill a silent promise he made—to return in one piece to Lillian. The entire town depended on this journey. But from what Griffin already observed, with ant-like figures in Scenic that grew larger as he descended, someone must have successfully notified them of the avalanche. He would now follow up with much-needed information to the powers that be.

The wire worked, and Griffin soon found himself safely down the path and headed for the depot. The place was a beehive of activity as workers assembled to hike up to Wellington on the path he had just walked. Talk swirled of the relief train that made it a few miles shy of Scenic, carrying supplies. Griffin stopped a railway worker for information. "Does the big boss know about the avalanche?"

"You mean O'Neill? He knows. Someone came in from Wellington and told everyone. But that fellow is in bad shape. Nearly froze to death trying to get here."

"How many are injured?" another man snapped.

Griffin recognized Dr. Stockwell, who had cases of supplies on sleds and several doctors and nurses with him. He did his best to give the man what information he knew, including the little boy's impromptu surgery in the dining room of the hotel by the chief telegraph operator.

"Well, I'll be. I always knew the folks of Wellington were resourceful and determined folks, and I've been proven right."

For some reason, his comment irritated Griffin. "But no one should have to go through this nightmare to prove who they are," he burst out.

The doctor gestured with his hand to calm him. "Wait, please. I do understand. But troubles happen. Each is a test of will and strength. And I know the people who survived this are in good hands with the people of Wellington."

"That may be. But they would be in better hands with you there. One woman can't move. She was in the snow for eleven hours. A baby's head is split open. Others need broken bones set."

Stockwell sucked in his breath and then shouted at his assistants and others that they must finish preparations and leave as soon as possible. Griffin felt a measure of relief that his trip had not been in vain, that help would come soon. But it would come even sooner if he could bring an eyewitness report to the big boss, Superintendent O'Neill.

Griffin inquired of Mr. O'Neill's location.

"He's at the hotel, directing operations from there. I'm sure an update from you would help immensely."

Griffin first went to the telegraph office with Lillian's message for her family, then left the busy throng in town and plodded through snow toward the hotel. The place evoked sweet memories of Lillian's delicately carved face and blue eyes staring at him from across the dinner table. How he wished for that time again and vowed that if God would avail him the opportunity, they would one day return here under better circumstances.

Arriving at the hotel and informing the clerk he had crucial news to deliver to the superintendent, he followed as the man led him to a large room where many from the GNR had assembled, looking over a large map spread out on the table. Griffin recognized at once the boss, the one who had spoken well of railway workers and thought enough of Griffin to outfit him in his associate's clothes and pay for his meal. Life and death now lay squarely on O'Neill's shoulders, and by the way he sat hunched over with the boisterous chatter of another man in his ear, O'Neill appeared to carry the weight of the world. But the weight of the calamity besieging the Cascade rail line was plenty.

Griffin wasted no time pushing his way forward and interrupting the meeting. "I just came from Wellington and have a report."

The talking ceased. The entire group looked up and gave Griffin their full attention. Mr. O'Neill stood and asked for the news. Griffin did his best to describe the scene—the wreckage, the people who survived, and the many who did not or were still missing. He ended with a plea for help for the wounded, the rescuers, and the recovery effort.

O'Neill stood silent for a moment, his face blanching to the color of snow. "My aide. . .the trainmaster, Arthur. . .have they been found? They were on my private coach."

"I don't know, sir. Most of the trains are still buried. We need a hundred men at least to help with the digging. We need supplies. Medicine. The workers are hungry. We need help now."

Griffin could clearly see the lines of anxiety and worry crisscrossing through the beard stubble on O'Neill's normally shaven face. "We have a medical team ready to leave. Supplies should arrive soon, as well as laborers. I will walk to Wellington myself once operations here are secured."

"Sir, children are dead. Some are gravely wounded."

O'Neill's face crinkled in a wince. He turned away, heaved a sigh, and then looked back at Griffin. "We can do nothing for the lost. But we can help the living, and we will, as God is my witness. I am a father too. And I am devastated." The final sentence came forth in a near whisper, but Griffin heard it plainly. The powerful man of the railroad stood enshrouded in a cloud of shock and grief. And for a moment, Griffin felt sorry for him.

He backed away, watched for a few moments as O'Neill's conversation to his subordinates turned frantic, then left, satisfied the superintendent knew the gravity of the situation.

In the crowded dining area, people talked at the tables with plates of food before them. The sight of it should have sent hunger pangs soaring through Griffin as he'd barely eaten anything all day. Instead he felt nauseous. The only bright spot he noticed was the table in the corner where he and Lillian had dined and where their relationship began, now occupied by several gents. *One day, Lord,* he prayed.

Just then the two men at that table looked over at him and, to his surprise, stood and made their way toward him. Large eyes and drawn faces greeted him. "We saw you around the passenger train," one of them asked. "Did you just walk from Wellington?"

"Yes."

"We heard the news. The train is gone. Hit by a slide. Many were killed."

Griffin could only nod, with the words of affirmation lodged in his throat.

The man took out a handkerchief and mopped his face. "I can't believe it. We would be dead too, you know." He gazed upward to the wooden beams of the ceiling as if searching heaven above. "We left the Seattle Express yesterday and walked here to Scenic." He looked over at his fellow passenger, who nodded with a downcast face.

Griffin leveled his gaze at him. "Then you should be thanking God for your life."

"Others wanted to leave, you know. But they decided to wait." He blew out a sigh. "Many more could have been saved. After we arrived and Conductor Pettit came in, it was discussed that they could safely evacuate passengers from the trains. The way off the mountain wasn't too treacherous with the route they had planned. Everyone could have come here for safety. Even the women and children. But it was a day too late."

"Is Conductor Pettit here?"

"No. He went back to the trains. He said he could not leave his post. Is he all right?"

Griffin shook his head. "He has not been found. I need to find the snowplow crew to see if another fellow is with them. His wife has been asking about him."

The man stood silent for many moments until he finally said, "I should feel glad to be alive, I suppose. But in some ways, I do not. There were women and children on that train. One young, feisty thing I kind of took a fancy to. Libby was her name. She was looking to walk out today."

Griffin shook his head. "Most didn't survive the night."

The men turned and shuffled away. Griffin stared into space for a long time after the men had vanished, thinking on their words. Just the thought others might have been saved by coming here...if only they knew...if only traveling parties could have been arranged ...if only there had been more time...

In an instant, the bit of faith he had mustered was shredded by the wind of anger.

Lillian never felt such relief when the group of medical personnel finally arrived from Scenic late that night consisting of several doctors, nurses, and supplies. She could barely stand but still did all she could to comfort the injured and the grieving. Dr. Stockwell immediately took charge, surveying the patients before him and commenting grimly on the mere twenty-three lives spared. Lillian couldn't help but agree. She had tried to keep herself busy so as not to mourn the fact that most of her newfound friends on the Seattle Express had lost their lives. She tried to force away the sights and sounds of the party last night when everyone had been so hopeful. The thought of them all retiring to their berths or other places for the night, only to wake up in eternity, continually filled her thoughts, even as she tried to fold blankets.

Just then she saw a hand. Mrs. Bailets had come to her side and now patted her arm. "You need to rest, dear. It's after midnight. Please go home and check on Elizabeth. We have plenty of workers now."

Lillian put the folded blanket on a pile. She knew she had a responsibility for Elizabeth's welfare, but her feet refused to leave this place. Especially the place where townsfolk had gathered together, becoming like a family to help the injured. "I do need to see Elizabeth, but we don't know yet about Clyde. I wish I had news to share."

"Even if you don't have news yet, she needs you."

Reluctantly, Lillian left the chores at the hospital and fetched her still-wet coat from the day's relentless activities. Despite it being the middle of the night, the town remained alive with lanterns flickering and men calling to each other in the distant ravine. A man brushed by her, holding a whiskey bottle in each hand, heading for the avalanche site. "Have you found more survivors in the wreckage?" she asked him.

"No. This is for the workers." He lifted the bottles. "No one can do the work down there when you're finding limbs and—" He stopped. "Beg pardon, miss."

Lillian gasped as the man stumbled through the snow, sipping on one of the bottles. *Did he really say what I think he just said?* Sickness rose up in her throat, and she managed to find an area of snow in time before she retched. *Oh God, I can't take any more of this!* She wiped away the sickness with a handkerchief from her skirt pocket and forced herself not to look down the tracks toward the ravine of death. Instead she kept her sights trained on the hillside in the area of her cousin's shanty, searching for a flickering light in the window. Elizabeth must have kept the lamps burning for her. She needed to devote time and care to her cousin and her baby. For all she knew, Elizabeth may have received word that Clyde was safe, even at Scenic this very moment. Maybe they would have a joyous reunion. The mere thought of them embracing each other shed a light of hope on this dark night.

She climbed the hill to the humble abode and peeked in the window before entering. The hope she felt for Clyde's return disappeared. Elizabeth sat in the rocker, the baby fast asleep in her lap, her eyes staring into space. Lillian inhaled a deep breath and prayed before turning the knob. Elizabeth sprang to her feet and rushed over.

"Clyde! It's about time. I've kept dinner waiting and waiting..." She paused, her eyes wide, then shook her head and held little Clyde Junior close. Her feeble voice asked, "Is there any news, Lillian?"

"No, not yet. But there still could be." She shut the door and stood there trembling, despite the warmth of the stove in the kitchen. "Clyde could very well be at Scenic. Griffin went to find out and hasn't returned yet. He goes there often enough when they need help..." Her voice faded as Elizabeth returned to the rocker.

"I made some stew earlier tonight," she said in an unemotional voice. "Clyde always likes a good hot stew. It will warm him when he comes back from that terrible duty of his. Why they make them work such outlandish hours is beyond me."

Lillian prayed her cousin's words would come true. It would be such a blessed miracle on a day that had seen precious little. Looking at the clock, she felt a week had passed rather than the hands closing in on the end of a terrible day that began before two in the morning. Exhausted and achy, she felt like she had walked twenty miles.

She went over to the stove to ladle up a small helping of stew. Even if she didn't feel like eating, she needed the nourishment to keep up her strength, especially for the days ahead. Returning to Elizabeth's side, she watched her cousin's fingers gently sift the downy brown hair of the baby as he slept. How she prayed the newborn would not be fatherless—that Clyde would be found safe, somehow, someway.

Chapter 18

Lillian heard a crash and awoke with a start, her limbs shaking, thinking another avalanche had raced down the mountainside to crush their town. Elizabeth had dumped a load of wood near the cookstove. She glanced out the window at an overcast sky with the promise of more snow. The mere thought made her depressed. If only time would return to February 28, before all this happened. In one frightful moment, life changed. Nothing would ever be the same.

"Let me help," she said to Elizabeth, forcing back a yawn and throwing on a work dress and apron before going over to feed the fire in the cookstove. The fitful night's sleep, marred by all the harrowing events whirling in a perfect storm, did nothing to help her regain her strength. She filled the coffeepot and heated water to make some porridge. Rubbing her tired eyes, she dreaded what this new day would bring.

Elizabeth's voice broke through the barrage of thoughts. "After breakfast is over. . .if you could go to the hospital and see if Clyde came in during the night. I almost went over there myself this morning. . ."

"I will but—" She paused. Griffin had all but said it would be nearly impossible to find anyone else alive after so much time had passed. The only chance they had is Clyde bunking in with a rotary snowplow team in Scenic. Until she heard from Griffin, hope must remain.

Her cousin's movements seemed forced and almost mechanical. Like many here in Wellington, shock infected every action and emotion. Soon that shock would give way to things she did not want to consider: the full effects of grief. Lillian had no choice but to take this moment by moment.

Drawing up a chair, Lillian sat down to the mush. Elizabeth returned to the rocker, leaving breakfast untouched. "You need to eat," Lillian said softly.

She shook her head. "I'll eat when that no-good husband of mine finally makes it back here. It's just like him to do this to me. All he ever thinks about is his snowplow." She rocked a little harder. "He's always cared more for that machine than me."

Lillian dropped her spoon into the bowl and sat back. She didn't know whether Elizabeth was deadly serious or making a joke. "You still need to eat to keep up your strength and have nourishment for little Clyde Junior. I'm sure Clyde expects a strong son when he returns." She uttered the last few words without the confidence in her heart he would walk through the door.

Elizabeth stood and made her way to the table to eat. "You are going soon to the hospital?"

"Yes. Just to make sure everything is all right."

"And you will check on Clyde?" she asked again.

"I will. But I won't be gone long today. More medical staff arrived late last night, so things are better at the hospital. I can help you here." Lillian managed a small smile and went to find her wraps. For a brief time the living awaited her care in the hospital, though she dreaded it with all its emotional upheaval in the last twenty-four hours. She shivered remembering the impromptu surgery on little Raymond and then caring for his mother, Ida Starrett. They had thawed her frozen extremities with heated bricks and blankets. Her cries had pierced the air, intermixed with cries for her baby. And then there was Oliver, who insisted she bring Griffin to see him as soon as she was able. The doctor finally set his fractured collarbone with the help of trained nurses. But any emotion of anxiety or distress from all this must be put aside and replaced by compassion and calmness.

Lillian put on her coat (which had finally dried out before the hot stove) and Elizabeth's boots, offered a farewell to her cousin, and ventured out into the snow and cold once more. Today she decided to see for herself the area of the avalanche and the sets of tracks that once held the mighty locomotives and three sets of trains. Even this early in the morning, men scoured the ravine for the living and the dead among downed trees and wreckage. At the moment she arrived, two men came huffing up the hill, drawing by a rope a sled containing a person wrapped from head to foot in the checkered blanket of the GNR. Lillian averted her gaze and murmured a prayer for the deceased's family before whirling about to walk to the hospital. The dead now became the prominent part of the recovery. Her eyes glazed over with tears, and she wished she hadn't gone to the scene of the tragedy.

At the hospital, several doctors stood around dressed in heavy coats, preparing to walk back to Scenic. Without the arrival of more wounded, and few requiring skilled care, extra medical personnel were not needed—a sobering fact to the effectiveness of the destruction caused by the slide. Mrs. Bailets and Basil Sherlock's wife remained to help the nurses, their faces worn and eyes bloodshot. Lillian wondered if they had gotten any rest at all. "I can take over," she offered.

"There's not much more to do," Mrs. Bailets said, wiping a hand across her face. "All the patients are stable, according to Dr. Stockwell. He's ordered most of the staff to go home. Broken bones have been set, and wounds are bandaged. As soon as they are able, the wounded will be transferred to hospitals."

"So no one else came in overnight?"

"Dear heart, no one has come in since Mrs. Starrett yesterday afternoon. I heard they are finding more of the deceased. But it's very slow work."

Lillian inhaled a deep breath with news of Clyde's well-being dimming. "Have you seen Griffin?"

Mrs. Bailets did not react for a moment. She then shook her head. "He has not returned yet from Scenic." Then she added quickly, "But I'm sure he's fine."

"No one can be sure of anything, can they? I had to tell my cousin that her husband is still safe somewhere, but I feel certain he was on the train. I'm still expecting Mrs. Covington to lay her hand on my arm and wish me well. I think I will see the children running around throwing snowballs and the women gathered in their circle, sewing clothing for the children." Her voice broke, and the tears came fast and furious. "I'm sorry." She quickly stepped outside before she erupted. The wounded had been through enough without seeing her emotional outburst.

Mrs. Bailets followed her. "Don't think I haven't had my crying spells in all this, Lillian. I know it's difficult. But we must stay strong for those who need us. It's all we can do."

Lillian nodded and blew her nose in the hankie that Mrs. Bailets pressed into her hand. She would go comfort Mrs. Starrett and maybe play a game with Raymond and hold the Grays' child. And pray that Griffin would soon appear with news to cheer them all and especially Elizabeth—that Clyde was safe.

Approaching Ida Starrett's bedside, she found the woman lying still with her gaze transfixed on the whitewashed ceiling above. When Lillian offered her some tea, her face turned to acknowledge her. "Are you taking care of my baby?"

Lillian bit her lip, wondering who she meant. She knew the littlest one, just eight months old, had passed away, trapped beneath his mother. Little Lillian was gone too. "Raymond is doing well. See? He is over there playing."

Ida shook her head. "No, no. My baby, Francis. I—I call him my little Frank." She then struggled to sit up. "He needs his bottle. Poor thing. He must be hungry."

Lillian didn't know what to do. Finally one of the nurses came to calm the injured woman as Lillian pulled away, too distraught to think for herself. Just then she heard a scream and knew the nurse had reminded Ida that baby Frank was gone. The pain in the mother's voice tore her heart.

Raymond sat opposite his mother, a large bandage across the left side of his head where the stick had been, holding a yo-yo in his hand. Lillian knew she needed to do something and approached the youngster to ask about his toy.

"Watch me," he ordered, showing her a trick by spinning the yo-yo. "One of those doctors taught me how." He paused. "The doctor said Mama is in shock. What's that?"

Lillian drew in a deep breath. "Well. . .your mama went through a very difficult time, Raymond. She was in the snow for many, many hours. Sometimes when you are hurting, your mind goes to sleep so you don't feel the pain. Your mama is going through that."

"Maybe because my baby brother died," he stated matter-of-factly, making the yo-yo swing up and down on the string attached to his small index finger.

"I'm sorry."

"I don't know where Lilly is either." He stood to his feet and looked around. "Where did that doctor go? I like him."

"He had to take care of more sick people." Lillian tried to fight back her emotion when Raymond mentioned losing his lost sister who shared the same name as her.

Raymond returned his gaze to her and stated solemnly, "I'm an only child."

Lillian looked at his one wide brown eye, the other eye cradled by a thick bandage. "You're a special child, Raymond. And your mama is going to need your help in the days ahead."

He nodded and continued to play with the yo-yo. Lillian looked over at Ida's bed, thankful she had drifted off to sleep. And right now Lillian had seen enough until she could gather her wits again. Maybe she ought to consider her own shock from what had happened. She certainly felt it.

With that, she fled the hospital for the fresh air outside, forgetting to even put on her coat. Suddenly she plowed headlong into a stocky figure covered in snow, who now embraced her tightly as her tears fell and her voice cried out the sorrow she'd kept bottled within.

———◆◆◆———

Griffin held the distraught figure in his arms as the snow fell, until he realized she had no coat. "You need to get your coat on, Lillian. You don't want to be sick. Then we'll go have some warm soup at the hotel."

Lillian disengaged herself from the embrace and followed him back into the bunk room to retrieve her coat. She stood there, fighting to put the coat on, every part of her trembling from cold and sorrow. Mrs. Bailets nodded when he told her they were going to get something hot to eat, then he led Lillian's sorrowful figure outside once more.

"I—I couldn't take it anymore," Lillian mumbled. Griffin said nothing as he guided her across the way and up the set of stairs to the hotel. "Hearing Ida calling for her dead baby. . .listening to Raymond tell me he's an only child. . ."

"I remember Ida when we found her in the snow, asking for her children. I felt the same way."

Lillian stared at him with eyes the loveliest shade of blue he'd ever seen, despite the color being muted by pain-filled reflection. They found a small table covered in a cheery checkered tablecloth. He saw her tremble as she remarked how she'd ripped up some of the tablecloths to anchor Raymond's limbs while surgery was performed on his head. Griffin listened patiently before offering thanks when someone brought them cups of coffee and bowls of soup. He encouraged her to drink the steaming coffee to warm herself.

She took one sip then set the mug down. "Did you find Clyde?"

Griffin shook his head. "There are many people in Scenic right now. It's possible he's there somewhere, but no one could tell me for sure." Watching her shake her head, he knew that she understood the likely conclusion. Clyde would have marched up from Scenic to check on his family if he were alive. His stark absence meant he must have been on the train when it fell into the ravine.

"Why didn't he come home that night?" Lillian suddenly whined. "He should have been here with his wife and baby son on such a stormy night. Elizabeth even cooked stew for him last night, his favorite." Her voice trailed off, and she sniffed, using a cloth napkin as a hankie.

"Clyde loved his work," Griffin said quietly. "I'm sure he thought that by morning his snowplow would clear the tracks for the trains. He wanted to be part of the crew to do it."

Lillian blew her nose. A cloud of sadness drifted across her face. He wondered if he would ever see joy ignite her blue eyes again. "I don't know what I'm going to do, Griffin, if we find out he's dead. Elizabeth will be so broken up. I heard Ida screaming about her dead baby before going into shock again. I couldn't take it. What if Elizabeth does the same?" She covered her face with her hands.

"Give this to God," he told her and gently took her damp hand in his. "He can carry it."

"I don't know what I believe anymore. I'm not a Christian like you. I—I just pretend to be. I don't know what to say. I don't know how to act. I can't even pray right now."

"You can't pretend before the Lord. He knows your heart, everything about you. He knows and He understands. You don't have to be anyone else but Lillian Hartwick."

"Does God truly understand though?"

Doubt bathed those words, and he had to admit, the doubts

circulated in him too. He spent a fitful night with other railroad workers who all pressed him for details about the avalanche. Some talked of buddies that worked on the fast mail train. All of them grappled with the anxiety and fear of having to head to Wellington to comb through a vast field of wreckage, looking for the worst of the worst. Despite that task, Griffin worried more over those like Lillian and how they would take the news of loved ones' deaths. Seeing her fragile state of mind, he worried that when Clyde was found, it might hurl her over the edge much like the trains—from an avalanche of despair into a pit. He worried she would give up on faith and on God. "I believe He does," Griffin finally said.

They ate their soup quietly for a time until one of the helpers came over and asked Griffin about his journey to Scenic. He dared not tell any of them, especially Lillian, what the two men at the dining room in the hotel had told him. That many might have survived if they had acted swiftly and walked the passengers from the train to safety. He made small talk about the visit, concentrating on his meeting with the big boss and the relief that would soon be on its way to Wellington. By tomorrow there ought to be well over a hundred men in the ravine, helping in the recovery. And he mentioned successfully notifying her family by telegram about her safety.

Lillian stood to her feet. "I should go comfort my cousin. She barely ate today, and she's nursing little Clyde. Who knows what the future holds."

"I'm sorry to make you sad, Lillian. I wish I had better news." He didn't care that this was one of the few times he used her first name. Too much had happened for formality now. They needed each other.

The snow-filled walkways became crowded with strangers arriving and work parties being formed to tackle the difficult efforts in the ravine. Lillian winced when they overheard men talk about how bad it was and how the new workers needed to prepare themselves for what they might encounter. "We had to ask Mrs.

Bailets for whiskey," a man said. "And not for pain neither but to deaden the gruesomeness of it."

Griffin abandoned propriety to put his arm around Lillian and shield her from the raw comments. He felt her slight form shake and heard her sniffle. "I don't know how I can make it through this," she mumbled. "How can anyone?"

"What is impossible to us is possible with God. Give it to Him."

She seemed to nestle closer to his protective care as they walked toward her cousin's home. "If only I could," she said softly.

When they arrived, Griffin asked if he should go in and help her share the news about Clyde.

"I can't tell her he may be dead. Not yet. He still could be alive somewhere. Until they—until they locate him, we have to keep the faith." As she stood there looking at him, frail and innocent, he couldn't help caressing her cheek. She took his hand, and to his surprise, gave an affectionate kiss on the palm. "Thank you for everything you've done. For going all that way to Scenic to try to find out about Clyde. For always being there." She managed a small smile, which to Griffin showed more hope than anything else he had witnessed these last two days. Despite the whirlwind of agony surrounding them, God seemed to be birthing a new miracle, one he prayed might happen in better circumstances. But the weight of adversity provided an open door, strangely enough. Where it might go from here, he had no idea.

Chapter 19

Lillian could not believe only a few days had transpired since the deadly avalanche. To her it seemed like a month. Every day the men dug through feet of heavy snow burying the crushed cars amid massive downed trees. The mere thought that snow could become powerful enough to overturn locomotives made her wonder if more tragedy lay in wait. A swift look at the formidable Windy Mountain did not show the crest of snow near its summit that had been the mountain's picture for a while. The crest was gone, surrendered to the force of a freak thunderstorm that caused it to break off, travel down the mountain, and consume families and friends in vengeful fashion.

Lillian inhaled another sharp breath when she saw a couple men lug up yet another sled bearing a deceased passenger. Mr. O'Neill had finally arrived from Scenic to take command of both the salvage operation and the dead, which would soon be dragged by sleds over eight miles and down Old Glory to the train at Scenic. Or as another man recently commented after downing his shot of mind-numbing whiskey, "More like going down Dead Man's

Slide." Word spread, and soon everyone began calling the pathway to Scenic by that name. Once there, the deceased would make a last train trip to their final resting place.

Lillian hurried on to the hospital for another day after a stone-faced farewell from her cousin, Elizabeth Hanks. No survivors had come in since Tuesday. No one in the rescue team that came to town had heard or seen Clyde Hanks in Scenic. But she went with the hope of some definitive answer to give her already grieving cousin, who held baby Clyde constantly these days.

Mrs. Bailets looked at her with dark circles under her eyes and wrinkled skin that showed her utter fatigue. Before Lillian could ask, she said, "No news."

"I know. But I wish there were." She looked about to see Ida Starrett sitting up against a mass of pillows, still staring into space. Her son, Raymond, sat beside her, trying to encourage her to look at the spinning top he had received as a present. "See, Mama? Wanna watch me?" He jumped off the bed, got down on all fours, and began spinning the top.

"Ida doesn't even acknowledge him," Lillian observed in a quiet voice.

"She's been that way for a while," Mrs. Bailets murmured. "The last time she spoke was to you, asking about her baby."

Lillian stared at the young woman, wondering if Ida might again respond, if not for her, then for Raymond's sake. She inhaled a breath and approached the bed. "Hello, Ida. How are you feeling?"

Ida stared fixedly across the room and said nothing.

"Mama won't talk anymore," Raymond declared, standing to his feet with the spinning top in hand. "I told some jokes, and she wouldn't laugh. Granny tried to get her to talk too. She won't say or do nothing."

Lillian watched the woman caught up in another world. And who wouldn't be, trapped for hours in an icy stranglehold, a tree pinning her from behind, her baby smothering beneath her, her extremities slowly freezing. And then the massive losses she had endured. First her husband, killed in a railway accident. Then the loss of two children and her father to the avalanche. Lillian came and patted Raymond on the shoulder. "I believe she hears us, Raymond, even if she isn't able to answer back right now. Just keep talking to her whenever you can." She wondered about the boy's own shock after the incident. Did he remember anything of that night? Did he feel himself tumbling around in the coach before being ejected onto the snow and getting the splinter lodged in his head? She wanted to know what he thought and felt but refused to broach that awful night. Instead she asked, "And what about you? Are you feeling better?"

"I'm okay." He paused. "Mrs. Bailets said my sister and baby brother went to heaven like Papa. And so did my grandpa. She said heaven is really pretty."

Lillian felt the tears enter her eyes and drew in a deep breath. "Yes. They are seeing God and all His beautiful angels. I can read to you from the Bible what heaven looks like, if you want."

Raymond nodded eagerly. Lillian found a Bible and encouraged him to sit on her lap. She opened it to Revelation and began reading about the mighty walls with many colorful jewels, the golden road, the fruit trees. She read it in a loud voice in the hopes it might give Ida comfort too—that her children and her father were in a sweet place with the Lord. Even if their manner of leaving was in the cruelest way imaginable.

"I want to go there," he said. "There's no snow or bad things, right?"

"Well, there could be snow, but it would be pretty snow like the kind we had when we made the snowmen. Remember? Not bad snow like what it did to the train."

Lillian looked up then to see several men in wool coats entering the hospital, their legs and feet covered in snow. She scooted Raymond off her lap, promising to read more later, and went over to greet them. The two men about her age took off their hats. They had obviously just walked the eight miles from Scenic. Probably reporters, as some had arrived in the last few days to cover the slide and its aftermath for the papers. One reporter had tried to get Lillian's statement, but she had begged off, unable to give any response to what she and the town had endured.

"Beg pardon, miss. I'm Luther and this is my brother, Frank. We are the sons of Sarah Covington, and we're praying she's here at the hospital."

Lillian stepped back, startled. Sudden tears filled her eyes. "I'm sorry. She—she is not here. They are digging. You may want to. . ." She motioned them to the cloakroom so as not to disturb the patients. "You may want to check the morgue in the baggage room of the depot. The deceased are being taken there."

The two sons exchanged looks of distress with faces reddening and eyes beginning to puff. They whirled for the door.

"Please. I can show you where the depot is." Lillian went to fetch her coat and scarf. They walked along the boardwalk toward the building, a distinct somberness filling each step. Just then Lillian caught sight of the gentle giant, Griffin, but to her dismay, pulling a rope attached to a sled that carried the deceased.

"Griffin, these two men are the sons of Mrs. Covington."

Griffin gave the rope to another man to continue with the solemn duty and came forward, removing his cap. "I'm sorry. We are still looking, but no one has been found alive now for several days. Have you checked the morgue?"

"I will go," Luther said, leaving his brother with a face set in stone. Luther wasn't gone long when he returned, shaking his head, his hand clasping a handkerchief. "She is not there."

"She must still be in the wreckage," Griffin said softly.

"What is being done?" Frank demanded. "It's been days and—" He stopped. "Where is this site?"

Griffin motioned to the men, who followed his tall form past the town to the silent tracks buried in snow and the activity of men crawling in and around the mass of trains and trees in the ravine below. "I'm truly sorry."

Frank groaned while Luther bowed his head as if in prayer. Lillian watched in pain the agony engulfing the sons, even as she thought about Sarah Covington's friendly smile and her strong faith. "She was a wonderful Christian soul," she told the men.

"We know that," Luther said.

"I don't just say those words. She—She was a good friend to me. We met at the beanery at the other end of the tunnel. She reached out to me when I was cold and alone. We shared nearby berths one night in the train. She—She told me about her family. How proud she was."

"There was no finer mother. . .or woman," Luther said, blowing his nose into a handkerchief. "She took care of our brother, you know. That's why she made this trip, to nurse him when he got an infection. She was going home to celebrate her fiftieth wedding anniversary today. We were going to have a fine gathering of family and friends." His voice trailed off.

Frank sniffed. "Mother loved to write too—poetry and stories and letters."

Just then, Griffin reached into his pocket and pulled out several written pages, torn loose from a book. "I nearly forgot. These papers were found in the snow. I looked them over, and they appear to be in fine handwriting, much nicer than a railway employee. I'm not sure but—"

"She told me she was writing a diary," Lillian said.

One of the sons took the papers, and a small smile formed on his drawn face. His finger traced the written lines. "It's Mother's handwriting. I'm sure of it. She loved to keep a written account of things." He shifted through the water-stained pages. "She talks about the long days on the train." He looked over at Griffin. "This means more than I can say. Even if we know she didn't make it, this is like her whispering to us from heaven. Thank you."

Griffin nodded, exchanging looks with Lillian who wondered at the finding that brought comfort to her sons. . .and to her.

"What happens now?" asked Luther.

"We are still looking," Griffin said.

"We want to help." Without another word the men stumbled down the bank of steep snow and tangled web of downed trees into the ravine.

Lillian watched the grieving pair. "And today is her fiftieth wedding anniversary." Her voice faded away, and suddenly she was crying at the thought of Mrs. Covington's poor husband without his love on their special day.

"I'm sorry, Lillian." Griffin stepped forward to comfort her with outstretched arms. For an instant Lillian wanted his comfort, but then she retreated at the last minute and stared at the snowy ground.

"Is there—is there any word yet on Clyde?"

"No. We found more wreckage earlier today, but one of the mail cars is still missing. Mr. O'Neill is down there taking charge and—"

"How fine of him to take an interest now," Lillian snapped. "He sleeps in a comfortable bed the night of the avalanche while children and their parents are smothered or ripped apart. I dearly love Berenice, but her husband did nothing and let people die. . ." Her voice trailed off into a whimper. She knew the words were wrong, but the pain ran too deep to stop herself.

"Lillian, he did the best he could and—"

"I expected you to come to his defense. You work for him, after all. What about Ida Starrett? Will he come and offer condolences for her child who suffocated under her? Or for the fact she can no longer walk or even communicate anymore? Or that she ignores her only living child?"

Griffin's face twitched. "Lillian, I helped find her. I know. I also talked to Mr. O'Neill. He's devastated." He paused. "And I believe it. His good friends and his aide died too. I have buddies gone from the mail train. Everyone has lost someone they knew and loved. Now we must find a way to go on."

He stepped forward again, but Lillian held out her hand to stop him. She knew he meant well, but the agony of the sons trying to find their deceased mother and her friend buried in snow framed every thought and reaction. Griffin left her to follow the sons to the wreckage. Lillian turned away, praying for another miracle for the sons. Though it had been days, maybe Sarah Covington lingered in a section of the railcar in the snow, kept alive by the many blankets she liked to use at night. She had complained to Lillian the night before the avalanche how cold she felt these days and must have plenty of blankets and a roaring fire in the stove to keep warm. They'd chatted a bit in the darkness of the sleeping car. She'd shared about her sick son, and Lillian had talked about life as an only child.

Lillian recalled something the older woman had told her.

"I hope you continue to communicate with your mother and father. There is nothing more precious than my children who reach out and offer me a note of remembrance. And being an only child, I'm certain it means even more from you."

Lillian swallowed hard when she thought of that, realizing she had not done well in recent communications with Mother. Ever since Christmas, the messages lagged. The heavy snows didn't help with the downed telegraph wires, but Lillian vowed to reestablish that binding tie with Mother and Father as soon as some kind of normalcy returned. She was thankful Griffin had sent word about her well-being while he was in Scenic. But after her recent outburst with Griffin, she knew now that normalcy would never happen. At least in the way she thought it might. No one knew what the future held. Even her future with Anthony. His proposal of marriage seemed like another time and place. And the woman who once agreed to it and waved farewell to him at the wharf in Everett no longer existed. What would become of them after all was said and done?

Lillian returned to the hospital to see if there was anything left to be done. Mrs. Bailets asked if she might check the post office to make sure nothing was amiss. "Did those two men find out anything about their mother? What a sad sight."

Lillian shook her head. "They decided to help with the digging. It's tragic, looking in the snow for one's deceased mother."

"I'm sure it is."

The words rushed out, along with the anger of grief. "I think about those still missing. Ned Topping, who now leaves his little boy an orphan. Little Thelma and her father. The pastor who led the service Sunday night. Ada Lemman, who used to scream to get out of there. Now she's gone."

"I remember," Mrs. Bailets said quietly.

"Everyone thought Ada Lemman was ill in the head, you know. Now I know why she did it. She knew she wouldn't survive. Somehow, she knew. And she was right." Lillian began to pace with the reality of it all hitting her with more force than the wicked avalanche. "I hate this place. I hate it. Sometimes I feel like screaming. As soon as the trains run again, I'm leaving. I can't take it anymore."

"I think you should. But you can't right now. The hurting need us too much." Mrs. Bailets gave her a gentle nudge. "Check the post office, would you?"

Lillian nodded, brushing the tears away. How she wished she was stronger, but the encounter with the mournful sons nearly led her over a precipice herself. It made her realize that maybe Sarah Covington was right. As the only daughter, her place was with her parents in Everett and not in some untamed wilderness beset with circumstances that went beyond human endurance.

She stumbled her way down the boardwalk and up the hill to the post office. There would be no mail to sort as they hadn't received any for a week. But to her surprise, a small bag sat there before the door—drenched, but still there. She hefted it up and opened the door to a silent and cold room. After lighting a lamp, she peeked inside and saw mail for Scenic. Someone had undoubtedly found the bag in the snowy ravine and decided the best place to bring it was here for safekeeping. Sifting through the envelopes, some with writing stained by the elements, she thought of the mail from the train still in the ravine and important letters for those who needed them. Tucking the envelopes back inside, she planned to head to the depot area and make certain the bag was returned to Scenic where it belonged.

For now she tidied up the place and swept the wood floor.

Memories of her time here, serving the townsfolk, even dear old Mrs. Winston who had lost her son, flooded her mind. But the good times did as well, like the reading lessons with Griffin after hours when she taught him the alphabet and how to sound out words. The day he read one of the readers that Mrs. Bailets lent her was like music to her ears. All had gone well here, despite the avalanche. Yet, she remained uncertain where her duty truly lay. With a besieged town or with her family, friends, and her fiancé, Anthony Travers?

Heavy footsteps pounded up the stairs and onto the small porch. She looked out the window to see Griffin. Shadows of the coming twilight had already begun to filter across the sky. She cracked open the door.

"It's getting late, and Mrs. Bailets said you were here checking things out. Is everything in order?"

"Except for this mailbag someone left. It's letters for Scenic." She handed him the bag. He nodded, though his face appeared haggard and his eyes downcast. "Is everything all right?"

"It was a difficult day," he said quietly.

Lillian stepped aside for him to enter. She lit another lamp and drew up a stool. "Are Mrs. Covington's sons still here?"

"They left about an hour ago so they would make it back to Scenic before dark. Soon after they left, we broke through to the Winnipeg sleeper car. It had been crushed under a locomotive. We had to go in on one end of it."

Lillian winced. She knew the Winnipeg well and the sleeping berths for many on the Seattle Express. She had stayed in it. "You found Mrs. Covington, didn't you?"

He nodded and looked down at his twisting fingers. "There was piping everywhere, and they were all trapped. We found many. Including the pastor, a whole family, another little girl in the arms of her father. . ."

"That must be Thelma. She had such a doting father. She wore a sweet party dress the night of the slide." Lillian gazed at the flickering flame in the oil lamp. And suddenly she heard a noise she hadn't expected. A man crying.

She quickly stood and came to him, her arm cradling his hunched shoulders.

"I feel like you did earlier, Lillian. I feel sadness, but I also feel anger. The superintendent was there when the discovery happened. I wanted to confront him. To ask him why. To ask why the passengers could not have left the trains and found refuge in Scenic." He wiped his face. "I saw the two lawyers that had left the train, you know. In Scenic. They told me it could have worked. They had made enough of a path, even down Dead Man's Slide, and could use ropes for the descent." He heaved a sigh. "But I don't know. I walked down that slide. It was very icy. I had a difficult time myself. But there might have been a chance had they left. Sitting helpless in those trains, there was none."

Lillian rubbed gentle circles on his upper back, feeling his muscles tense into tight ribbons. His breathing turned ragged. "Griffin, if we had only known beforehand. But no one knew. No one knows the future."

Griffin wiped his face again and stood to his feet. "It makes for some really tough questions. And I have many." He picked up the lantern. "You should be getting back home."

"We still don't know about Clyde, do we?"

Griffin stared, his eyes luminous in the light of the lantern flame. "The last mail car hasn't been uncovered yet. It's under all the other trains. We have to dig through mountains of metal and wood and snow and three-foot diameter trees. But I think when we do find it, you will have your answer."

Lillian could not say any more but followed Griffin out into the cold darkness to go and comfort her cousin.

Chapter 20

～◦～

TUESDAY, MARCH 15

The train whistle tooting as it exited the Cascade Tunnel was a welcome sound after nearly three weeks of being stranded from unrelenting snowfall that buried everything and anything. Just two days ago, the first train from Scenic managed to slowly crawl into Wellington, bringing much-needed supplies that earlier had to be dragged on toboggans up the steep incline of Old Glory—now called Dead Man's Slide. But the initial train run was short-lived as crews again had to unbury a section of track caught under another slide. Griffin was called upon to help with the task, as many of his fellow workers still laboring at the accident site were sick, mentally or emotionally exhausted, or had quit outright to seek warmer ground elsewhere. Griffin couldn't blame them. He felt like a war-weary soldier fighting battle after battle for weeks on end, only to be faced with a massacre under the terror of the avalanche. At least most of the passengers had been accounted for. They'd had their answer for Lillian's cousin Elizabeth a week ago when Clyde was found in the mangled mail car along with other missing men.

The time had come to move on with life as best they could, even if one wondered how that was possible. Griffin now watched a few people disembark from the latest train, including a gentleman dressed like a city slicker in a dark wool coat and tall hat. So many relatives, friends, news reporters and others had descended on Wellington that the regular townsfolk were difficult to find. Early on, the lack of transportation kept most curiosity seekers away, not wishing to make the eight-mile journey by foot from Scenic. But now with the tracks finally set free from their snowy imprisonment and train travel beginning again, Wellington would likely get inundated from the lowlands. This new arrival fit the picture of another reporter or even a lawyer. Rumors circulated of such men descending on the town to begin their cases. It seemed inevitable that lawsuits would happen due to the loss of life and that the blame would be placed squarely in the lap of Superintendent O'Neill and the GNR.

Hefting up his shovel that had seen too much action of late, Griffin shoveled away some crusty ice, watching the man look around in puzzlement. Had the gent gotten off at the wrong stop? He pitched the shovel into a snowbank and approached. "Do you need help?"

"Yes. I'm looking for a Lillian Hartwick. Do you know her?"

The mention of Lillian's name sent the hairs rising on his arms. It had been a sad day not long ago when the workers finally uncovered the crushed mail car and found all aboard dead. Including Clyde. Griffin left Lillian alone to grieve with her cousin in isolation. He'd seen her once, when he brought them fuel and fresh water. She looked like one in mourning, with deep black circles under her eyes, her black dress all wrinkled as if she had slept in it. "Yes, I know her."

He removed his hat. "Allow me to introduce myself. Mr. Travers, President of the Northwest Timber Company. Miss Hartwick is my fiancée, and I would very much like to find her."

Griffin nearly lost the grip on his shovel. He recalled the name belonging to the fiancé that was to meet her that one time in Scenic when his duties kept him away. And the lost moment had become a moment of gain for Griffin. "She is not well," he said, wondering why the man came now. Unless the vast coverage of the disaster in the press spawned guilt in him to finally pay a visit after all this time.

"How do you mean? Is she ill?"

"None of us are well, sir. Surely you heard what happened."

"Of course. It's all over the papers. I sent several telegrams, but—"

"The wires have been down for days because of the slide. We only just got them back."

"I would have come sooner, but of course there have been no trains to this area. And I had no intention of walking that eight miles."

"There were trains back in November—" Griffin began, then looked away under the man's baleful stare, wishing his irritation had not gotten the better of him.

"I won't pretend to believe you are privy to mine and Miss Hartwick's communications, sir. Unless you work for the telegraph office." The man surveyed him from the top of his felt cap to his muddy boots. "However, I can see you're a common laborer. So before you return to your shoveling, if you would point me in the direction of Miss Hartwick's lodgings? She is supposedly staying with her cousin, Elizabeth Hanks." His gaze encompassed the few buildings of this simple railway town, still buried in snow, and he grimaced. "It shouldn't be too difficult as there's not much here."

"If you would follow me." Griffin wanted to engage the man in small talk, but nothing came to mind. From the ravine in the distance came the loud sounds of metal on metal and the strain of pulleys. An earlier train brought mechanical winches to begin heaving the train parts out of the ravine. Some workers on the trains still remained unaccounted for, and Griffin was glad not to be a part of this operation. Even if it meant guiding Lillian's fiancé to her cousin's home. He wished he could warn her of this pending visit, knowing as a woman she might want to primp. But inwardly, he was glad for an impromptu meeting. Maybe the harsh realities of this place would send the dapper gentleman back to his fine surroundings and leave them here to rebuild life—and hopefully nurture love.

Griffin led the man up the hill toward the shanty still covered in white. He gazed behind to see that Travers had stopped as if pausing to take everything in.

"She lives here?" he asked.

"These are the railway dwellings for the workers. Her cousin's late husband worked the rotary snowplow until he lost his life in the avalanche."

The gentleman sighed, adjusted his hat, and took thoughtful strides up the hill to the dilapidated dwelling. Griffin made a mental note to help fix the roof corner that was sagging from all the snow. He ventured up to the door and knocked. A woman answered, her hair bound up in a tight bun, wearing an apron smeared with food and dirt over a black dress. Lillian.

"Griffin, I don't have time—" she began.

"Uh. . .Miss Hartwick, I brought a visitor who came on the train today."

Her blue eyes focused behind him and onto Travers, who returned the stare as if equally astonished. "Anthony! What are you doing here?" She looked down at her soiled apron covering the black dress and turned away. "I—I can't be seen like this," she whispered.

No one said anything for an awkward moment until Griffin intervened. "I'm sure Mr. Travers knows you are caring for a grieving widow and her baby son. Isn't that right, Mr. Travers?"

Silence ensued. Griffin wondered what might break the stalemate of speechlessness. Finally Lillian said softly, "I—I will meet him at the hotel in an hour." She said it as if Griffin stood like an acting telegraph operator between the two. The door now shut.

"I suppose you heard her, sir?" Griffin asked Travers, who looked as if he had turned to stone.

"I did. But. . .was that Lillian Hartwick?"

"Yes."

Travers shook his head and turned to descend the hill. "That woman was a stranger," he mumbled, loudly enough for Griffin to hear.

"We all become strangers when confronted by things too terrible to consider." Griffin acknowledged the ravine to their left as they made their way down the hill. "I have unburied the living and the dead from that rubble. The young and the old. And it makes strangers out of us all until we can heal." He then added, "If we ever can."

Travers wiped a hand across his face. "But I made a commitment," he said, more to himself than anyone in particular.

Griffin at least commended the man for remembering his promise, despite what he'd just witnessed. But Griffin couldn't help letting a part of him hope and pray that the strangeness of the encounter would steer Lillian toward him and away from this fancy man of the coast. And likewise, send the man back to where he belonged.

Somehow, someway.

———— ◆●◆ ————

For an instant, Lillian felt caught up in another world. Never in her life did she expect Anthony Travers to appear on the doorstep of Elizabeth's ramshackle home. The sight of this place—and her—must have sent shockwaves coursing through him. She'd heard the whistle blow announcing the beginning of passenger service once more to their town, but never did she think Anthony would come to a mountainous region that had just seen untold devastation. Perhaps it spoke more about his character than she ever realized. Though they had lapses of silence and hadn't laid eyes on each other in many months, he still cared.

Lillian examined herself in the mirror and gasped at the stranger staring back at her. Except for the color of her eyes and hair, little compared to the regal lady who arrived many months ago, ready to help her cousin in her time of need. Wrinkles marred her complexion. Deep-set eyes stared back with dark circles beneath that went along with the color of her dress. Mourning had aged her—and how could it not? Everything had been turned upside-down. What was to be a joyous completion of a difficult winter season in the Cascades had disintegrated into grieving for friends and loved ones lost. Most everyone in town wore black these days or at least a black armband on their coat sleeve, sharing in the sorrow.

But Anthony's impromptu arrival and the meeting to come thrust her back into a life she'd forgotten. One of propriety, class, and perfection with dress and attitude. While she ought to look nice for their meeting at the hotel as an intended should, she merely dispensed with the apron and kept the black dress. Anthony might as well face the facts. They were a town and family in mourning.

Elizabeth stood in the doorway, a sleeping baby Clyde in her arms—where he remained from morning till night unless Lillian stole the babe away to give her cousin a needed break. "Is that the man you told me about?"

The question startled her, as Elizabeth had barely uttered a word after being told that Clyde had died. "Yes."

"I'm surprised he came. It says a great deal if you ask me."

Lillian remained uncertain exactly what Anthony was saying but would find out soon enough. She took up her small handbag. "I'll be back as soon as I can."

"Don't worry about us. We aren't going anywhere."

But Lillian did worry. She worried what would happen now that Anthony had arrived. A person couldn't go through these horrific circumstances and not be changed by them. She kept her sights on the hotel perched on the side of the hill, thinking of Anthony inside its shabby interiors. She glanced behind her at the salvaging operations and heard the shouts of men working to begin clearing the train debris. The heavy pack of snow created by the avalanche remained, but the cleared tracks revealed that life was slowly returning to a new normal, evidenced by Anthony's unexpected arrival. The bunk room used as a hospital ward had seen the last of its patients released or go on to other hospitals. She wished then she had said farewell to Ida Starrett, Ida's mother, and Ida's son Raymond before they left for a hospital in Spokane. But she could not leave Elizabeth in her mournful state. It took all her wherewithal to see to Elizabeth's

198

comfort and make certain little Clyde was cared for.

Lillian mounted the bank of stairs and walked into the hotel. Anthony sat at one of the tables covered in a checkered cloth, a small glass of amber liquid before him and a plate of food to one side, staring at nothing in particular. She inhaled a deep breath at the pensive display and approached. Immediately, he leaped to his feet and pulled out the chair for her. The last they had seen of each other was on a damp and cold day on the wharf with him waving farewell, ready to oversee a shipment of timber to San Francisco. It seemed like another lifetime, and in many respects, it was.

"Do you want anything?"

She ordered tea from the young server girl who appeared.

"How are you?"

She shrugged. "Not well."

"I heard about the avalanche, of course. It's all over the papers."

She said nothing and just watched the flame lick at the oil in the lamp.

"I sent several telegrams, but the worker said the lines have been down for some time. So I decided to come as soon as the train began running."

Lillian's gaze drifted over to meet his. She appreciated the sparkling of his dark eyes staring into hers, reflecting the candle's flame. He seemed sincere, but he knew nothing of the tragedy here and what they had endured. And the grief that overwhelmed them.

"I saw your mother. She is well, though she misses you. She thanks you for the telegrams you were able to send. I will send word today that I have arrived and you are well. Unless you want to say otherwise?" He continued to stare at her, his forehead furrowing. "Are you all right?"

"You may tell her Elizabeth's husband is dead. I—I have not told her yet." She paused and looked away to a window. "And no, I'm not all right. No one can be all right after going through this."

Anthony flinched and stirred in his seat. He said nothing for a few moments, as if analyzing the situation presented before him.

As the president of his own company, much like Jim O'Neill with the railroad, Anthony had to contend with situations and responses among the workers and the general public. Undoubtedly, he'd never encountered anything of this magnitude, unless he had dealt with catastrophes at sea with his shipping vessels. *But none would have consumed families who went to sleep and never woke up, would it?*

"This must be difficult," he admitted in a morsel of genuine empathy. "But you need to consider your future, Lillian. And us. If I had known we would be kept apart this long because of my business and the weather, I would have insisted you come to San Francisco. Now you can return to where you belong."

"Elizabeth needed me then and still does. Now more than ever."

"We'll have time to talk about that." Anthony went on to discuss his business while they had been separated. Lillian's gaze drifted to the open doorway that led to the lobby and caught sight of a familiar figure standing there, conversing with Mrs. Bailets. She would know his hulking form anywhere. When he turned, their gazes met for only an instant. And to her shock, he lifted his hat before turning to leave.

"Something catch your eye?" Anthony wondered.

"Just Mr. Jones, picking up a few supplies. He's the one who showed you where I live. Everyone here knows each other. We have all become friends through this tragic time."

He said nothing, only stared at his meal after only taking a few bites before pushing the plate away to indulge in his glass of liquor. Sitting there in his presence, Lillian felt more and more like a stranger. Whatever may have once been kindled between them had been snuffed out.

Anthony now stood. "It's been a long day, and I will retire. I will see you again tomorrow."

"How long do you plan to stay?"

"Until you're ready to leave. Which I pray will be soon."

Lillian balked. "I can't leave now. Elizabeth and her baby need me."

"You are not the baby's nurse or a lady's maid. You have a life you are meant to live, Lillian. I understand you went through a terrific ordeal here. While terrible in its aftermath, you cannot bring the dead back to life or find happiness in a damaged railway town. And I know your mother misses you. You're her only living child."

Lillian chewed on her bottom lip at the thought before rushing to offer a good night and hurrying from the hotel. Stepping outside into the blustery cold wind, she noticed the area had grown dark with the falling twilight—and she had forgotten to take a lantern. Then she spotted Griffin in the distance, gripping the handle of a lit lantern that flickered madly in the wind.

"Do you need an escort home, or is Mr. Travers escorting you?" he asked.

"He's too tired." She walked beside him as he led the way. "And I'm tired too."

"I'm sure you are. Everyone is. Grief does that to you." The area remained busy with men working well into the night, as they had since the incident. Lillian thanked the men for their steadfastness. Many labored long and hard to try to free the trains so they might get out from under the menacing shadow of a snowy Windy Mountain. But the relentless storms that pounded day after day made it a losing battle. And it made her wonder, too, if any battle was worth it, or if the losing side proved inevitable.

"You look deep in thought," Griffin noted.

"I was thinking how hard everyone worked to get the trains moving the day of the avalanche. Or at least they thought they would get them out in time."

"Everyone did their best," he agreed. "It was not meant to be."

"I don't understand. Why would God allow everyone to work hard but the ends not justify the labor? Why do anything, then, if it's doomed to fail? I think of Clyde working day and night with the rotary snowplow. Elizabeth told me how his machine had even broken down, trying to cut through the heavy snow with big trees embedded in it. The trees ruined the machinery. When he got it working again, they were hours away from probably getting the trains freed. He went to bed that night in the mail car, ready to tackle it at first light, not even going home when he could have. And then the slide hits and he's dead." She stopped in her tracks. Tears fell fast with heaves gripping her breathing. "Why?"

Griffin stood silent. Whether he matched her consternation over this or he wanted her to grieve, he said nothing for many moments. They then continued walking. "You're not alone in your questions, Lillian."

She wiped the tears from her face. "I feel alone. Anthony wants me to go back to Everett. He says Mother misses me. I am her only child, you know. Seeing families ripped apart makes one think. A part of me wonders if it might be a good idea to return home. At least for now." She wondered too, with her husband gone, if Elizabeth might consider leaving Wellington and seek another life. The only reason she even lived in such a remote place was Clyde's work. But now there was nothing to keep her here. And nothing for Lillian either. Was there?

Griffin's walk turned to a shuffle. "I—I wish you would stay. This town needs you." He paused. "I—" He hesitated. "I know you're engaged. But I need you, Lillian. We need each other. We've been through many bad things. Your Mr. Travers doesn't understand that. He may try to change you into someone you're not."

"I don't know who I am. And maybe I won't know unless I leave. And for all I know, Elizabeth might want to leave too." She looked up to see the light reflecting on his face from the lantern. "You've been a good friend, Griffin. I'll never forget it." She considered if she had been born differently, with different means, she could see herself in love with his caring attitude and helpful heart. With the man himself. But Anthony's dark eyes gazing steadily at her told her she could not run toward Griffin, despite what her heart said. She had duties, and as he reminded her, duties also as the only child of her parents that she had neglected for far too long.

Lillian moved on with Griffin beside her to light the way. He said nothing verbally, but she could tell what he wanted to say. That he loved her and by the grace of God, they would make it through.

When they arrived, Griffin caught her by the arm, and she turned. "I would never keep you here, Lillian. You must do what you think is right. But I'll be here if you ever need me." With that, he lumbered off, his giant form seemingly shrunken by a foot as he walked with his shoulders hunched over.

------◆●◆------

Griffin knew this day would come but had high hopes it wouldn't. Especially with everything he and Lillian had been through. But hearing the concern in her voice for her parents and on the heels of the visit by her intended, the past pulled at her heart with a strength neither of them could stop. What did he have to offer a woman like her anyway—one who had grown up among the elite and now had a fiancé the caliber of a company superintendent at her beck and call? He was uneducated, with little money to his name, living in a bunkhouse, uncertain what the future held. But he also knew they had been through the valley of the shadow of death together. They had heard and seen things no one should. They had felt the power of God's might and tasted His wrath. They had touched eternity with those swallowed up by a wave of white, who had entered a place mortals could only imagine.

He kicked up slushy snow, returning to the bunkhouse for an early night to find Oliver and a few of the men gathered around a deck of cards. Oliver still sported his arm in a sling and talked of pain in his side from cracked ribs. When he saw Griffin, he pointed to a chair. "Come join the game, Griff."

Griffin welcomed the bit of warmth the invitation generated. In the old days, a haughty and evil Oliver would have continued ensnaring him with his lack of education as a display of mockery for all to see. Instead he thanked Griffin many times over for risking his life to save his lowlife neck, as he called it. Just the other day, he showed Griffin a telegram sent by his mother. Griffin would never forget the tears welling up in his old nemesis' eyes when Oliver's mama told him to thank his rescuer—that without Griffin, her only boy would be gone.

Right now, though, Griffin wasn't in the mood for a hand of harmless poker where the men gave away matches rather than their hard-earned cash. Griffin had suggested using the matches as a substitute, and Oliver pounced on the idea. This night he remained too burdened in his heart with his thoughts a jumbled mess.

"You don't look so good," Oliver observed. There was yet another trait in the man Griffin thought he would never see in a million years. Oliver caring for someone else—and especially him of all people.

Griffin fell on top of his bunk and shut his eyes. "Just worn out," he muttered.

"We're all that way. I wish I could help and not be laid up with this arm." He acknowledged the sling. "Have you run into that gal again? The one who was teaching you?"

Griffin flopped a hand across his eyes. "Yeah. Looks like she's going home to Everett." He blinked open one eye to see each of the men look at him. Heat entered his face.

"Probably better. This place is too badly damaged. Many people are leaving. If I could start over somewhere else, I would." Oliver turned away to rejoin the poker game. Griffin couldn't blame him. Oliver had seen death flash before his eyes and his buddy Beau disappear into a crevasse, only to be pulled out a few days later when it was safe, a look of utter disbelief frozen onto the man's face. Oliver had been changed in ways Griffin never would have believed. Griffin paused to consider it. Dare he give the Lord thanks for the new friendship and changed heart of his persecutor, the one who had caused such turmoil in his life? He watched Oliver, cards in hand, interacting with the other men. No longer did the man possess the boisterous, commanding, lording-it-over-others personality. The self-confidence built on misery had melted away, as sure as the heaps of snow gave way to the warmth of spring, with concern and kindness taking its place.

Watching Oliver's changed heart gave Griffin hope for the future. Lillian may feel in turmoil right now. She may have to go back to where she once came from for a season, to set things right in her heart. But anything could happen. Anyone could change. And if by some miracle Lillian did return by the mercy of God, he would be ready.

Chapter 21

EARLY APRIL

Lillian wondered if she was doing the right thing when the conductor strode through the train, announcing their arrival to Everett in a few minutes. Nervous jitters assailed her from the moment she boarded the coach. Seeing the passengers in their seats, some traveling with children, sent tears springing into her eyes with the reminder of the times spent on the stranded Seattle Express and the passengers who had tried to make the best out of a difficult situation. The trembling increased when she thought of it and then the pain-filled aftermath. A groan of despair escaped, sending an eyebrow rising on Anthony's face. She wished now she was in the other coach with the third-class passengers, where cousin Elizabeth and her baby sat at this very moment. She didn't feel a part of velvet luxury. The thick, ruby-red curtains and plush seats seemed out of place in her life. She wondered if Elizabeth would feel similarly, stepping into her parents' sanctuary of large rooms filled with furniture, paintings, and the like. At least the atmosphere would be friendly enough. Lillian had telegrammed Mother to inform her of her arrival time and to ask if Elizabeth could come as well. Mother responded with great enthusiasm, inviting her and the baby to stay as long as they wanted.

"I don't think I'll ever return," Elizabeth said, looking at the simple furnishings in the tiny dwelling before they left Wellington. A small family, the husband a survey worker, had already laid claim to the furnished home, making it an easy affair to move while leaving behind possessions for the new inhabitants. With salvage work at the avalanche site well underway and the tracks repaired, the time had come for new beginnings and a departure for a different life. "I just hope Clyde isn't looking down on me, disappointed that I have given up on the life we built together," she mourned.

"You're doing what's best for baby Clyde," Lillian said. "It's too difficult living here alone with a baby in these mountains. In Everett you have family."

Elizabeth nodded, closed her trunk with a decisive thump, and made final preparations to leave the tiny home she had shared with Clyde for three years. The old had passed away, as sad and brief as it was, and the new had come.

Lillian considered her life as she gazed at Anthony Travers sitting across from her, stuffing papers in a leather case before the train came to a stop at the Everett depot. Anthony had left for a few weeks while Lillian and Elizabeth readied themselves for the move to Everett. He then returned to Wellington to officially escort them back home. Observing him on the ride here, she found herself comparing him to Griffin. Shorter in stature and leaner. Clean-shaven but for his crisp mustache. Smartly dressed and carried himself with authority. Griffin was much taller, stouter, with beard stubble on his wide chin, a lumbering walk, and the ability to bear loads that no one ought to carry. They were like night and day.

But Griffin had been an ever-present help during the long days since the avalanche struck. While he remained busy, he never wasted an opportunity to see her and Elizabeth, bringing them needed supplies or offering up the latest news. Once, he had asked if Lillian cared to walk with him for a spell. They did, along the trodden path that had seen many travelers in recent weeks walk between Scenic and Wellington. Arriving at Windy Point, she glanced down the steep terrain of the path now called Dead Man's Slide and inhaled a deep breath. She thought of those poor deceased souls in sleds, making their final journey from a night of terror to the train in Scenic that would take them to their final resting place. For certain, most never thought their journey here on earth would end at Wellington. But some had an inkling of the disaster, and the thought bothered her.

Lillian stood to retrieve a small case from the upper rack and then followed Anthony to the door. "I must wait for my trunk at the platform."

"Henry will be here," he said, referring to his aide. "He will fetch your trunk and take you to your mother's. I must go to the office. I've been gone far too long with these many trips to the middle of nowhere."

Lillian tried not to take offense, even if a part of her wanted to ask why he must leave now when she had only just arrived back after months of absence. But she kept her lips pressed together and waited for her cousin to alight from the coach.

"It's busy here, isn't it?" Elizabeth observed, her voice betraying her anxiety over the rush of workers and passersby, some yelling to each other. She cuddled her baby close. "I'd forgotten the smell and the noise of a city."

Lillian had too after the many months spent in Wellington, except the odor of burning coal from the trains. But soon the smell would dissipate, and the air would teem with the fragrance of pine drifting up from the valley below. After the wheels of the trains moved onward to their destinations, the pleasant sound of Haskell Creek gurgling beneath the bridge and traveling toward the Tye River, soothed her. But all that was gone by their arrival in Everett, replaced by a life she once knew and had nearly forgotten.

Henry delivered them safely to Mother's. After hugs and tears for both her and Elizabeth, Mother gestured them to the sitting room for tea. The vastness of the room—with shelves of books, huge vases, and paintings above the wainscoting—nearly made Lillian dizzy. One could put most of Elizabeth's shanty inside the sitting room alone. She had forgotten how large the house was, and even that would pale in comparison to the home Anthony planned to buy them. She suddenly yearned for the coziness of the old sitting room in the shanty, beside the warmth of the coal heater, working on her embroidery near the lamp light.

Mother did her best to make everyone feel at home. "Gretchen would be glad to look after the baby," Mother told Elizabeth. "I've already made inquiries for a suitable nanny."

Elizabeth shook her head. "I'm fine, Aunt Claire. I will take care of little Clyde. I don't need a nanny."

Lillian watched Mother squirm and could guess her thinking—that a proper woman living under her roof employed a nanny to care for a little one. Lillian had a nanny, though only for her younger years. She barely remembered the woman except she had flaming red hair and a thick Irish accent. Lillian thought once she would burn her fingers if she touched the nanny's hair.

"I only think it will give you time to—" Mother began.

Lillian flew to her feet. "Mother, may I have a word?" If Mother objected to Elizabeth caring for her child, what would she say when she found out Lillian had worked as an assistant postmistress, taught a railway worker how to read, and associated with the rabble of second- and third-class citizens? They entered the dining area where Lillian told Mother that life in Wellington was not like here and not to change Elizabeth's ways to suit their way of living.

"I was only trying to help her fit in," Mother said softly.

"We've been through a great deal. We had to manage on our own." An unexpected tear entered her eye which she wiped away.

"I know you have. I'm so glad you left that horrible place. My daughter is home now, and everything will be just lovely."

Lillian offered a weak smile and returned with her to the sitting room, where they made small talk and enjoyed the tea. But inwardly, she felt a part of her was missing. Maybe her mother's words affected her in a way she hadn't expected. While the situation in Wellington certainly was horrible, the people she had come to know and work with were the best of human compassion and concern. An image of Griffin flicked across her mind until she forced herself to listen to Mother drone on about life in Everett in her absence. She had no choice but to make this work with Elizabeth here, at least for the time being.

———◆•◆———

Lillian sipped on her tea, trying to give the impression of regality with her back straight, her dress neat as a pin though black in color, while the women spoke in soft tones about their individual lives. Mother thought it would cheer Lillian while introducing Elizabeth to society by offering a community tea. She invited all her friends. But to Lillian it seemed a dishonor while Elizabeth remained in mourning. When she took a delicate bite of a diamond-shaped piece of bread spread with flavorful cheese, she thought back to the trains of Wellington and how the passengers subsisted on greasy bacon and mealy potatoes when food became scarce. Even in Elizabeth's house, food was parceled out to make it last. Here, food was plentiful. And Elizabeth appeared to enjoy the gathering, with Mother convincing her to allow little Clyde to go with a part-time nanny so that she could sample the lifestyle of being a carefree young woman. Seeing her laughing away at a story Lillian's friend Helen told, Lillian thought Elizabeth already appeared a different person than what she was in Wellington.

The only one of Lillian's circle of friends who had not come to the gathering was Berenice O'Neill—the very person she was most eager to see after her long absence. Her heart fell when Mother told her Berenice had a previous commitment. For an instant, Lillian wondered if she could be avoiding her in the aftermath of the avalanche, knowing her husband's involvement in the sad affair. Did she worry Lillian would become too emotional? Lillian certainly did. These were emotional times, and no one knew how to act.

Lillian looked at the light reflecting in her tea until she felt one of the women jostle her arm. "You haven't said anything, Lil," Helen noted.

"You're seeing an absentminded fiancée pining away for her husband-to-be," Mother joked.

"Have you made any plans yet?" Helen inquired. "I'm sure you received the invitation for my wedding in May. Did you set a date?"

"Heavens, I've only been back a week," Lillian said, a little sharper than she would have liked. Not that she'd seen much of Anthony to even ask about dates, an engagement ring, or anything else, as he'd been away on business for a few days. Everyone went on with daily life as though nothing had happened in some obscure town way up in the Cascades. Maybe she ought to as well. It had been six weeks since that terrible day, but still she dreamed of the hand as she had long ago, before leaving Everett. The rescuers had shared about dragging victims out of the snow. In one dream Lillian had pulled on the hand caught in the snowbank, and it belonged to Sarah Covington who asked her the question, *Why?*

Lillian had screamed and wakened from the nightmare, her skin sticky with sweat. Mother had come rushing into her room, asking if everything was all right and then fetching her some warm milk, which soothed her a bit. But the vision remained. Now she sat with a china teacup and a party of gossiping ladies, wondering what to do with her life and with her grief. It didn't feel right to be in the company of smiling faces and cheerful conversation after the terror that had enveloped Wellington.

"I'm sure Mr. Travers is very happy to have you back," Helen commented, drawing Lillian into the conversation. "It was chivalrous of him to let you go to that wild place for so long." She paused, her eyes darting back and forth when Lillian and Elizabeth centered their gaze on her. "I meant no disrespect, mind you."

"No, you are right," Elizabeth interrupted. "Wellington was

indeed a wild place. And dangerous. I should have never let Clyde talk me into living there. Now he's gone, making me a widow with a baby."

No one knew what to say after that, so Mother changed the subject with a few mundane questions of each lady present. When the gathering ended, Elizabeth apologized for her outburst.

"You have every right to say what you feel," Lillian said. "That place took away the one you loved."

Elizabeth wiped a stray tear. "I shouldn't blame Clyde for doing his job. I only wish he had thought more of us. He didn't need to sleep on the mail train that night."

"I slept on the Express the night before it happened," Lillian reminded her. "If the slide had hit that night, I wouldn't be here. The Winnipeg car was crushed, and many of the passengers from the Seattle Express were found dead there." When she considered the magnitude of her words, she took a step back and bowed her head.

"Lillian, we'll have none of that!" Mother announced in a sharp voice.

"But it's true, Mother."

Mother placed her hand firmly on Lillian's arm. "God heard my prayers and kept you safe. And now you're back with me. And that's all we're going to say about it."

Lillian knew she might physically be in Everett, but inwardly her heart and mind remained in the mountains and the site of the calamity that had branded a lasting mark on her heart. She wondered then how Griffin was getting along, with all the hardship he had endured during the crisis. When Elizabeth disappeared to check on baby Clyde and Mother gave instructions to Gretchen, the maid, to clear the plates and teacups, Lillian slipped away to her room and the small wooden desk. She took out a piece of cream-colored paper, thought for a moment, and then penned a note to the gentle giant.

Griffin Jones
Wellington, WA

I hope this message finds you well. I think often of the mountains—but not the calamity we faced, which seems like a lifetime ago. I hope this finds any of the remaining wounded healing. I also hope there is no more snow. It rains here quite often, but I must admit I don't miss the big snowbanks nearly three times my height. No one here would believe it. I find myself strangely missing Wellington, though—my work there and, yes, our reading lessons. I hope you find the time to read when you can. If you can do it every day, you will get better at it.

Give my fond affection and good wishes to Mrs. Bailets.

Yours,
Lillian Hartwick
Everett, WA

Lillian read it over but found nothing amiss, only remembrances and an interest in the welfare of a few injured railroad workers left behind. The hospital had long since closed, but some like Oliver remained in town to finish healing, if that were possible. Ida Starrett, still paralyzed from the waist down, and young Raymond, bearing the wound from the wood lance, along with others, all left several weeks ago for other hospitals. The memories of times spent with people like the Starretts still weighed on her, leaving her to wonder if she could ever move on.

Lillian took up the note and told Mother she was going out for some fresh air. Once outside, she hailed a streetcar that took her downtown to the post office. Inside the establishment, thoughts assailed her of her work at the post office, the townspeople she helped, the card given to Mrs. Winston, the reading lessons with Griffin. Now she observed a worker sorting mail into boxes. "Can I help, miss?" the gentleman inquired.

"I did such sorting," she mused, "but at a very small post office in Wellington."

The man stared at her. "Wellington! The avalanche town. Were you there when it happened?"

"Oh yes. A dreadful time."

"It was all over the papers. They just had an investigation into it a few weeks ago." Word soon spread throughout the post office of an eyewitness to the disaster, and people began congregating to hear the story and pepper her with questions. Lillian felt her grief eased by talking about difficult times with those who had no idea what happened. She described the power of snow hurling locomotives off the tracks, and her friends and others—men, women, and children, even a baby—losing their lives on the eve of their rescue. "A heartbreaking tragedy."

The people stared wide-eyed. A few women took out their lace hankies to dab their eyes. Lillian took comfort in the reactions of empathy and was glad she had come to mail the letter to Griffin. God indeed worked in mysterious ways.

When Lillian arrived home, Mother was in the middle of conversing with two young men in the sitting room. They stood and bowed when she entered. "These two men are from the newspaper," Mother announced. "Where did you go?"

"To the post office." Lillian did not wish to tell her mother how she had lingered downtown afterward and taken a walk near the wharf where she once said farewell to her intended, Anthony, before he set sail for California with a load of timber.

A man slipped off his hat. "We were informed you were an eyewitness to the avalanche in Wellington and survived. My sister overheard you at the post office and rushed home to tell me. I hope you'll pardon the intrusion, but I had to talk to you."

Lillian's face grew warm when she noticed Mother look at her with wide eyes. "I lived in town, yes. But I was not on the train when the slide hit."

"Please, may we interview you for a news story? Since the inquest into the avalanche a few weeks ago, we need a new angle."

She untied her hat and made her way to a chair. For the next hour, Lillian engaged the reporters in details of life in Wellington and all that the people had endured. The man wrote furiously on a notepad while the other reporter took a photo. She liked bringing the stories of her friends to life and prayed the reporter would remember the suffering. She wondered then if Elizabeth would like to tell her story, but Mother interrupted by saying she had gone to lie down.

"I wish she was here," Lillian told the reporters. "She lost her husband in the disaster."

"Maybe I can return at another time to interview her for an article," the reporter said, standing to his feet. "I believe we have an excellent story here. If you don't mind, I'd like to type this up immediately."

The maid showed them to the door. Lillian turned to see Mother staring at her thoughtfully. "I can see this whole thing has affected you greatly," she said quietly.

"Yes, it did. I don't know when I'll truly recover from it. Or what that would even feel like." She took off toward her room to see Elizabeth in the hallway. "Oh Elizabeth, I wanted to tell you. Two reporters were here to interview me about the slide. I told them you might want to talk about Clyde. They hope to come back—if that's all right. It made me feel a little better to share about the ones we loved."

Elizabeth's eyes narrowed to mere slits. "Clyde would be fit to be tied if he knew I told nosy reporters about our private life. I hope you didn't tell them anything."

Lillian felt the heat enter her face. "Only that I stayed with you and that Clyde gave his life trying to dig out the trains. The reporter was touched by the story. I could tell."

Elizabeth stomped her foot, and her hands flew to her hips. "Lillian, that is a private matter! How could you tell perfect strangers my business?"

Lillian felt a wave of anxiety course through her. "I'm sorry. I thought it would be all right to share about his life."

"It wasn't." Elizabeth whirled and hurried away.

Chills swept over Lillian. The avalanche was happening all over again. The good she thought she had mustered by sharing in the heroic deeds of others suddenly evaporated, leaving behind destruction. Now she wished Griffin were by her side, giving her advice on what to do or how to even feel.

Chapter 22

"You are not to speak about it anymore. And you are not to be involved!"

Lillian blinked at the accusatory tone hurled at her when Anthony Travers arrived back after his short business trip. He waved the newspaper, rough lines creasing his face, his mustache twitching. She patiently told him how the people appreciated hearing stories of lost friends and family, but he threw the paper on the table.

"Don't you see what you've done? You implicated me and my business in this whole disaster." His fingers smacked the paper.

"I did no such thing!"

"It's right here—'Miss Lillian Hartwick, fiancée of Anthony Travers, president of the Northwest Timber Company'—in print for all to see. My name and the company name. My picture even. And then a picture of a tree on top of a train car! I had investors wiring me in worry, asking if the company was involved in the avalanche. They said rumors were going around that lumber operations on the mountainside set up the calamity!" He paced before her, his breathing turning rancorous. "This could ruin me!"

For an instant the outburst reminded her of poor Ada Lemman on the train in the days leading to the avalanche, certain she was going to die. The passengers deemed her crazy. But in the end, elements of her fear proved true. She died, as did her husband.

"I'm sorry Anthony. It was not my intent to blame anyone or anything."

"I'll need to meet with my lawyers and call a meeting of the board to fix this. But they will inquire of my association with one who speaks so candidly to the press without my consent." Lillian watched his face redden. Gone was any semblance of the man with a calm demeanor, who had given her the cameo pin for Christmas, who was once concerned for her welfare or so she thought.

"I don't see the problem."

"Then I will tell you plainly. My investors will run if they catch even a whiff of trouble or that timber operations were to blame. Then it's over."

"Anthony, there is no justification in blaming the lack of trees for the slide. It's not even in the article. The snowfall was terrible and the slide itself took out many trees that. . ." Her voice trailed away. She might have stood strong under any other turbulence, including a mighty avalanche, but under the onslaught of this tidal wave of anger, first from her cousin and now from the man she was supposed to marry, she felt weak and useless.

Lillian swiped up her coat and left the room, despite his voice demanding that she return, that he had not finished, that there were legal ramifications in all of this. She couldn't bear hearing any more, lest she start screaming like Ada Lemman for relief. Inside her, though, the screams had long since commenced. Between Elizabeth and now Anthony, everything was falling apart. The only consolation she found was her fingers discovering the envelope tucked in her coat pocket. Another letter had arrived from Griffin. He had sent two since her arrival back to Everett, and this was his third. But Anthony had sent a message asking her to meet him at his office as soon as possible. She had folded the letter in half and stuffed it in the coat pocket. Now she felt a strange sense of warmth when she touched it. If only she could tell Griffin how scared she felt under the angry countenance of her supposed fiancé. That she missed the kindness in Griffin's eyes and the way he used to direct her where to go in the coming darkness, both within and without.

For a long time she walked, trying not to make eye contact with anyone for fear someone would recognize her and call her out for the article. But it wasn't her picture in the paper. They chose to print one of Anthony. And beside his photo, one of a large tree that had smashed a train car. Now she had the memory of Anthony's anger to add to her pain.

Why did I ever leave Wellington? she mourned, even if peace there stood on shaky ground. There seemed no place for her to rest her head. No serenity. No resolution. She found a bench overlooking the sound and sat down to listen to the bells and then a horn as a cargo ship approached. Now she withdrew the envelope that had her address in Mrs. Bailets' handwriting. Griffin only managed to write two- or three-word sentences in big block letters, telling her in his last letter that he and Mrs. Bailets had constructed his previous communication. The mere thought of their effort on her behalf, to ask about her welfare and to wish her well, made her feel warm inside.

She opened the letter to see huge scrawls of simple words, much like a child's—

How are you?
I am good.
I work hard.
I miss walks.
I miss you.

Then followed Mrs. Bailets' fine handwriting and composition for the rest of his letter to her—

The work goes on here. They have completed taking most of the

train wreck from the valley. There is talk now of constructing
snowsheds so this never happens again. There are so many
strangers here in town now, it's hard to find a friendly face.
Mrs. Bailets misses your work at the post office that is starting
to pick up again with the fast mail train coming several times
a day. I hope one day you might be able to visit and say hello.

Yours,
Griffin
Wellington, WA

Lillian couldn't help smiling at the sweet letter and Griffin's effort to try to write part of it. She brought the paper to her lips and kissed it. He and Mrs. Bailets were her true friends in adversity. Friends who did not cast blame as many had in recent days. Friends who cared about her. And truth be told, friends she thought of day and night.

"Hello, Lillian."

Lillian looked up to see a young woman dressed in a coat and a large hat with a light whisper of a veil covering her face. A man in a dark coat stood back in the distance. When the woman lifted the veil, Lillian gazed into the face of Berenice O'Neill, the wife of the railroad superintendent Jim O'Neill. Immediately, she tucked the letter in her coat, stood, and gave the woman a light embrace and kiss on the cheek. "It's good to see you."

"Welcome back. I'm sorry I couldn't make it to your mother's tea the other afternoon."

"It was a pleasant gathering. Mother is trying to help me adjust back into society, I guess." Her gloved hand crinkled the letter in her pocket. "But I don't think high society suits me anymore."

"I'm surprised. I'd thought you couldn't wait to return here after everything that happened and wed your Mr. Travers."

"Mr. Travers and I are no longer suited for each other, I'm afraid."

Berenice stared for a moment then placed a gloved hand on her coat sleeve. "Let's go to my house and have some tea."

"That would be lovely." Lillian was grateful Berenice chose not to avoid her. She wondered, though, at the many emotions circulating in the woman's mind and all the burdens Berenice must be carrying. She wondered too about the man in the dark coat following behind.

When they arrived at the house, an envelope lay on the front step. Berenice ignored it, but Lillian picked it up. She saw the name O'Neill with a drawing of a skull and crossbones, and a sudden chill raced up her spine.

"Give it to me," ordered the man in the dark coat.

"Just throw it away," Berenice said softly, removing her coat to reveal a black dress. "The note is like all the others condemning my husband. Some are calling him a murderer after what happened in Wellington."

Lillian felt shock and dismay. "How awful!"

"For a time I didn't dare leave the house. I was too frightened for our Peggy Jane. When Jim was here giving his testimony a few weeks back in the preliminary inquest about the disaster, we had an armed bodyguard." She nodded at the man who was giving his coat to the butler. "Lloyd accompanies me on errands or if I need a breath of fresh air."

Lillian stared wide-eyed, realizing at once her troubles hardly compared to what poor Berenice was suffering.

"Jim hired both Lloyd and the butler to watch over everything while he's gone. Reporters continue to ask for my views, which I have never given." She paused. "But I see from what I read in the newspaper that you talked openly about it."

"I realize now I should have never done it. What was supposed to help my healing has caused others pain. Anthony is furious with me. Since there are rumors that the cutting of timber in the mountains made a natural path for the slide, he thinks his company will be blamed." She lowered her face and stared at her folded hands in her lap. "Now you're getting hateful letters."

"I've been getting letters ever since the accident. The timber industry is not to blame. The Great Northern Railway is not to blame either." Berenice drew a hankie from her reticule and dabbed her eye. "But I will say that Jim and I are devastated by what happened. I didn't sleep for many nights. I asked God every day why it happened, especially to the innocent children. I know how hard my husband worked to clear the snow. He wrote me often how he labored night and day to get those tracks cleared before the slide hit. He'd get one part of the line cleared, and then another slide would come or a snowplow would break down because of a fallen tree. And it never stopped snowing. He would send telegrams saying how bad it was. He said how much he wished he were home, but he could not leave if the children in that passenger train weren't home in their beds. But in the end, it did nothing." She again dabbed at the tears and blew her nose.

Lillian remained still, unable to think of what to say. She wished she had an answer, but the truth be told, her questions mirrored Berenice's in many ways. For some unknown reason, God allowed it to happen.

"I know scripture says all things work together for good. But it is difficult to find consolation in that with the losses people have suffered." Her tear-filled eyes focused on Lillian. "And your cousin lost her husband. I'm certain she is grieving."

Lillian nodded and clasped her hands in her lap even tighter. "Clyde was a good worker. He took pride in his snowplow, maybe more so than his family. He wanted to see those trains moved. And in the end, he gave his life doing it."

"Please extend to your cousin my heartfelt sympathy. Tell her too that Jim cares deeply about the sacrifices the railway workers made to help those in need."

"They are still working hard," Lillian mused, thinking of the letter in her coat pocket. "I just got a letter today from a worker. He said they are planning to build a snowshed over that part of the track to prevent any further incidents from happening."

Berenice nodded. "There are many plans being drawn up now. For the snowsheds and perhaps one day, even a different way to bypass the Windy Mountains. A new tunnel, perhaps. Jim talked of it. He doesn't want the trains to go through the Cascade Tunnel anymore. But don't let it go any further than that. All it is, is talk."

"But if they built a new tunnel—" Lillian began.

"It would be very expensive, so it's only talk. But if it comes to pass one day, Wellington and other rail towns would cease to exist. Although things are already changing. It will never be the same."

"Neither will we, I expect." Lillian stood. "I should be going. Mother is probably wondering where I am."

"I'm sure your intended is happy you are back, even if things are a bit strained right now. Love has a way of enduring. And love becomes stronger during trials. Will you set a date for the wedding?"

After what happened between her and Anthony, Lillian remained uncertain about anything. "We'll see."

Berenice ventured forward and gave her an embrace before they parted. At least Lillian could find thanks in their friendship that had helped in times of need, like the midwife who came on her husband's private train to help Elizabeth and the meal at the hotel paid for by her husband, along with the nice jacket he insisted Griffin wear. Now she wondered where the future might lead, and the sudden realization this trip to Everett may not be the awakening she thought but rather a long farewell.

———◆•◆———

Lillian paced back and forth in the foyer, pausing at times to stare at her reflection in the mirror. The dress was luxurious enough. Tonight she had dispensed with the black she had worn since Clyde's demise and chosen a blue velvet dress and jacket, with a long beaded necklace and earrings to match. Gretchen had fashioned her hair into a soft bun, with ringlets framing her face. But the nerves within made the reflection in the mirror seem to jump, as did the worry creases on her face and the dark circles persisting under her eyes. She tried to cover it all with some powder, but it did nothing to hide what she felt. After the episode when Anthony shouted his anger over the news article, she'd had no contact with him until, out of the blue, he'd invited her to this dinner.

"Hopefully you will set a wedding date," Mother cooed, helping her adjust a jeweled butterfly comb in her hair. "Everything will be better once that happens." Mother seemed oblivious to the goings-on between them, and probably for the better. Lillian did not believe anything would proceed with the marriage until they first reconciled. His silence spoke so loudly that a pathway forward had been brought to a dead halt. And to Lillian, it may be a blessing in disguise. She had no interest jumping feet first into this relationship. She didn't love him, nor did she want the strain of being a boss' wife. She had witnessed Berenice's suffering with her husband and the avalanche, and it tore her heart. Every day, she thought of the envelope bearing the skull and crossbones lying on the O'Neill stairstep and Berenice living in fear. Lillian could never endure such a life, waiting for some unseen axe of anger to fall from the disgruntled and the hurting.

"Mother, I hope you will abide by whatever happens tonight," Lillian now told her.

She stepped back. Her blue eyes that Lillian inherited grew large. "You aren't confident, then?"

"No. I lost that a while ago."

A knock came on the door. Gretchen opened it to reveal Anthony's aide, who would take Lillian to the hotel. Putting on her coat, she wondered why she'd even agreed to this dinner. She knew she'd never eat one bite as she tried to control her trembling fingers inside the long gloves. It made little sense for her to order extravagant food, only to watch it grow cold under his baneful stare. How she wished she were transported back to that time at Scenic, with Griffin fidgeting in his too-tight dinner jacket, enjoying a meal he had probably only ever dreamed about.

"You look beautiful," Anthony said when she arrived.

Lillian managed a small smile but kept her gaze averted, unable to look him in the eye. He had already chosen wine for them, given the crystal glasses half-filled with ruby-red liquid. The paper menu at her place setting began to waver as tears glazed her eyes. She inhaled a breath and tried to concentrate but could not. "Anthony, I'm sorry. I can't go through with this."

He sat quietly, his gaze never leaving her face.

"I visited Berenice O'Neill the other day. What she is going through is terrible, and I simply can't live my life like that."

"What are you trying to say?" he asked simply.

Lillian shared about her visit with Berenice—the letters, the threats, and the guards, all in the aftermath of the avalanche and the inquest that followed. "I came back here to find out what to do with my life. I realize now it isn't about marrying you and living in Everett. And it never will be."

She expected his fingers to tighten, for anger to distort his features, and for his tongue to lash out. But he only sat back in his chair and let out a loud sigh. "Well, this makes it much easier, I must say."

Lillian blinked at his quiet tone that took her by surprise. "What do you mean?"

His gaze shifted to his place setting where he began to reset the spoons. "I didn't know how to tell you this. We made a commitment, after all. Granted, it was made many months ago, but it was still a commitment. But...I'll just come out with it. I met another woman while working in San Francisco."

Lillian sat frozen in her seat as he explained about the woman who had captured his interest. When he finished, she said slowly, "So you would have married me but kept her as a mistress?"

His face reddened. "Of course not. I would have called it off with her. I had my private assumptions, but I needed to hear from you what was in your heart. And you said it loud and clear, that marrying me is not what you want either."

At first Lillian wanted to be angry at this seeming rejection. But in all honesty, she had rejected him long ago. Like him, she had tried to keep a commitment severely tested and tried during their absence. And like him, the void created in the heart became filled by another.

"I do hope we can part as friends," he added. "I know I was hot under the collar the other day about the article in the newspaper." He paused. "The truth be told, I see how that place and the whole disaster affected you. I believe you were changed by it, maybe in ways you haven't even realized."

"I realize it very well. But I thank you for noticing. And for being honest." She paused. "Is this lady of yours of a good reputation and sound heart and mind?"

He nodded. "She is. But so are you, Lillian. Look at all you have been through. And I know there is a fine gentleman ready to call you his own. One who will give you peace and contentment and be the perfect one for you."

Lillian felt her face heat at the words. The meeting had gone far differently than she ever expected—and with words she never thought would be expressed. While they parted ways early, forgoing the dinner, she knew now that God was guiding her onto the right path for His name's sake. If it was not too late.

Chapter 23

MAY

The sound of rushing water greeted Griffin as he came out of the bunkhouse into the bright rays of morning sunshine. Haskell Creek had risen dramatically over the last week as the heavy weight of winter rapidly declined under spring's warmth. He couldn't have been happier to see all the snow begin to recede, even if it made for tumultuous creeks and rivers. At least the bridge over the creek in town was high enough and sturdy enough to take the swiftly running waters with all the snowmelt. A bird flew down and landed on a fence line, tipped its head casually, and opened and closed his beak, the musical chirp drowned out by the sound of rushing water. To Griffin, all these were encouraging signs that some semblance of spring was beginning to return after a deadly winter season.

He walked along the boardwalk to see workers gathered to finish salvaging the wrecked trains. For weeks they labored, using tall winches to drag up train parts and load them onto flatbed cars. The men worked carefully, as passengers in the deadly wrecks still remained unaccounted for. He hated to think that the last might not be discovered until the snow finally melted away, but the reality of it seemed likely. The burial by the Windy Mountain avalanche had been deep and traumatic, and it would take a long time for Wellington to resurrect from the grave—if it ever did.

He thought of Lillian then and blew out a sigh. While he missed her, he didn't blame her in the least for fleeing. Many had done the same thing, too overcome by the death and destruction to remain here. Others were plain fearful of snow burying them in another avalanche, and again, Griffin couldn't blame them. Even though Windy Mountain stood serene with its snowcapped peak, it remained a symbol of deadly strength.

Griffin walked down to where the trains had stood that fateful night and looked at the steep terrain devoid of the conifer tree cover that once existed, mowed over by nature's wrath. Down below, a few hardy souls still looked around in the melting snow at the scrap metal, but most of the larger pieces of the wreckage had been removed.

"Hard to believe it happened."

He glanced over to see that Oliver McCree had joined him in his thoughtful perusal of the ravine area. Over these many weeks, the once-vicious enemy and he had become friends. They both shared in the loss of good friends in the battle of life and death. Oliver rose from the snowy grave, grateful for his life. He still sported issues due to his injuries, but he and Griffin worked together at times with the heavy parcels that came in, including construction materials. Rumors circulated of the Great Northern Railway erecting snowsheds over the area where the trains stood to protect the tracks from future avalanches. Some men had come to survey the land and take the needed measurements. Materials began arriving, with machinery arriving first to accept the steel girders that would form the skeleton of the structure, and then the tens of thousands of pounds of concrete in barrels to build the barrier. Wood also arrived to construct buildings to house the workers, and the eating bunkhouse needed to be expanded to feed everyone. Wellington began rising from its pit of destruction by the arrival of workers and materials, ready to become an active rail town once again. "Don't think I'll be able to do the kind of work they expect around here," Oliver had bemoaned to Griffin, upset that his body seemed to take forever to heal from the fractures. The railroad bosses were gracious, giving him only duties he could handle, but he talked often of leaving.

The two men now stood in silent respect over the slide area. "Soon there won't be time to think anymore with all the building coming," Griffin mused.

"You think any more about that gal? The one you liked? Can't think of her name."

"Lillian. Sometimes. But this place is not where she belongs. She was meant for better things in life." His voice trailed off.

Oliver nudged him. "C'mon then. Mrs. Bailets just had some new girls arrive to work in the hotel. Let's go say howdy to them. I could use some flapjacks that are better than what they cook up at the bunkhouse. Rumor has it one of the gals is German, and she asks the cook to put sweet apples in the flapjacks. Sounds good to me."

Griffin thought on it but then shook his head. Oliver mumbled something about his refusal being his loss and strode off whistling. It might be good to get his thoughts away from Lillian and on to other things. If only he didn't keep her memory alive with her letters hidden away in his pocket or under his pillow every night. He thought of them working together to help those in need and then the dinner at the hotel. He'd been back to Scenic a few times since the tracks reopened, visiting the hotel and even the hot springs that Lillian never had a chance to see before her beau tore her away. He thought how he would like to take her on a day excursion to see nature's marvel. . . Then he chastised himself. Lillian was not coming back. She and the fancy timber tycoon had likely set a date and their marriage loomed, even though her last letter didn't mention it. Instead, she described the emotional meeting with Berenice and how well her cousin Elizabeth was adapting to life in Everett. Fine womanly conversation, even if Griffin desired to know the unspoken thoughts that lay between the lines.

Griffin returned to the main bunkhouse to eat his usual fare of greasy bacon and dry flapjacks before the fast mail train was scheduled to arrive. He still missed seeing the friendly faces of Joe Walters and Matt Weiss greeting him as the mail train pulled into town. At times their loss was like a knife stabbing him. The men that manned it now were all businesslike, tossing out a modest mailbag for the town before disappearing inside the train without so much as a greeting. While he thought the removal of the trains from the ravine and all the chatter of rebuilding would help mend the hurt, it did nothing. The town still received visitors who offered farewells before a mountain that had claimed the lives of their loved ones. One man even brought a bouquet of flowers from the city and tossed it over the embankment, spreading the vibrant color across the stark, gray snow. Grieving took on many forms, some in quiet mourning and reflection, others in outright anger and brawling in the saloon, with fellow workers grieving their dead brothers on the railroad. Wellington had seen it all.

Inside the eating bunkhouse, Griffin sat at his own table, not in the mood to converse with others. The flapjacks tasted like sawdust. Even Lillian's burnt ones from long ago would make a pleasant change. He decided to try to compose another letter to her. Maybe Oliver would help him write it. Or Jack McClintock. Mrs. Bailets was up to her shoulders in work, so he dared not ask her anymore. Occasionally, she mentioned how she wished Lillian were here to run the post office. "I miss her," she had said dolefully.

Griffin would have echoed a similar sentiment but only nodded and turned away before his feelings became too obvious. But to the woman's keen eye, he could hide nothing.

"You'll meet another fine woman, Griffin," she had told him. "You're a nice man with a good head on your shoulders." But right now his shoulders remained hunched over with emotional burdens he wondered would ever be lifted.

Griffin headed back to receive the mail when the train whistle interrupted the sound of the running creek and the chirping birds on this early spring morning. He made sure the hook was ready for the bags, but today the train drew to a stop. Men began unloading heavy barrels, all labeled CONCRETE for the new snowsheds. The men said little to Griffin, even when he greeted one young man with fiery red hair who only grunted and rolled barrels off the train to an awaiting rail cart. Griffin swallowed hard. Memories of Joe Walter's grin flooded him, and instant tears made his eyes blurry. There was no getting over this. Even if the railroad thought the coming snowsheds would help and life would appear to have moved on, it would never make up for the loss that proved too raw and too real.

Once the train moved out with great speed as if it couldn't wait to leave under the watchful eye of Windy Mountain, Griffin set to work using the rail cart to move the heavy barrels toward the storage sheds at the passing tracks where the work would commence. A miniature mountain of steel girders stood ready while several fellows examined the blueprint for the massive structure to be built. Everything appeared in order for the snowsheds. He blew out a sigh. But nothing else in life.

"Hello, Griffin."

A feathery-light voice filled the air. He shook his one ear until the voice called out again. A small woman in a thin coat and large hat stood there, accompanied by a grinning Oliver.

"I told you to come to the hotel for those fancy flapjacks filled with apples. Look who I found eating there."

Griffin blinked rapidly to make certain this was no dream. A smile lit her face as she stepped forward. "How are you?" she asked.

He tried to speak but could not. Finally, he cleared his throat and managed to find his voice. "Miss Hartwick. What a surprise." He wanted to ask what in tarnation she was doing here. Or if she had gotten on the wrong train that ought to be heading back to her fiancé, wherever he dwelt at that moment.

"I got in last night, on the eastbound train. I spent the night at the hotel, of course." Lillian giggled. "Mrs. Bailets wanted to find you outright, but I told her to keep it a secret." She acknowledged

Oliver. "He told me you were a little down today, so this seemed as good a time as any to surprise you."

"I—I'm certainly surprised. Did you rest well?"

"As well as can be expected." She nodded at the building materials. "It looks like the railroad is moving heaven and earth to change things around here."

"Snowsheds will be built to protect the tracks and the trains."

"I remember you mentioning that in your letters." She gazed beyond Griffin to Oliver who still stood there, smiling from ear to ear. "Thank you so much for showing me where to go, Oliver. I'm sure more of Anna's apple flapjacks are waiting for you."

He swept off his cap and bowed before wheeling around and heading back in the direction of the hotel.

"He's a different man than the angry one in that fake courtroom," she murmured, watching him walk back to the center of town.

"People are different," Griffin said slowly. "Life goes on, but it's been changed and everyone with it." He walked along the pending construction site that bordered the ill-fated ravine.

Lillian heaved a sigh as she gazed out over the area. "It's hard to believe what happened here just a few months ago. I see a lot of the debris has been removed. There's still so much snow. In Everett, we have sweet spring flowers. But here, winter won't let go."

"Not for long. The birds are singing. The snowmelt is well under way. The streams and rivers are running high."

She glanced back toward town. "When I left here, the town was still buried. It's nice to see the buildings again, and it looks like they are building even more bunkhouses."

"For the workers who will be building the snowsheds. The GNR is spending a lot of money. They are making changes so Wellington lives once again."

Lillian turned quiet, and he wondered what her demeanor meant. Most of all, he wondered why she had returned. To finish offering her farewells to this place? To continue with personal grieving, as others had done? Or something more? He wanted to ask her outright but kept the questions to himself as they walked along the boardwalk.

A ball suddenly bounced before them. Griffin picked it up with a flourish and tossed it back to the young boy.

"How sweet to see young faces again," she said softly. "That's what I missed in town. The children."

"With the new engineers and builders coming in, there will be plenty of families. They want to build a schoolhouse here. I hope on Sundays we will have church."

Lillian whirled then, and for a breathless moment he thought she might embrace him. The idea gave him tingles. "How wonderful, Griffin."

"You should consider teaching. You're excellent with teaching someone how to read." He halted and felt his face grow warm. "Not that you haven't a life already in Everett, but—"

"I *had* a life in Everett. I went back to see if any of it remained." She paused to savor the warm breath of wind across her face. "I have some good friends still. Mother was ecstatic I had returned. But…" She paused. "All I could think about was Wellington. And you."

"I'm sure your Mr. Travers is not pleased."

"He's found another woman in San Francisco. He was glad to hear it when I told him things would not work out. I told him I could never become the wife of an important businessman, like Berenice O'Neill. Remember? She is the wife of the railway superintendent. It would have been the death of me. Truly." Her cheeks took on a rosy tint, and her hands folded over each other across her handbag. "It was a difficult lesson to learn. Like Anthony said, we had made a commitment months ago, standing there on the wharf. He was ready to fulfill it, even saying farewell to his beloved in San Francisco." Their gazes met. "But I wasn't willing to go that far. I could never really say goodbye, Griffin."

Her blue eyes began to shimmer with what could only be tears. He'd never known anyone who cried for him. Or cried over a reason to be with him. Who would want to? "Why?" he finally asked. He had to know the truth. It wasn't money. Or a lavish lifestyle. Or living in the snowy Cascades. His life radiated the meagerness and the mundane life of a common laborer.

"Because you spoke the truth to my heart. You showed me a God who wasn't some steeple or pages in a book but a living Person who cared." She hesitated. "I don't understand everything. I don't know why He allowed a terrible slide to happen that sent people to heaven early. Even a baby. But I do know that when you spoke about Him, something inside me came alive. I wasn't just living each day for the sake of living. I anticipated each day and what it brought, both in joy and in sorrow."

"Lillian." He didn't stop to consider what he was doing as his lanky arms swept her up and his lips captured hers in a lengthy kiss. How he loved the feel of her tender form against him. The words she spoke were like the added sweetness of icing to a scrumptious cake. He couldn't believe his blessings, and when nothing had made sense. But this made perfect sense and in the most perfect timing, on the heels of great change and the warmth of spring that finally made the chilling cold of death and destruction wave a flag of surrender. He stepped back but kept her hands in his. "How long do you plan to visit?"

Lillian laughed. "As long as possible. My trunk is at the Bailets Hotel, and my heart is right here."

Griffin opened his mouth to respond when several men called out for him to leave the lady alone and lend a helping hand. Grins decorated the workers' faces. "Forgot about my job," he said sheepishly. "I better get back to work."

She giggled. "Go on with you then, and I'll see what Mrs. Bailets is up to today."

He continued to observe her lovely, sculptured face, wishing he could stare at her for the next hour, but earning a paycheck beckoned to him. And when the men saw him dance a little jig as he returned to help move the barrels of powdered cement, they inquired of his happy mood.

"Nothing can be that good," one grumbled.

"Oh yes, it can. Love."

———◆◆◆———

"There must be a mistake with the ticket," the conductor said, looking at Griffin from the top of his felt hat to the bottoms of his shiny shoes. "It shouldn't say THIRD CLASS. You are hardly going far either. If you would follow me, sir."

Griffin chose not to argue with the conductor leading the way to first class, as this night he felt like a gentleman. And he owed it all to William Bailets, whose wife Susan cajoled her husband into finding him suitable eveningwear. After asking around, the man located a dinner jacket, trousers that Susan let out, and even shoes. The shoes themselves probably weren't the best selection with snow still lingering about, but he would take his chances at looking his best. Just the notion they were able to even find suitable clothing that could partially fit his tall stature showed the goodness of God in the smallest details of life.

Settling into the plush velvet seat, he hoped Lillian had received the invitation Susan Bailets penned for him, inviting her to this dinner and an excursion afterward to see the famous hot springs. Griffin looked for Lillian's arrival, wondering what she would say to seeing him seated in first class. Would her lovely blue eyes widen in surprise? And would she take the seat opposite him?

On the final call of *all aboard,* Lillian scampered in, and to his surprise, scurried on by, her large hat blocking him from view. He inhaled a deep breath. At least she was here. And he would not worry that she failed to recognize him. Who would in this prim and proper eveningwear when she expected a torn shirt and pants, a muddy cap, and a third-class status? It would make for a fine surprise when they arrived.

Not twenty minutes later, after the train wound its way around the still-snow-covered Windy Mountain range and past Windy

Point to descend to Scenic, he disembarked the train at the depot along with several passengers. He waited patiently for Lillian to alight from the coach. When she did, her eyes widened.

"My goodness, Griffin! You were seated in first class? Why, I didn't even see—"

He only offered her his arm. "It was a last-minute change. The Bailetses helped me dress as a gentleman, and the conductor agreed. But come, let's find a ride to the hotel." Thankfully a small wagon and driver sat there to take passengers over to the hotel along the muddy and snow encrusted road. "It's a much different town than when I was here a few months ago to see Mr. O'Neill after the slide happened."

"You helped everyone, Griffin." He loved her smile that jolted when the wagon hit a rift of ice then drew to a stop before the hotel. He slipped a coin to the driver and again offered her his arm. Thankfulness filled every part of him as they walked into the hotel dining room. Instead of feeling out of place like he did on their first meeting here, he never felt more at peace. Lillian removed her coat and hat, giving it to a nearby attendant. The dress she had selected, a singular silky affair tied with a wide bow, accompanied by a long necklace and gloves that reached to her upper arms, left him tongue-tied and sensing how little he deserved her beautiful presence.

"So how did you get the dinner jacket this time?" she asked with a laugh as they were seated.

"From the Bailetses. Susan is very happy to make everything go well. They wanted me to look the part and act it."

"You have only ever been genuine, Griffin. There is no actor in you."

Griffin stared at her face, searching for any crossed lines, a furrowed forehead, or anything else that spoke otherwise. She only sat with a small smile on her lips, perfectly composed as if she truly loved to be here—a fact that both amazed and humbled him.

Griffin reached across the table to grab her hand, soft and warm in his large one. He had held back his intentions ever since she arrived in Wellington a week ago. Now, every part of him cried out to make things permanent before she slipped out of his grasp. He never wanted her to leave him again, not for the big boss of the timber industry or anyone else. "Please, Lillian, marry me." Suddenly he let go of her hand and straightened in his seat, stretching out the collar of his tight shirt. "That came out too fast. I was supposed to say more. I'm sorry."

"At least you're a man who knows what he wants." She laughed before a serious expression overtook the smile on her lips. "Yes, I'll marry you."

Griffin could not believe the words that floated across the table. A nearby waiter began to applaud. Griffin grinned, as did Lillian, and soon a good deal of the dining room broke out in applause when word spread of their engagement.

"Goodness, I never expected this," Lillian said with glee. "It's like I'm marrying the most famous man of the Cascades. Which I know I am."

"No. I'm the luckiest. And a grand cheer for us." They reached across and touched lips in a grateful kiss. He then sat back and looked at the menu, his lips turning into a gigantic smile with all his dreams coming true. "I'm happy I can read the menu, thanks to you. Let's have a good supper."

Lillian laughed along with him.

Chapter 24

FOUR YEARS LATER

"Any news yet?"

Lillian heard this question nearly every day inside the post office as she handed Oliver a piece of mail. "Not that I'm aware of. I'm sure the telegraph office will let us know as soon as word arrives."

He glanced at the envelope. "I still have trouble remembering that this town is now called Tye. I keep thinking the mail's been misdelivered."

Lillian recalled the fall of great change in October of 1910, when she and Griffin had wed before a backdrop of beautiful-colored leaves and a crisp scent in the air. During that month, the powers that be decided in hushed tones to change the name of the town from Wellington to Tye, after the raging river in the ravine. They hoped the stigma surrounding the town would lift and folks would not look at it as some forbidden place no one dared stop to visit. Susan Bailets hailed the decision as a success due to a dramatic increase in passengers coming to the hotel for a bite to eat or to spend the night. Since the name change, folks appeared to breathe easier with patrons at the hotel, general store, and saloon—and the town began to lift out of a dark and gloomy pit.

Oliver cackled then as he snapped a suspender. "I remember giving Griffin a whipping when mail was misdelivered to here instead of Scenic." His smile disappeared. "I sure was an angry old man then. Even if he and I are the same age. Hate makes you old."

"Yes, until we know the saving peace of the Lord," Lillian said with a smile. "And remember too, Oliver, the old man has passed away. The new has come."

"Yeah, it sure has. Anytime I see someone at work picking on someone else, I let 'em have it." He then added quickly, "In a friendly way, mind you. And I tell them to come to church on Sunday and get right with the Lord."

Lillian chuckled. With the building of the schoolhouse a few years back, church services were heavily attended on Sundays. She would never forget, though, the church service on the ill-fated train the day before the avalanche, led by Reverend Thompson who, like many others, did not survive. A tear still entered her eye at the thought of Sarah Covington's sweet voice singing her favorite hymn and her words of confidence that the Lord would deliver them. Only sometimes it happened in ways not entirely understood.

"Well, I better be getting back," Oliver said. "Anna will wonder what's keeping me." He waved the letter. "Her ma writes every week, but it's in German."

Lillian laughed and returned to the sorting. The place had grown these last few years with the town tripling in size as many new families arrived. Houses had been built, and the town of Tye thrived.

But now all eyes were on Olympia, where the superior court was in its final days of deliberating the verdict in a lawsuit over the avalanche. At first the GNR was found guilty of negligence. Lillian often prayed for Berenice, wondering how she was enduring all this with her husband being scrutinized for contributing to the effects of the slide that killed over ninety souls. The debate of negligence raged around tables at mealtimes, and even over their humble table at the tiny house where she and Griffin lived. Being a railway worker caught in the thick of it all, he believed it unfair to heap blame on the GNR. All that could be done was done, according to Griffin. For Lillian, she had no dealing with handling the massive burden to free the tracks and trains from relentless snow like Griffin had done. She'd been among the frustrated passengers, with those helpless and innocent ones who knew they faced peril, and then with the injured. She said little of her feelings to Griffin, but deep inside she often questioned if something else could have been done to save the people.

Lillian sighed and forced the arguments away. What happened, happened. A guilty or not guilty verdict would do little. Some talked about money, but she knew well it would never satisfy a hurting heart. She came from a well-to-do family and nearly wed a booming lumber tycoon profiting off the earthquake disaster in San Francisco. No money, no prominence in society or in social circles could bring peace to a hurting heart. Only God could bring it.

The door bumped open, and Griffin walked in with a little girl toddling beside him. "Look who wanted to see Mama working."

Lillian's whole being warmed. She stepped out from behind the counter and gave the little girl a big hug. "And how is my sweet little Sarah Jane today?"

She held out a piece of paper. "Look what I did, Mama!"

Lillian took it to see the drawing of mountains and flowers and sun and even a train, accompanied by the endearing words of *I love you*. "How lovely."

"I wrote the words," Griffin said with a chortle. "Not that long ago, I couldn't write a thing."

"Now look at you. A dispatcher in training."

He laughed. "I never would've believed that either. Reading time charts and plotting arrivals and departures. And learning Morse code."

"And you do it well. They ought to be happy to have such a hardworking man in charge of the trains." She looked lovingly at her daughter. "Isn't your papa hardworking, little one?" The little girl hummed as her tiny hand ran across the smooth wood counter.

"So there's still no verdict," Griffin said, finding a chair to sit.

"I hope it comes soon. Do you think there will be issues here and more changes if the court rules against the railroad?"

Griffin shrugged. "There are rumors. Some say the GNR will have to cut back. Others talk about them doing alternative runs. But the mail and the passengers need to get from Spokane to Seattle and back again. They can't do anything about that line or the mail train, which provides them a lot of money."

"Will you have to give up your training?"

"I don't think so. Dispatchers are needed so everything runs. It's important communication we didn't have with the slide." He then scooted Sarah onto his lap and gave her a hug.

"I don't know what I would do if I lost Sarah," Lillian said, then slapped a hand across her mouth. Her pensive thoughts had escaped before she realized it. Griffin stared at her with a questioning glance. "I'm sorry. She's Thelma's age, the little girl who died in the wreck. I can still see Thelma skipping around the coach in her party dress the night of the terrible slide. She used to ask every lady there if she could be her new mama. I guess because she was missing hers." Her voice broke. "I can't imagine how her mother feels."

Griffin stroked Sarah's hair. "We can't, Lillian. But we can pray. And trust. It's all we can do."

Lillian swallowed down her emotion, knowing she shouldn't have brought up such things. But with the pending verdict, of which many families looked for restitution and maybe a final closing of this terrible book, it all came to the surface again. Not long after Sarah was born, Lillian had managed to locate Sarah Covington's family's address. She sent her husband and sons a note, telling them she had named her newborn after their courageous wife and mother—one who never lost hope, even when everything appeared bleak. Luther wrote back on behalf of all of them, grateful to receive her message and for the honor in his mother's memory. And Lillian did remember whenever she said Sarah's name and told her little daughter about God's love. She knew somehow that Sarah Covington looked down on her with that friendly smile that warmed her heart to this day.

Lillian busied herself with the final sorting of the mail, assembled some outgoing mail that she gave to Griffin, and then closed the office. Griffin took the mail bag while Lillian grasped little Sarah's hand, and together they stepped out into the warm sunshine. Even though it was late summer, Lillian never ceased to give thanks for the lovely weather. But the coming of fall, though it brought their wedding anniversary of four years and the pretty autumn colors, also heralded the arrival of another winter season. And with that, she couldn't escape the nagging fear. Even to this day when she heard a strange roar, albeit the distant engine of a locomotive or the revving of the snowplow, she would dash out to see if Windy Mountain had again unleashed a wild fury. But seemingly serene, the mountain stood there, even if a side of it remained devoid of vegetation, reminding her of its fatal contribution to their town.

"I wonder if I will ever get over this," she said softly to Griffin.

"What?"

"The fear of winter. The weather is lovely right now, so nice and warm, but soon the snow will come again."

Griffin sighed. "My offer is still there. We can leave here and return to Everett to live. Your mother would love to see Sarah more often. And I can easily get a job."

Lillian said nothing. She knew Griffin would do whatever she asked because that's the kind of man he was. But moving back to Everett would stir up more issues than she wanted to deal with. Although her parents reluctantly gave their permission for their union, she always felt in their hearts they were sad their only daughter never married the president of a timber company. She didn't want Griffin to live under a cloud of disappointment in anyone's eyes. When her parents came to visit a month ago, they showered their granddaughter with presents and spoke kindly to Griffin. Maybe the doubt over Griffin's acceptance was her own overactive imagination. Like the fear of another avalanche.

"You're quiet all of the sudden," Griffin observed. "You must be thinking about it."

"No. I'm thinking how it would be a mistake to leave here because of fear." She looked down the tracks to the huge concrete shed that shielded the trains from winter's fury. The sheds gave the workers less backbreaking work of shoveling too. But it remained a stark gray reminder as a stone and steel monument of a stretch of track where passengers in three sets of trains went to sleep and never woke up. "We have to live," she pronounced.

Now as Lillian surveyed Tye with its many new buildings and heard the gleeful screech of children running about in play, the town felt renewed, just like a forest in springtime after the snows left. The church was crowded on Sundays, the people friendly and helpful, and Lillian could not think of life anywhere else. Just like the decision she made four years ago to return here under Griffin's startled expression that melted into a kiss of promise and an agreement to marriage. Her heart belonged to the Cascade Mountains. . .and to him.

The whistle blew with the arrival of the fast mail train, ready for pickup and drop-off. Lillian stood by as Griffin hurried to the depot to deliver the small sack of mail and retrieve the new one. He didn't need to do the transfer as others had been assigned the task, but some duties were just a part of his nature from the work long ago.

The train tooted again, signaling its departure. Griffin returned with only a few letters this time. One in particular caught Lillian's eye, addressed to Susan Bailets, but with the return address of Ida Starrett, British Columbia, Canada. "Oh my goodness, it's from Ida!" Griffin looked at her questioningly. "You remember Ida? The last one pulled alive from the wreckage."

"Of course. How could I forget? Her son Raymond had that huge stick in his forehead." Griffin placed a hand on his own head as if reliving it, wincing as he did.

"I must take this over to the hotel right now. Can you take Sarah home?"

Griffin nodded as she walked swiftly down the boardwalk for the hotel, her skirts swishing. They had heard precious little from the passengers and crew, except in the early days of pilgrimages here or yearly anniversaries of the avalanche when some came to pay their respects. The last meaningful message Lillian received was from Sarah Covington's son Luther when he responded about naming her daughter after his mother. And now with the verdict pending, most decided to let this place go and try to move on.

Lillian looked again at the envelope, wondering what the letter contained. She had heard nothing about Ida since that final day at the hospital, before she left by train to seek better medical attention, accompanied by her mother and son. Absent from the woman was her father, baby son, and little Lillian, along with her husband in another accident—precious losses that no doubt ached to this day.

Lillian climbed the stairs and burst into the hotel lobby to be greeted by several folks she recognized. Immediately she asked for Susan—who insisted that Lillian call her by her first name after her marriage to Griffin. "We're equals now," she had said with a laugh. "Two married women trying to keep our men in line."

Susan Bailets came hurrying down the stairs, her arms full as usual. Lillian could probably count on one hand the times she had witnessed the hardworking woman *not* bearing a burden. "Well, what brings you here, Lillian? Don't tell me something has gone wrong at the post office."

"On the contrary. Special delivery." Lillian held out the envelope.

Susan handed the stack of towels to another housekeeper. "My land, it's from Ida Starrett." She motioned Lillian over to the corner of the modest lobby and two chairs. Her fingers shook some as she opened the letter. Scanning the contents, a smile broke out on her face. "Well, isn't that something?"

Lillian tried hard not to fidget, but her curiosity climbed so high that she dearly wanted to rip the letter out of Susan's hands and read it for herself. Then the woman cleared her voice and began reading it aloud.

> Dear Mrs. Bailets,
>
> My son Ray reminded me today that we owe a great deal to you and the people of Wellington. Though it's been several years, I've been unable to talk about what happened. But I would be at fault if I did not at least offer my sincere thanks for everything you've done. My dear son and my mother would not be with me today without your effort and the kindness that you and others have shown. The railroad too has been very kind to us, and we look forward now to the continued blessings of God in our lives as we keep the faith. Thank you again.

Susan Bailets wiped a tear from her eye and waved the letter like a banner. "Would you look at this? Here's someone who lost practically everything but remains grateful, even if she cannot speak about that gruesome slide that tried so hard to wreck us." She looked over at Lillian. "You know how hard it is sometimes to thank God that He spared the hotel but then wonder why a trainload of people died?" She shook her head. "That slide came so close to this building. But it's like the mountain had its eye on the trains. I can never get that out of my mind."

"I don't think we should," Lillian said. "You never forget. You find ways to live with it." She pointed at the letter. "And Ida did. She found ways to let go of her pain and move on. Even offering a blessing to the railroad that some think took their loved ones away."

"I'll never understand it."

"I guess what's impossible for us to understand is possible for God. He understands why it happened. He understands the loss. He understands the pain. I think that's what we have to hold on to. His understanding is a picture much bigger than ours. And we can leave our hurting questions with Him."

Susan sniffed, taking up the corner of her apron to dry a few stray tears. "Sounds like you've been listening to that preacher husband of yours again," she said with a laugh.

"Well, Griffin does have a better understanding of things than me. Probably because he has God telling him loud and clear. He would like that you called him a preacher. But he wants to be a dispatcher and help the trains."

"And he will make a fine one too. I miss him running these horrid errands though. He did every kind of miserable thing the railroad needed." She reached out her hand. "At least I'm glad to still have you at the post office."

"I wouldn't be able to if one of your gals here couldn't keep an eye on Sarah those few days I work. She loves playing with your grandchildren."

"What's one more? We love Sarah."

Lillian loved her too and, with that, told Susan she'd better get home to put on some supper. Walking onto the street, she saw folks begin to hurry to the telegraph office adjacent to the depot, craning their heads to hear. One after another relayed the message.

"What happened?" she asked a passerby.

"The court has announced their ruling. The railroad has been found not guilty. The slide was ruled an act of God."

Lillian did not know whether to celebrate or not. Surely her friend Berenice and her husband Jim O'Neill would be relieved. For that she was happy. But for those seeking monetary restitution beyond the railroad compensation, and for those seeking closure, what would it mean to them if they could not hold anyone at fault? Except to shake a fist at the Almighty.

Lillian took her time returning to the house, perusing all this in careful thought, to see Griffin standing on the front porch with Sarah playing at his feet. "Did you hear?"

He nodded. "Yes. Not guilty. Ruled an act of God."

They sat together in rocking chairs on the front porch, watching townsfolk along the boardwalks with talk of the verdict in the air. "It's like Ida knew what would happen," Lillian murmured.

Griffin turned, his eyes narrowing. "What do you mean?"

Lillian told him about the contents of the letter from Ida Starrett. "She thanked the railroad for their kindness. How about that?"

Griffin exhaled through pursed lips in the sound of a whistle. Sarah looked up and laughed, wrapping her tiny hands around her papa's leg. "Ida decided to think about what's important. Being thankful. Even with her losses, as terrible as they were. What a gift that is." He reached over and took Lillian's hand in his. "And I'm thankful. Very thankful. Without all this, we would not be together, Lillian. Or have Sarah Jane."

Lillian couldn't help but agree. While tragedy appeared to tear lives apart, it also had a way of knitting people together for God's great purpose. "I guess all of this was an act of God," she mused. "From allowing us to think and choose, to the snows that came, to welcoming life and saying goodbye in the sight of death, to saying *I do* at the altar... All of it.

Thank You, God."

Author Note

Thank you for journeying with Lillian and Griffin through a difficult time in American history. The Wellington avalanche was precipitated by historic snowfall in a short amount of time and, due to the cold and warming conditions, led to multiple avalanches in the area. One can always look back to consider if something might have been done to move the trains before the main avalanche struck. But as the extraordinary circumstances surrounding the week the trains sat on the tracks showed, not much else could have been done that hadn't already been done. In the end, the Washington State Supreme Court agreed, absolving the Great Northern Railway of all responsibility for the accident. Eventually the GNR opened a new tunnel through the Cascade Mountains in 1929, rerouting the railroad away from this deadly stretch in Stevens Pass. Wellington (or Tye) ceased to exist. Now a quiet trail, the Iron Goat Trail, wanders through vegetation and remnants of the snowshed built shortly after the avalanche, covering the tracks that once held the ill-fated trains.

I endeavored to bring to life the passengers who did exist on the trains wrecked in the avalanche—those who lived, breathed, worked, and died during this time. Many of the rescue attempts and the care of the wounded actually occurred. The telegraph operator, Basil Sherlock, really did perform the surgery on the little boy to remove the huge splinter from his forehead. Susan Bailets and her husband, William, did much in town to keep things going, giving goods and services from their hotel and general store during this time. The people in Wellington banded together in those crucial hours after the avalanche to pull passengers and train crews from heavy snow and train wreckage, doing what they could on their own with no outside help. Miraculously, they managed to save twenty-three people from certain death. Many more likely could have been found if there had been more rescuers, but to surmise what lives might have been spared is simply conjecture at this point. For certain, trains falling on top of trains from a tonnage of snow and massive trees are ingredients for a deadly result.

It is difficult as a writer to come up with a satisfying resolution to a catastrophe. But there is something about a disaster that brings people together when the days are filled with heartache and grief. In the end, they and us find a reason to "give thanks: for this is the will of God in Christ Jesus concerning you" (I Thessalonians 5:18).

Lauralee Bliss

Lauralee Bliss is a published author of many romance novels and novellas, both historical and contemporary. Lauralee's prayer is that readers will come away with both an entertaining story and a lesson that speaks to the heart and soul. When not writing, Lauralee can often be found on the trails where the author has logged over 10,000 miles of hiking. She makes her home in the Blue Ridge mountains with her family. Visit Lauraleebliss.com for more information about the author and her adventures.

A Day to Remember

A series of exciting novels featuring historic North American disasters that changed landscapes and multiple lives. Whether by nature or by man, each of these disasters altered history and was a day to remember.

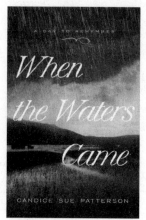

When the Waters Came
By Candice Sue Patterson
May 31, 1889

Relive Friday, May 31, 1889, in Johnstown, Pennsylvania, when the South Fork Dam failed. As Pastor Monty Childs and nurse Annamae Worthington work together to help the survivors, a kindship forms that may soon be torn apart by unburied secrets.

Paperback / 978-1-63609-758-9

When the Flames Ravaged
By Rhonda Dragomir
July 6, 1944

World War II Gold Star widow Evelyn Halstead is taken in by her brother and soothed by the love of his wife and children. Evelyn refuses to cower in grief, so on a sweltering July day in 1944, the family attends the Ringling Brothers and Barnum & Bailey Circus in Hartford. When a blaze ignites the big top, Evelyn fears she will lose all that remains of her life, while Hank Webb, who hides from his murky past behind grease paint as Fraidy Freddie the clown, steps out of the shadows to help save lives and return hope to Evelyn.

Paperback / 978–1–63609–786–2

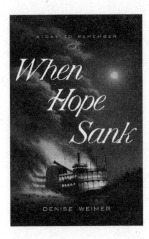

When Hope Sank
By Denise Weimer

April 27, 1865

The Civil War has taken everything from Lily Livingston, leaving her to work for her uncle at a squalid inn along the Arkansas riverfront that is overrun by spies and bushwhackers. Her only hope of escape is a marriage promise she is uncertain will be fulfilled. When on April 27, 1865, the steamboat Sultana, overloaded with soldiers, explodes and sinks, Lily does all she can to help the victims, including Lieutenant Cade Palmer. But what would the wounded surgeon think of her if he knew she could have prevented the disaster—and may have knowledge of another in the making?

Paperback / 978–1–63609–829–6

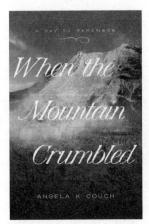

When the Mountain Crumbled
By Angela K Couch

April 29, 1903

Relive Wednesday, April 29, 1903, when Turtle Mountain collapsed upon the town of Frank, Alberta, Canada, causing both chaos and solidarity. A Canadian Mountie and a strict schoolmarm must find a way to work together to help survivors, including the children in their care.

Paperback / 978–1–63609–922–4

JOIN US ONLINE!

Christian Fiction for Women

Christian Fiction for Women is your online home for the latest in Christian fiction.

Check us out online for:

- Giveaways
- Recipes
- Info about Upcoming Releases
- Book Trailers
- News and More!

Find Christian Fiction for Women at Your Favorite Social Media Site:

 Search "Christian Fiction for Women"

 @fictionforwomen